A PLACE TO DIE FOR

ALSO BY A.M. STRONG AND SONYA SARGENT

Stand-Alone Psychological Thrillers

The Last Girl Left

Gravewater Lake

The Patterson Blake Series

Never Lie to Me

Sister Where Are You

Is She Really Gone

All the Dead Girls

Never Let Her Go

Dark Road from Sunrise

I Will Find Her

PRAISE FOR *A PLACE TO DIE FOR*

"Strong and Sargent's *A Place to Die For* drips with dread and delivers chills on every page. This is a beautifully sinister twisted tale of love, loss, and a building that refuses to give up its secrets—claustrophobic, haunting, and absolutely unputdownable."

—Kaira Rouda, *USA Today* bestselling author of *We Were Never Friends*

"*A Place to Die For* is a fast-paced, twist-filled psychological thriller that will keep you reading way past bedtime and leave you breathless until the final page. Sonya Sargent and A.M. Strong once again prove themselves masters of the genre. This book is brilliantly crafted, relentlessly suspenseful, and impossible to put down."

—Elise Hart Kipness, *USA Today* bestselling author

A PLACE TO DIE FOR

A.M. STRONG
SONYA SARGENT

THOMAS & MERCER

Published by Thomas & Mercer, Seattle

www.apub.com

EU product safety contact:
Amazon Media EU S. à r.l.
38, avenue John F. Kennedy, L-1855 Luxembourg
amazonpublishing-gpsr@amazon.com

ISBN-13: 9781662533006 (digital)
ISBN-13: 9781662532993 (paperback)

Cover design by Faceout Studio, Molly von Borstel
Cover image: © Stephen Mulcahey / ArcAngel Images; © macrostudio99, © elegeyda, © caesart / Shutterstock

Printed in the United States of America

For Grace Strong, who has been with us longer than we ever thought possible at 104 years old

1

Him

Then

I watch from the darkness, enthralled. You are everything to me . . . at least in this moment. It's a character flaw, I realize, that I become enamored so quickly. No, *enamored* isn't the right word. Neither is *obsessed*. I'm not *that* kind of guy. A better word might be *intrigued*. Which is exactly what I am right now as you move through the apartment, not even bothering to turn a light on when you head into the kitchen, go to the fridge, and grab a bottle.

Petite sirah.

Nice choice. A lesser person might have gone with a cabernet. It's the most popular wine by far. I read that somewhere, and it's stuck in my mind. Not sure why. But you're different. You don't follow the herd. And maybe that's what I find so fascinating.

You're at the island now—a clean expanse of luxurious quartz with flowing crystalline veins that meander like small dark rivers. You pull the cork. It comes free with a reluctant pop, as if the bottle wants to stay as it is for a little while longer, eager to extend the anticipation of that first, perfect sip. And I understand, because I feel the same way.

The anticipation is almost better than the act. A delicious longing. But every bottle has its time, just like your time has come.

Almost. Because I'm not quite ready. I want to savor these last few exquisite moments we have together. You don't know it, will never know, but you've become a force in my life over the last three months. Besides, there's the wine you just uncorked. It would be a shame to waste it.

After removing a glass from a cupboard near the fridge, you turn back toward the living room with your precious cargo in hand. I might as well be invisible, standing in the dark hallway, clad as I am in black pants, shirt, sneakers, and gloves. As you pass the door, I shrink back anyway, pressing myself flat into the shadows, against the wall. I would hate to ruin our last minutes with screaming and running. Not that I would let you do either of those things. Instead, I would slip the knife from my pocket before you even registered what was happening and let my blade do the rest. It would be a messy, sloppy, hurried end. Not the magnificent finale I have planned. But you *don't* see me, because you're not even looking. After everything I've done to you over the past few months, you are convinced of your safety inside this apartment. Maybe it's the swipe-card entry on the lobby doors or the electronic keypad dead bolt that you place far too much confidence in. Or could it be the pistol stashed in your bedside drawer? A pistol that is completely, utterly useless so far away from the living room, where you are now sitting back down on the couch. Not that it matters. I removed the bullets on my last visit to the apartment a couple of nights ago, while you were out to dinner with that irritating friend of yours who laughs at things that aren't funny and tells you to *find a good man*.

Well, what does she know, because you've found one already—not that you realize it yet—and I'm excited to spend some time with you, even if our relationship will be nothing but a memory by dawn.

A good memory.

Even better than the one we are making now as you put the wineglass down on the wood-and-metal coffee table with the designer dings and dents—factory-added scrapes that don't quite look real—and pour yourself a huge glass that would get any bartender in the city fired.

I let you drink it, pour another, and drink that one, too. Then I make my move.

You register my presence a moment before I reach the couch. You turn your head, eyes flying wide behind those little round wire-framed John Lennon–style glasses that first drew me to you. Quirky spectacles that most young women would never choose to wear. It's those little nuances of character that always suck me in. But there's no time left to bask in your uniqueness, because I can tell you're about to scream.

My hand flies over your mouth in an instant. I lean in low so that my lips are next to your ear. The lingering scent of the perfume you put on before you left for work this morning is a pleasant, if momentary, distraction until I compose myself. Then I whisper, "Make a noise and you're fucking dead."

After that is when our best memories are made.

2

Jordan

Now

Life is weird. One moment, you're on top of the world, and the next, it all comes crashing down to leave you standing amid the debris and wondering how you ended up there. Which is where my fiancé Sam and I find ourselves one sweltering Friday lunchtime in August, as we listen to the loan officer tell us that our dream home is suddenly and inexplicably out of reach.

"I don't understand," I say to the woman across the desk from us at the bank. "We were approved for the mortgage weeks ago. We've done what you told us and provided everything you asked for. We *had* the loan. It was a done deal. How can there be a problem now?"

"Your credit reports," the loan officer replies. Her name is Joy, which I find ironic under the circumstances. "There's an issue with—"

"No." I cut her off sharply. "You pulled our credit when we applied. We're good. No debt. No late payments. Both our scores are over seven hundred." My voice rises as the shock bubbles through. "There's nothing wrong with our credit. How can there be—"

"Jordan!" Sam shifts in his seat, places a calming hand on my arm. "Let the woman speak, or we'll never find out what's going on."

I clamp my mouth shut, even though I'm far from done.

Sam pulls his hand away, runs it over his hair, as if he doesn't have a care in the world. But to me, the gesture says something else, because I know him so well. He can't keep still when he's stressed.

"Thank you." Joy looks at Sam, then back to me, her face creasing with sympathy. "I understand what you're saying, and I agree. Both your credit reports came back great when we ran them for the application, but it's our policy to pull your credit again before closing on the loan to make sure nothing has changed. It's a formality. People don't usually go out and run up a bunch of new debt in the middle of getting a mortgage."

"We didn't," I say. "I haven't even put a cup of coffee on my credit card in the last eight weeks."

"Which is great, but *you* aren't the problem. It's Sam."

"What about him?" I ask. Sam is Black, and at the moment I can't help wondering if that has something to do with it, because it wouldn't be the first time we've faced discrimination. Before I was one half of an interracial couple, such concerns never crossed my mind. I wish they still didn't, but my previous naïvety has been tempered by experience. In this case, though, it appears that the reason is more mundane.

"I told you both not to open any new accounts or increase your debt. I was very specific about that." She turns her attention to my fiancé. "Which is why I was so surprised to see that you opened a new account right after we ran the report."

"What the hell?" Sam glances at me, deep-brown eyes full of confusion. "I didn't open any new accounts. I swear." He turns his attention back to the loan officer and repeats the assertion.

Joy sighs. "That's not what the report we ran yesterday says. Even then, we might have been able to work around it, but not with the balance you're carrying."

Sam's back stiffens. "I don't know what you're talking about."

"Here." Joy pushes a sheet of paper across the table toward us.

It's a page from Sam's credit report. There's a line item marked in yellow highlighter. I stare in mute disbelief. "Twenty thousand dollars? That's not possible."

Sam picks up the report. "I have no idea how this got on my credit. It's obviously a mistake."

Joy takes a deep breath. "Look, I can only go on what I see in front of me, and right now, there's no way we can proceed. Not until this is resolved. My advice would be to reach out to the credit bureaus. Dispute the record. If you really didn't open that account and put all those charges on it, then you might be a victim of identity theft."

"I told you already, it wasn't me," Sam says. "There must be something you can do."

"There isn't." Joy shakes her head slowly with pursed lips. "Not until that record is off your credit report."

"That could take months," Sam says, sounding deflated.

"What about me?" I ask, looking for any way to salvage the situation. "My credit is fine. Can we get the loan based on that? Take Sam off the application?"

"In theory, but it wouldn't help. We'd have to start the process all over again, and honestly, I don't think you'd be approved on your own."

"Why not?" I ask, even though I know what she's going to say.

"Well, there's the fact that you're self-employed. And you've been running the business for less than eighteen months. That's not enough time to show a steady income. And even if we did overcome that, you wouldn't get approved for anywhere near enough."

"But—" I want to say more. I'm just not sure what.

It doesn't matter. Sam hammers the final nail into the coffin himself. "Jordan. We're done here. It's over."

"So we just give up?"

Sam leans back in his chair. "I don't see that we have any choice."

I look at Joy for something . . . anything . . . to refute his assessment, but she says nothing. The conversation appears to be over. I stand and jerk my purse from the back of the chair, grab the laptop bag sitting at my feet, then stomp out of the cubicle, ignoring the cold, hard lump that rises in my throat.

Moments later, we're outside on the sidewalk.

A swell of tears push from the corners of my eyes.

"Hey, it'll be all right." Sam touches my face, brushes the tears away. "Look, I have to get back to the office, but I'll make some calls, talk to the credit bureaus, see if this can be fixed."

I don't think he'll get anywhere—not in time to salvage our loan application, anyway—but there's no point in stating the obvious.

Sam puts his arms around me, holds me tight. "You'll be okay this afternoon?"

I nod and pull away, assure him that I will, which is not at all true. He lingers, as if he senses that I'm putting on a brave face, or at least trying to. But nothing else he can say will make me feel any better, and he's already used up his lunch hour. The last thing we need is more trouble, so I tell him to go, saying, "We'll talk when you come home tonight, okay?"

Now it's his turn to nod. He kisses me quickly, then turns to make the short three-block walk back to the downtown office building where he works, leaving me alone and fighting back a new wave of tears.

3

I can't dwell on this all day. I have work to do. An appointment in a swanky suburb of the city called Newton. The same neighborhood I grew up in and where my parents still live. I'm meeting one of my mother's friends. Her name is Hillary. She's in the middle of a remodel and wants help picking out the fixtures and fittings. The new furniture that will go into the place once it's done.

That's what I do. I'm an interior designer, not that you'd know it from the state of our own apartment—the ratty old couch, side tables that we plucked off the curb when a neighbor was moving out, and a secondhand IKEA coffee table. That's what happens when you're saving every penny for a down payment. We promised ourselves that once we own our own home, we'll buy a new couch and a mattress that doesn't dip in the middle. Maybe even get a dining room set instead of sitting in the living room and eating off cheap tray tables from Walmart.

After our meeting in the bank, all of that feels further away than ever, and to make matters worse, we have to be out of our current digs by the end of the month, which is only a week away. My mood turns darker. I'm not sure I can deal with being bright and chirpy in front of a client right now. I phone Hillary and make my excuses, promising to stop by early the next week. She has an electrician there anyway, and he's taking longer than expected, so it's no big deal, much to my relief.

Having cleared the only item on my schedule, I catch a train back to Jamaica Plain, an eclectic neighborhood of Boston that's popular with college students and twentysomethings, where I share an apartment with Sam on the third floor of a converted house. But that's not where I go, because I can't face the long, empty hours until Sam comes home from work with nothing but my own dark thoughts for company. Instead, I make my way to the Morris Tavern, an Irish bar a few blocks from our building, to drown my sorrows.

I almost order a pint of cider, but then I stop. It's barely two o'clock. What am I doing? Day drinking? Really? I change my mind and get a cup of coffee instead—a poor but responsible substitute—which I sip in the corner of the bar, watching the other patrons who don't share my hesitation about alcohol so early in the afternoon. I'm glad for the company, but it doesn't lift my spirits because I can already feel the hopelessness creeping around the edges of my mind, which scares me. I don't want to be in that place again. If I don't do something, and quickly, this could turn into a full-scale panic attack.

Take it easy, you can get through this, I tell myself. *Remember your calming exercises.*

I close my eyes, force myself to breathe from the diaphragm. Slow, steady inhalations and longer exhalations. I focus on my happy place—

Sam and I holding hands and walking in the park with our future children, a little curly-haired boy and his older sister. They run ahead of us to see the ducks in the pond, a bag of crackers clutched tightly in the girl's hand to feed them. It's a beautiful, perfect, sunny day, and the sound of laughter fills the air.

The pit in my gut loosens. I take another deep breath, hold it, count to five, exhale. I keep this up for a few more minutes until my mind quiets and I'm centered again. Calm. I open my eyes and bring myself back to the present. This situation sucks, but it's nothing compared to what Sam and I have already survived. We will be fine.

I finish the rest of my coffee, and I'm glad I didn't order a cider. Alcohol is the last thing I need right now. I gather my laptop and purse, then hurry from the bar. But when I get home and climb the stairs to the apartment, my newly found sense of calm evaporates in an instant. Because our front door is open, the frame around the lock splintered and cracked. And when I look past the door at the mess in our apartment, it only takes a moment to realize why.

We have been robbed.

4

I stand frozen by inaction and fear. Someone broke into our apartment and trashed the place. Are they still inside? Will they come charging out at me when they realize I'm home?

I take an instinctive step backward.

The hallway is swamped in a gloomy half light thanks to the busted light fixture at the top of the stairs. We've been complaining to the building manager about it for weeks, but he hasn't lifted a finger to fix it.

I reach for my phone to call 911, but it won't connect.

Shit. *Shit. Shit. Shit.*

This is a common occurrence in our building. I often lose service as I climb the stairs, only regaining it once I'm inside the apartment and close to a window.

I should get out of here. Turn and run and not stop until I'm back outside, on the sidewalk, where it's safe and I can call for help. But then, before I can flee, my eye catches a glint of silver on the floor outside the door. I step toward it and reach down, pick it up.

A single small diamond stud earring.

I recognize it as one half of a pair that Sam bought for me when we were first dating. They weren't expensive—he was broke at the time—but I've always loved them. I'm overcome by a sudden, white-hot fury. How dare a stranger come into our personal space and take the things we cherish. I forget all about fleeing. Enraged, I push the door wide and step into the apartment. It's only then, after I've put myself in danger, that I realize how stupid I was. What if the apartment wasn't empty? I could have come face-to-face with whoever broke in . . . I could have ended up shot or stabbed. Stuff like that happens all the time in the city. Thankfully, there's no intruder lying in wait. But they have left evidence of their presence everywhere I look.

The apartment is a mess.

The seat cushions have been pulled off the couch and flung aside. The lamp that previously stood on our end table now lies on the floor, bulb smashed. The intruder also sprayed graffiti in red paint on the coffee table and TV screen. I rush through the apartment, checking every room. There's more graffiti on my desk in the breakfast nook—our apartment is so small it was the only place I could put a desk—and on the kitchen cabinets. The bathroom mirror has been similarly vandalized. But it's when I enter the bedroom that my heart falls. As I suspected from the earring in the hallway, my jewelry box is open and empty. They took everything. The only reason I still have my engagement ring is because I'm wearing it. A small mercy. When I check the nightstand next to Sam's side of the bed, I see that the automatic watch he inherited from his great-uncle Albert is missing, too. I return to the living room, go to the coat closet next to the front door, and open it, already knowing what I will find. My Burberry jacket is gone. The one my parents bought me for Christmas three years ago. So is the case containing Sam's personal laptop. I turn to survey the chaos that has descended upon our apartment and fight back a scream of rage. I want to lash out, punch the walls, do anything to release the pent-up frustration and sense of violation that boils within me. But none of that will do any good, so instead, I cross the room and step close to the window where the reception is best, rest my laptop bag on the floor, then dial 911. After that, I call Sam and tell him what's happened. Then I pick up a seat cushion, put it back on the sofa, and wait for help to arrive. And in that moment, I wonder how my world could have come crashing down around me so quickly.

5

I have never felt unsafe in my home before, but now I can't stop shaking as I sit in the living room among our ruined furniture. I don't even want to think about what would have happened if I'd come straight here instead of going to that bar. Would I have walked in on the intruders? What would they have done to me? A host of scenarios tumble through my head, each more frightening than the last. I push the dire thoughts from my mind as best I can and wait for Sam.

He arrives home around the same time that a pair of uniformed police officers show up. They look around, ask for a list of missing items, take statements from us, and that's about it. When I inquire if they're going to dust for prints or do anything beyond the bare minimum, they exchange a weary glance and tell us that we shouldn't hold our breaths. And as for recovering our stuff . . . not likely.

After they leave, I go straight to the kitchen with tears brimming in my eyes and return with a roll of paper towels and a bottle of window cleaner. I scrub at the TV screen in an attempt to remove some of the graffiti, which comprises a four-letter description of female anatomy that begins with a *c*, no doubt meant to shock in its vulgarity. The thieves got more creative with our coffee table and opted for a badly executed yet recognizable drawing of male genitalia. Why whoever broke into our apartment bothered with these crass acts of vandalism, I don't know, but they leave me feeling violated. And maybe that's the point. Whoever did this wasn't just content to take our possessions; they wanted to make sure we wouldn't ever feel safe here again. And it worked.

"Hey, take it easy," Sam says, coming up behind me as I drop a spent paper towel on the floor and tear another one off the roll, going back to my task in a frenzy even though it's clearly not working. The spray paint won't come off. He puts his hands on my shoulders, turns me around, takes the paper towels and cleaner away from me, and sets them aside. "This isn't getting us anywhere."

"I have to do *something*," I tell him with a sob. "Look at this. It's ruined."

"We'll get another TV." Sam steers me toward the couch and sits me down, then does the same. "It's just stuff."

My gaze drops to the coffee table, where more disgusting language awaits in bold red strokes next to the dubiously drawn artwork. My skin crawls. "I can't stay here tonight."

Sam's voice is soft when he replies, "Then we'll go to a hotel and deal with it tomorrow."

"No. You don't understand. It's not just one night. I can't stay here, period. I don't feel safe anymore."

"We can stay in the hotel for as long as necessary."

"With what? The money we saved for the down payment? We need that cash, every penny of it, if we're ever going to get out of places like this."

"Well, there's Rob. I'm sure he'll let us crash at his place."

"Hell no." I shake my head. Rob is Sam's friend. They met in college and were roommates for a while, until he dropped out. "I've seen Rob's apartment. It's awful. He hasn't cleaned or vacuumed since the day he moved in, and he doesn't flush the toilet." *Not to mention all the pot he smokes.* I take a deep breath. "We can go to my parents'. I mean, if you're good with that."

"Of course. It's . . . it's fine." Sam glances sideways at me. "I'd say we could stay with my folks, but . . ."

"They live in Chicago."

"Right."

I wipe my eyes. "I'm sorry about this."

"What? The credit thing? Getting broken into? That's hardly your fault."

"No." I shake my head. "Going to pieces. Bawling my eyes out. I don't know how you stay so calm."

Sam shrugs. "Guess I just internalize instead."

"That's not healthy."

"I know." Sam reaches out. He takes my hand and squeezes it. "You want me to pack us a bag?"

"Maybe." I stare at the coffee table. At that foul graffiti. And then I remember something. A cold dread envelops me. "Shit."

"What?"

I jump up, race into the bedroom, past the dresser and the small mahogany jewelry box that now sits open and empty. I rush to my nightstand but don't see what I'm looking for. Desperate, I pull the drawer open, even though I know it won't be there. There's a pair of nail clippers, a flashlight—because the building is old, and the breakers trip all the time—and a bottle of over-the-counter sleeping pills. But not what I'm looking for.

"What's going on?" Sam stands in the bedroom doorway.

"It's not here," I reply, a glut of panic welling inside me. I push the items in the drawer aside. It's a futile gesture. "My Tiffany bracelet. The one with the angel charm that you gave me to honor our baby after the miscarriage." I turn to him in anguish. "It was here this morning, and now it's gone. They took it."

"Are you sure?" Sam steps into the room.

"Of course I'm sure. I took it off this morning before my shower and left it on my nightstand. I forgot to put it back on." This is too much. It means everything to me. A beautiful silver bracelet with round, flat links and a charm that Sam had custom made of an angel holding a heart-shaped opal, the birthstone for October. That was when our own angel would have been born. The bracelet was a symbol of love and loss, and a testament to our strength as a couple to overcome anything life throws at us. It also had a little compartment to hold some of her ashes. I turn and look at Sam, shoulders slumped, arms at my sides, and ask the question that's been running through my mind since the moment I found our front door busted open: "Why is this happening to us?"

6

I'm in the middle of packing bags for myself and Sam so we can get out of here, when my phone rings.

It's Jinny, our real estate agent.

She's the last person I want to hear from, under the circumstances, and I can guess what she's calling about, so I ignore the call. When a message comes through moments later, my suspicions are confirmed.

"I'm so sorry," she says without bothering to elaborate, then goes on to tell me that it's nothing to worry about in the grand scheme of things. There will be other condos. In the meantime, she'll talk to the sellers, see if they would be willing to wait while we resolve the issue, but imparts in the same breath that it's unlikely. Boston is a hot property market, and they have backup offers.

I really couldn't care less about the loan or the condo we were buying right now. Our home has been violated. My bracelet—the only link I have left to the child I will never meet—is gone. All I want to do is get the hell out of this apartment and go somewhere I will feel safe. Jinny can wait.

We take an Uber to my parents' house. As we ride, I phone ahead and tell them about the break-in. When we arrive, they're waiting at the front door. My father scurries down the steps to the car as it pulls up into the driveway, and insists on grabbing our bags, then hauls them into the house and deposits them at the bottom of the stairs. After that, it's nothing but sympathy and questions for the next hour. When Dad finally declares that he's going to throw some steaks on the grill—and a chicken breast for me because I don't eat red meat—it's a relief. Sam accompanies him, beer in hand, and leaves me alone with my mother.

She flits around the kitchen, preparing a salad to accompany the steaks, and talks over her shoulder. "Next week you'll be in your new home, and that nasty apartment will be nothing but a memory." She dumps lettuce into a bowl, then turns to face me. "Honestly, I never liked the place. And the less said about that neighborhood, the better. It was only a matter of time before something like this happened. Thank heavens you weren't home, or it would have been so much worse."

Shit. With all the stress and upset of the break-in, I haven't told her what happened at the bank. "Mom, about the house—"

"Yes, dear?" She grabs an onion.

"The loan fell through. We aren't getting it."

There's a moment of silence. My mother's hand hovers midair above the onion, knife poised; then she slowly puts it down. "I don't understand. You were approved already. You're closing on Tuesday."

"I know that." Why did I mention the loan right now on top of everything else? Today has been stressful enough. It's Friday, which gave me the whole weekend to break the news to my parents. But it's too late now. "There was an issue with Sam's credit."

"Ah," she says, as if this were a foregone conclusion. "I was telling your father only last week that—"

"Mom. It wasn't him. Someone must have stolen his identity, opened a credit card, and ran it up."

"There's no need to interrupt me. I was just going to say that we should have loaned you the money instead of the two of you going to all that trouble with a mortgage. That's all. I wasn't casting aspersions on Sam."

Of course she wasn't. I love my mother, but she can be a little . . . judgy. "Look, it doesn't matter. I just wanted you to know what's going on. We might have to stay here for a week or two, just until we find alternative accommodations."

"You can stay for as long as you need, honey. Both of you. Honestly, I'm happy to hear that you're not going back to that dreadful place."

"Thank you." I swallow my annoyance at her phrasing. *Both of you.* As if there was ever any question that Sam would be here with me. My parents would never say it, at least not outright, but they have always been unsure about Sam. He checks all the boxes on one level—he's a lawyer and comes from a good family—but he also works for a lowly nonprofit when he could be in the private sector earning five times as much. They see this as a character flaw. Especially my psychiatrist father, who defines his very existence by billable hours. Plus, I'm pretty sure my mother is just a teeny bit racist and doesn't love the idea of her daughter being in an interracial relationship, no matter how amazing Sam is.

"And in the meantime, you can call Jinny and tell her you'll pay cash for the house." My mother picks the knife back up and takes aim at the onion once more. "It's a little more than we have on hand, but we'll talk to the bank on Monday about taking out a home equity loan to cover the rest—just until your dad can liquidize some of our investments. Problem solved."

"No!" My response is a little sharper than I intended because I'm still irritated by what she said about Sam. "I'm not taking your money."

It stops my mother in her tracks, giving the onion another temporary reprieve. "Don't be silly, of course you are. It's the logical solution. When you get sorted out, you can pay us back."

I take a deep breath, because I know she's trying to be supportive, even if her methods are a bit blunt. "I appreciate the offer, but we can't let you go into debt like that for us. It's too much—and honestly, Sam and I need to make our own way."

"Like you're making your own way with all those clients I've been sending you?"

Touché. My interior design business would be more like a hobby if it weren't for my mother's friends, but considering the circles she moves in, I tell myself they would have hired me eventually either way. And soon, once people see what I can do, I won't have to rely on family connections to keep the proverbial lights on. "That's not the same thing. I'm still doing the work. It's still *me*."

"Whatever you say, my dear." My mother brings the knife down, and the onion's luck finally runs out. "We'll talk more tomorrow, when you're not so cranky."

I bite my tongue, a common occurrence around my mother. Considering how often I've bitten it over the years, I'm surprised I still have one.

7

We spend the night sleeping in my parents' guest bedroom, which used to be my room when I was living here. It hasn't changed much, except that the trappings of a teenage girl are gone: the boy band posters, teddy bears, and cheap mall jewelry. We're both adults, but it's almost like I'm seventeen again and I sneaked him in—not that I ever let a boy into my room back then, because I wasn't that kind of girl.

On Saturday morning, I'm awakened by Sam slipping out from under the covers, even though I know he's trying not to disturb me. Hardly surprising, since we're crammed into a full-size bed. There's barely room for the two of us. We spent the whole night waking each other up every time someone shifted position, and I'm exhausted.

"What time is it?" I ask groggily, rolling over and rubbing sleep from my eyes.

Sam slips a polo shirt over his head. "Seven thirty. I'm going over to the apartment with your dad."

"Why?" I'm still half asleep.

"Because all our stuff is there, and we need to get it."

That makes sense. There's no way I'm ever living in that place again. Not after what happened.

"Hang on." I push back the covers reluctantly. "Give me a minute to get dressed, and I'll come with you."

"No need. Go back to sleep." Sam leans down and kisses my forehead. "We've got this covered."

"Are you sure?" I ask, even as I pull the covers back up and snuggle into them.

"Positive." Sam laughs and steps toward the door. "Love you."

"Love you more," I mumble, closing my eyes and spreading out in the bed.

When I wake up again, it's much later. I reach instinctively for Sam before I realize he's not there. All that's left of him is a dent in the pillow and a faint scent of aftershave. I haul myself out of bed and stumble, bleary eyed, to the bathroom. I look awful, possibly thanks to how little sleep I got. My hair, which normally falls below my shoulders in cascading fiery-red waves, looks dull and flat. My eyes, which Sam once described as a pair of sparkling emeralds, have lost their luster. They're sunken and weighed down by heavy bags.

I pull myself away from the mirror, then shower, get dressed, and go into the kitchen to make a cup of coffee. That's when I find it. A folded sheet of paper with my name on it propped up against the coffee maker, because Sam knows I can't function before caffeine.

It's a note.

Try not to let yesterday get you down.
We'll get through this. Promise.
Love you lots!
Sam

I read the note a second time and smile. Sam is the most positive person I know. His cheery disposition and never-say-die attitude have made him a rising star at the Preservation Project, a nonprofit dedicated to saving historic buildings from the wrecking ball. He took the job right out of law school. Of course, he could earn a heap more money at a corporate law firm. Somewhere that has actual, paying clients and the opportunity for him to make partner one day. But he loves the job, and I love his passion for saving the beautiful historic buildings in our city.

I drop a pod into the coffee maker, my eyes still on the note, and open a couple of cupboards until I find a cup. Once it's finished brewing, I take the cup and grab my laptop before settling down at the kitchen table to check my email.

It's mostly spam, which I consign to the junk folder. What's left are automatic bill payment notifications and messages from mailing lists I've joined at one time or another. There's also an email from Jinny. She's spoken to the sellers, and they're going with a backup offer. I'm not surprised, but it's disappointing. Up until now, the door was still open, if only a crack. Now it's been slammed firmly shut. We're done with buying a place of our own, at least for the foreseeable future.

I sit at the table and finish my coffee, staring at Jinny's message as if I can change the words contained within the email simply by force of will. When that doesn't work, I trash the message, go back into the kitchen, and make another cup of coffee.

At that moment, my mother appears, and any hope of a quiet morning spent wallowing in self-pity evaporates.

My father and Sam are gone most of the day. They make several trips between Jamaica Plain and Newton, boxing up our possessions and stacking them in my parents' garage. Except for the furniture that isn't worth keeping—the ratty old couch, ruined IKEA coffee table, my desk, spray-painted television, and lumpy mattress, among other items—which they drag down to the sidewalk and drop at the curb for apartment-dwelling scavengers or the trash pickup.

After that, Sam hands the apartment keys back to the building manager, who tells him that we won't be getting our deposit back because of all the damage. It wasn't our fault, which sucks, but even Sam's lawyerly protestations fail to change his mind. The money is gone. Just one more consequence of the robbery that further sours my mood.

By Sunday evening, I've reached my low point. We'll have to start apartment hunting in the coming week, which fills me with dread. Boston is not a cheap place to live, and I fear that we'll end up back in Jamaica Plain, which I used to love for its eclectic vibe and young energy but now view through a different lens. And if we can't find affordable housing in JP—as the locals refer to it—or another neighborhood in the city, then we'll have to look farther afield.

I decide to call Jinny first thing on Monday morning and see if she knows of any apartments that would be willing to do a lease shorter than a year or let us go monthly—both of which are unlikely—so that we can start looking for another place to buy the moment Sam's credit is fixed. But she beats me to it. Sam has left for work and I'm about to sit down at the kitchen table with my laptop and a cup of coffee when the phone rings.

"Jordan? Are you sitting down?" she gushes when I answer. "Because I have some news, and I think you're going to like it."

8

Him

Then

It's been six months, and I've thought of you often. The way those small round spectacles drew attention to the jade sparkle of your eyes. Even at the end, after your light had gone out, they shone for a while longer, almost as if you were still in there somewhere, looking back at me. But now the memory is fading, and I can feel my need growing once again. The desire for a new love. Even if my affection goes unrequited until those final, delicate moments when our fates become tangled for a few glorious hours.

I think I've found my next relationship. I've been looking for a few weeks. At first it was halfhearted, because turning my affections to someone else meant letting go of you, my jade-eyed love. Admitting that our moment had passed. I still remember the first time I saw you on a sun-drenched Saturday morning at the farmers' market on the bank of the Charles River, with the grand old buildings of Cambridge in the distance across the water. You were carrying a cloth bag from the bookstore in Davis Square that isn't there anymore. It had a picture of an owl wearing spectacles on it, and I wondered briefly why owls, above other birds, are associated with reading. Perhaps it's because they are seen as wise.

I followed you for a while, compelled by some unknown force. You stopped at a produce stand, purchased some apples from a local orchard. When you put them in the bag and looked in my direction, I saw another pair of spectacles. Those small round glasses balanced so perfectly on the bridge of your nose. From that moment on, I was enthralled.

That's how it always goes. Some little quirk that sucks me in. A chance encounter that leads to happiness. I went back to that same market last week, perhaps believing that if I met someone else in our special place, it would be a sign from beyond that you were good with me moving on. But no one caught my eye.

Today, though, it's different. I spotted her a few minutes ago standing at the counter in the coffee shop and waiting for her order. She's nothing like you, Jade. You had a nerdy aura. You dressed like you didn't know the power of your beauty. You wore jeans and baggy T-shirts. Flannel pajamas to bed. Kept your hair in a ponytail.

This one is your exact opposite. She wears a knee-length black skirt and tube top that offers a glimpse of her pale, thin belly. The clothes look casual, but I can tell they're expensive by the way they fit. Her hair is loose and free. A cascade of black silk that tumbles over her shoulders and reaches halfway to her waist.

At first, I'm not sure if she's the one. A worthy successor to you, Jade. But then she reaches for her coffee, and I see the tattoo. The little thing that makes her perfect. It's on her forearm, right above her wrist. The dark outline of a raven sitting on a branch and silhouetted within a crescent moon. In Greek mythology, ravens are considered messengers of the gods. Is this a message from you, I wonder? The approval I crave.

I can't help but stare, fighting the impulse to move closer and get a better look. There will be time for that soon enough. When she leaves, I rise from my table in the back corner, drop my half-full cup into the trash, and follow her out onto the street.

She steps toward the curb, and for one terrible moment I think she's looking for a taxi. A ride that will whisk her off to somewhere unknown and out of my life before we've even had a chance to connect. But then she hurries across the street, dodging cars and a bicycle, before vanishing underground into the subway station.

I trail her down to the platform and watch her sip coffee as she waits for the train. Is she on her lunch hour and heading back to work? I doubt it. Not dressed like that. I mean, sure, there are places where such an outfit would be appropriate, but I'm not getting that energy. So maybe she's a student. Besides, most people don't take the subway on their lunch hour. They go somewhere local. Quick.

When the train breezes into the station, she moves forward to board. I do the same. Then, as I'm about to follow her onto the train, a high-pitched beeping sound distracts me. My pocket vibrates. Shit. It's work, and at the worst possible time. I'm in my second year as a resident physician at Mass General, which is shorthand for "trainee with a degree," and even though it's my day off, I'm on call.

I pull out my beeper—yes, I know the device is an anachronism in the modern world of cell phones, but for some reason hospitals still use them—and check the message. Code Orange. Mass casualty event. That sounds ominous, but it's probably a pileup or a bus crash. Maybe even a train derailment, which is unsettling, given my current location.

Regardless, it's inconvenient, because if I respond to the Code Orange, I'll lose her, and I don't know what to do. But then, as she steps onto the train, I catch another glimpse of the tattoo and my heart beats faster. It *is* a sign from you. I'm sure of it now. You're telling me what I need to do.

Pushing the pager back into my pocket, I follow her onto the train. I might take some heat for ignoring it, but this is more important. Then I stand, enraptured, and watch her from the other end of the carriage as the train starts to move. Because she's the one. I don't know her name. Not yet. But it doesn't matter, because from now on, I'll think of her only as Raven.

9

Jordan

Now

News? My heart leaps. I wait for Jinny to elaborate with growing excitement. Has the bank reconsidered our loan? Or maybe the sellers decided to give us time to work things out after all? But when she speaks, my bubble bursts.

"There's an opening at the Glendale, and I think you might qualify."

I place my coffee cup down on the table, try to mask my disappointment. "What's the Glendale? I've never heard of it."

"Only one of the most exclusive cooperatives in town," Jinny says with more enthusiasm than I've ever heard from her. "Almost impossible to get into. It's located in the Back Bay, near the Public Garden. The smallest apartment is two thousand square feet, and all the units have a view of either the Charles River and Cambridge or the Boston skyline."

"Really?" I don't know anything about cooperatives, having never lived in one, but it doesn't matter. "A two-thousand-square-foot apartment in the Back Bay with a view? Sounds expensive. Like, 'Way out of our price range, why even bother looking at it?' expensive."

"That's the thing. It really isn't. The price for each unit in the Glendale is determined by the amount of the building it takes up, and you purchase the relevant percentage of shares in the corporation that owns the place. That's what gives you the right to live there. It's sort of like a permanent rental for as long as you hold the shares. That's how cooperatives work."

Jinny seems to be forgetting one thing. "We can't purchase anything right now. No mortgage approval, remember?"

"That's just it. You won't need a mortgage. Not with the way this deal is structured. The apartment is financed by the board that runs the Glendale. And here's the best thing. Because you're buying shares instead of real estate, the closing costs are minimal. There's no title insurance or mortgage taxes, and the down payment is only five percent. You just commit to paying a monthly maintenance fee, which I hear is quite reasonable."

"Five percent?" We'd saved twenty for a down payment. Depending on the asking price, we might actually be able to keep some money in the bank. "That's incredible."

"Right? It's an almost unheard of down payment for a co-op unit. You'd be nuts not to pursue this."

"I don't know." I'm still not convinced, because there's always a catch. "Those shares must be super expensive."

"They are, and normally you wouldn't come close to qualifying. But the board are looking for certain qualities in a tenant. I think you and Sam would be a great fit. And if they like you, they have discretion to provide financial assistance from a fund set up by the family who built the place. From what I've heard, that assistance can be *extremely* generous . . . for the right tenants."

I'm confused. "It's a new building?"

"Goodness, no. The building has been there forever. It's sort of a fixture. It was built back in the early 1900s as rental apartments by an industrialist who wanted to get into real estate. It's been in the same family ever since. His descendants converted it into a cooperative about ten years ago and changed the name." Jinny takes a breath. "Look, none of that matters. What's important is that there's an opening. The previous occupants of the apartment are moving to California, or so I've been told. Something to do with their work."

"Then why is the board selling it instead of the owner?" I ask.

"Because you can't sell your shares in the Glendale on the open market. It's a limited equity cooperative, which means you have to sell them back to the executive board at the price you originally paid, plus a percentage on top for each year you owned them linked to inflation. It's in the rules when you purchase." Jinny takes a quick breath. "Look, we can talk more about this later. It could all be moot. The board might not approve you to live there. Like I said, it's super hard to get into. But we might as well put an application in. What do you say?"

I think about the apartment we just fled. The graffiti and the busted door. The idea of renting somewhere like that again twists my stomach into knots, so there's really only one thing I *can* say. "Okay. We'll give it a go."

10

After Jinny puts the application in, we wait. When a week goes by and we haven't heard anything, I start to think that we never will. This was a stupid idea. We're clearly not suitable tenants for a place like the Glendale. But then, on the following Tuesday, we receive an invitation to attend an interview. I'm beyond excited, even though Sam cautions me that this is far from a done deal. They might not like us, and even if they do, there are other considerations. We still have no idea how much the apartment will cost, and even with financial assistance, it could still be out of reach.

But Jinny is optimistic. She tells us that the odds are good. If the Glendale's board didn't like us, they wouldn't waste their time on an interview. Even so, I'm nervous as we drive across town the next day and meet her outside the building.

It's an imposing six-floor structure with a sandstone facade, arched windows on the second floor, and colonnades supporting a decorative plinth. The building would not be out of place in a European city like Paris or Rome, which only makes me more nervous. Will the board that runs this place really let us live here? Being turned down based on the application is one thing, but to lose this opportunity after we meet with them and see the apartment would be so disappointing.

Jinny isn't fazed, though. She leads us up a set of granite steps to the front door and presses the buzzer to let the doorman know we've arrived. After a brief conversation, the door unlocks. But Jinny won't be joining us. She has another appointment a couple of blocks away and will meet us when we're done. "Don't worry," she says. "You've got this." Then she departs.

"Ready?" I ask Sam nervously.

"As I'll ever be." He takes my hand, pushes the door open, and we step into the Glendale.

The inside of the building is dripping in prewar opulence. A floor of inlaid marble tiles reflects the light from a huge chandelier hanging down from a vaulted ceiling that rises through the second floor. English oak wainscoting adorns the walls. A dark-wood staircase with posts topped by frosted glass lamps winds around a central birdcage elevator. To our right is a door that leads into a small mailroom with gold-colored boxes built into one wall. To our left is the doorman's desk, and beyond that, an office. A plush red couch sits against the wall near the desk. The doorman motions to it and asks us to wait, then makes a phone call. Ten minutes later, we're escorted along a corridor behind the staircase and into a reception room, where the board members are waiting.

And what I see takes my breath away. A huge fireplace with an impressive brownstone mantel occupies one wall. Floor-to-ceiling bookcases wrap around the walls, their shelves packed with antique volumes. A pair of arched windows spill dappled sunlight across a dark oak floor. A pair of chandeliers, smaller facsimiles of the one in the entrance lobby, hang from a coffered ceiling. Two men and a woman sit in wingback chairs arranged around a low coffee table. They face a couple of empty chairs, clearly placed there for us.

After we take our seats, the woman speaks. "My name is Catherine Cole. I'm the great-granddaughter of the man who built the Glendale." She nods toward an older gentleman with thick white hair and a beard sitting to her right. "This is my husband, Ronald."

He raises a hand in greeting but remains silent.

Motioning to the other man, Catherine says, "This is Dr. Andrew Burgess."

Dr. Burgess is younger than his counterparts by at least a couple of decades. He has wavy blond hair, brown eyes, and the enviable good looks most doctors seem to possess.

"So, what do you think so far?" he asks, with a faint smile that somehow feels hollow.

I take in my surroundings, overawed. "This place is fantastic."

"I'm pleased that you like it. I've been here since the building was first turned into a co-op, and I wouldn't live anywhere else."

"I can see why," I say, my eyes roving across the shelves packed with books. "It's like I'm inside some Gilded Age mansion. It's just . . . wow."

Catherine beams with pride. "We feel this room is a suitable introduction to the grandeur of the building. The couple who built the Glendale, John and Kathy Putnam, were huge supporters of the arts, including literature. John even ran a publishing house for a while, although his other ventures did better. They had this library installed to provide somewhere for the residents to sit and reflect . . . to find a measure of peace from the bustle of the city beyond these walls. It's an unusual feature, but one that we're proud of at the Glendale."

"I would be, too," I say, in a hushed tone. It feels wrong to raise my voice too loudly here, even though no one is trying to read.

Catherine nods knowingly, as if she understands. "There was also a telegraph office and gymnasium on this floor, and two reception chambers, a dining room, and a sauna on the second floor. They even had plans for a ballroom at one point. It was luxury living back then, for sure, which was how John envisioned it. Of course, most of that is long gone, converted into apartments."

"Except for the library," says the doctor. "We couldn't bear to part with that."

I look around, imagining myself living here and relaxing in this room on a cold winter's evening with a fire roaring in the grand fireplace while I work on my laptop. It's hard not feel a twinge of excitement, and we haven't even seen the apartment yet.

11

The interview goes well. At least I think it does. At the end, they inform us that they still have three more applicants to interview. Then Catherine offers to show us the apartment, which feels like a tease, given that we don't yet know if we'll be allowed to live there.

I've already decided, based on the common areas alone, that should we be offered the place, it's a resounding yes. The building is a dream, and the terms are so reasonable that we actually could afford it.

The Glendale has four apartments on each level, except for the second floor, which has two because the lobby rises up through it, and the ground floor, which has only one. The top floor is a penthouse occupied by Catherine and her husband, Ron. The apartment we're looking at is on the fourth floor, taking up a quarter of the space on one corner of the building.

We ride up in the antique birdcage elevator, which makes me feel like I've fallen back in time to an era of flappers and gangsters. When we arrive at the fourth floor, I'm no less enamored. The landing is full of vintage charm, with brass sconces topped by milk glass shades that cast a warm glow, a smaller version of the chandelier in the lobby hanging from the ceiling, and a black-and-white-tile patterned floor. But what really draws my eye is the painting hanging between the apartment doors opposite the elevator. It's an impressionist-style street scene with a building I recognize instantly.

"Is that the Glendale?" I ask.

Catherine nods. "Yes. My great-grandfather visited Paris several times in the 1890s and fell in love with the art there. According to family lore, he met Édouard Manet at the Folies-Bergère and asked him to paint this from a photograph he took with him."

"It's not signed," I say.

"Manet also died in 1883," Sam says dryly. "Which means this can't be his work."

A faint look of displeasure crosses Catherine's face. "You are correct."

Sam shuffles his feet. "Sorry. I didn't mean to offend you."

"No offense taken. The problem with family stories is that the details have a habit of becoming less distinct over the years." Catherine walks us to a door opposite the painting. "Shall we proceed?"

Sam nods, shooting me a pained glance as Catherine unlocks the door.

We step inside, and I'm surprised to see that, in contrast to the old-world charm of the common areas, the apartment is bright and modern. We enter through a square foyer illuminated by concealed lighting. Two huge oil paintings—swirling explosions of color that dazzle the senses—hang on opposite walls in slim aluminum frames. They're so large that they practically stretch from floor to ceiling. More concealed lights shine down on them. The floors are light wood planks with a distressed finish. A thick orange-and-black wool rug with a swirling pattern that complements the wall art fills the center of the room.

"The paintings come with the apartment," Catherine says. "It's part of our commitment to my great-grandfather's mission to support the arts. They're on loan from the family's private collection. Unless you prefer to install your own pieces, in which case I can have them removed."

"They're beautiful," I say, wondering what Catherine and the other board members would think of the cheap Van Gogh prints we purchased from HomeGoods when we moved into our previous apartment. It was the best I could do at the time, given our limited funds. "And I love the floors."

"Me too," Sam agrees. "They offset the modern renovation beautifully."

"Thank you. They're original. We deliberately kept them this way to showcase the building's character." Catherine leads us into a living room with a stacked stone fireplace flanked by built-in shelves. This room has more light wood floors, and one of the biggest brown leather couches I've ever seen. There's a glass-and-metal coffee table—nothing like our old IKEA one—and two side chairs that match the couch. A huge TV hangs over the fireplace mantel. Despite the size of the furniture, everything fits comfortably into the space. I feel like I've walked into the pages of an interior design magazine.

A huge quartz island dominates the space between the living room and a gorgeous kitchen that even I would want to prepare meals in . . . And I loathe cooking. The fridge is an enormous, gleaming stainless steel monster. Another smaller fridge is built into the island, which has racks for wine.

After stepping back out of the kitchen, Catherine leads us across the living room and into a dining area with an oblong table and eight chairs. The wall to our left is taken up by a built-in hutch with shelves behind glass doors on the top, and four rows of drawers on the bottom. Like the floors, it looks original to the apartment. I can almost see the fine bone china and silverware of days gone by displayed in this hutch.

Catherine steers us through the room and past the hutch to a set of sliding doors.

"I think you'll love this," she says, parting the doors and ushering us onto a wide balcony with stunning views of the Back Bay and the city skyline beyond. "Well? What do you think?"

"I love it," I say, turning to Sam. "Isn't this fantastic?"

"It sure is," Sam replies, but there's an edge to his voice. A cautionary note. He casts me a quick look that drums home the message. *Don't get too attached. We don't have the place yet.*

But I can't help it. I *am* attached, even though I know we aren't the only applicants, and we stand a good chance of being turned down, regardless of our tour guide's upbeat, friendly demeanor.

We go back inside, where Catherine leads us to the left and into another room, which is empty.

"This is the guest bedroom," she says. "But it would also make a great office or even a meditation area."

An office, I think to myself. *I can finally have a real office.*

Then, as if Catherine is saving the best for last, we find ourselves in the main bedroom, which puts our previous digs to shame. There's a king-size bed, and another TV mounted on the wall. An en suite bathroom boasts a glass shower cubicle with four heads, and a soaking tub.

"The entire building was renovated ten years ago, before we converted it to a cooperative," Catherine says. "We spared no expense, as you can see."

I almost wish she hadn't shown us the apartment, because now that I've seen it, I'll be heartbroken if we aren't approved. It's so much more than we could ever have imagined to be within our reach.

Sam leans close to me and whispers, "Just keep in mind, it won't look anywhere near as good with *our* furniture in it."

Somehow, Catherine hears him, even though she's on her way back out of the bathroom. She turns to us. "Actually, the previous owners left the furniture behind. They didn't want the expense of moving it all the way across the country, so whoever we approve for the apartment will have the choice of keeping it."

"Really?" I step back into the bedroom and look at the bed, resist the urge to flop down on it and see if it's as comfortable as it looks. "All this stuff?"

"All of it," Catherine says in a chirpy voice. "Unless the new tenant doesn't want it."

"It's great," I say quickly. "We'll keep it . . . I mean, if we're approved, that is."

"Excellent." Catherine smiles and claps her hands together. "I believe that concludes the grand tour."

We follow her back through the apartment and ride the elevator down to the lobby, where Jinny is waiting and chatting to the doorman. I don't want to leave. I'm falling in love with this place despite my best efforts not to get excited. Catherine bids us farewell and says that we'll be informed of the board's decision soon.

Once we're out on the sidewalk, Jinny turns to us. "Well? What did you think?"

I look up at the building, and the balcony of the apartment on the fourth floor. I imagine myself standing up there and gazing out over the city on a balmy summer evening. Only two words can do this place justice. "It's perfect."

We hear back from the board of the Glendale a week later. During that time, I'm on tenterhooks, unable to think of anything else, even though Sam tells me repeatedly not to get my hopes up. There were other applicants, and they probably don't have credit issues like we do. But then Jinny calls with the news. We're in. The board has approved our application. All that's left to do is sign the paperwork, which will happen at noon on Friday, just a few short days away. I want to pinch myself, make sure this is real. But it is. After everything we've gone through over the last few years—the miscarriage, my struggling business, the loan falling through, and finally the robbery that's left me shaken to the core—our luck is turning around. We've done it. The apartment is ours!

12

I stand in the living room of our new home and take in my surroundings, barely able to comprehend that this is actually happening. That we are really going to live here.

It's Saturday morning, and a long day of moving in stretches ahead of us. Even though we have the whole weekend, I really want to sleep here tonight. I appreciate that my parents have been letting us stay at their house, but I'm ready for some alone time.

Sam must be thinking the same thing, because he turns to me, hands pushed deep into his pockets, and says, "Ready to get this done before we end up back in your childhood bedroom for another night?"

So that is exactly what we do.

When we first arrived, we were met by the doorman, an older gentleman named Angelo with a shock of thick silver hair. He greeted us with a smile and a housewarming hamper, courtesy of Catherine and the Glendale's board. He also offered us a luggage cart, which we gratefully accepted. We don't have much heavy furniture, but I was already exhausted just thinking about carrying everything up to the fourth floor by hand.

We bring the first load up in the fantastically retro birdcage elevator and wheel it to the apartment. That's when we hit a snag. The cart is heavy, weighed down with boxes so high that we can barely see past them, and when we roll it into the apartment, the wheels catch on the thick orange-and-black wool rug in the foyer and refuse to move another inch.

Sam backpedals, dragging the cart away from the offending rug. "Probably should have moved this first."

He's not wrong. Even if the cart had traversed the rug with ease, the wheels might have damaged it. I join him at one end of the rug, and together we roll it up and push it aside.

That's when we see it. A large, uneven dark-brown stain in the middle of the floor, marring the otherwise gorgeous light oak planks.

I stare at it. "No wonder they put a rug here."

Sam nods in agreement. "I bet that stain has soaked all the way down into the grain. Practically impossible to get rid of without replacing the boards."

"I wonder what it is?"

Sam shrugs. "Who knows? The building's been here a long time. Looks like someone spilled something. Maybe old varnish, or paint?"

"Well, whatever it is, the rug is going right back over it once we're done," I say, grabbing the cart again and wheeling it past the rolled-up rug. "I don't want *that* to be the first thing everyone sees when they come here."

"Agreed." Sam pushes the cart forward. "Let's hope we don't find any more nasty surprises waiting for us."

"Even if we do, how bad could they be?" I ask. "This place is unadulterated luxury compared to all our other apartments."

"We're living the dream," Sam replies, flashing a grin as he steers the cart into the living room and brings it to a halt. He grabs a box marked *Bedroom* and sets off with it in his arms. I head in the other direction with one marked *Dining room*. Once the cart is empty, we wheel it down to my dad's car, which we've borrowed for the day, and head back to my parents' garage for more stuff.

We do this five more times, driving back and forth through the clogged Boston traffic. On the last load, my dad drops us off, saving us the trouble of driving his car back to Newton and taking the T home.

Thank goodness for that. I carry the last box into the bedroom, then retreat to the living room. Exhausted, I flop down on the sofa. It's now seven o'clock at night, and we have so much left to do. But after a brief discussion, we decide that all but the essentials can wait until morning. One of those essentials, Sam declares, is a celebratory bottle of wine, which he grabs from the welcome hamper.

We spend the next couple of hours sipping prosecco and basking in the beautiful silence and understated opulence of our new swanky digs. At nine thirty, I declare that I'm done, and we make our way to the bedroom. He comes up behind me, slips an arm around my waist, cups my breast, and nuzzles my neck. But the gesture is halfhearted. I can tell that he's dead on his feet.

"Maybe we christen the place tomorrow night?" I suggest, twisting around and giving him a quick kiss.

Uncharacteristically, Sam looks relieved. "Tomorrow night."

With that settled, we undress, make up the bed, and climb between the sheets. The mattress is even more comfortable than I expected. We've barely turned out the lights before I'm fast asleep. As I drift off, a warm and fuzzy thought rolls through my head. That *this is it.* We're finally where we should be, and from now on, our lives are going to be different.

We spend most of Sunday settling in and putting stuff away. My parents insist on helping, and I don't argue, because we have so much to do. For once, my mother doesn't complain about my living arrangements. In fact, she gushes about the doorman and how we are in *a nice area of town.* She can now rest easy knowing we won't be murdered in our sleep, she informs us a little too dramatically.

In the afternoon, Sam and my dad drive back over to my parents' house to get an antique desk that my father is gifting me for my new office, which we're going to set up in the spare bedroom.

While they're gone, Mom and I unpack the last of the linens, then give the main bath a good scrub-down, even though it already looks pristine. After that, we retreat to the living room and have already poured ourselves glasses of well-deserved wine when the men reappear, puffing and panting, and carrying the desk between them.

Fifteen minutes later, after the desk has been installed in its new home, Sam orders pizza. It's ten o'clock by the time my parents leave, and we decide to get an early night. I rinse the glasses and leave them drying next to the sink; then we make our way to the bedroom.

This time, when Sam slips his arms around me, I can tell that he's up for it. He undresses me slowly, savoring every moment. First, my top. I raise my arms, and he slides it over my head and frees it. My jeans are next. I discard them and stand before him in nothing but a lacy white bra and panties. When he reaches for me again, I step back, running a finger up and under my bra strap.

Sam's breath quickens.

I smile. "Not yet. Your turn."

He doesn't need to be told twice. His clothes come off so quick it makes my head spin. There is no teasing. No seduction. *Frantic* would be a better word. One moment he's dressed; the next, he isn't. He stands there, arms at his sides, without an ounce of self-consciousness. I take in his body, his obvious desire, and a faint heat touches my cheeks. Sam has always kept himself in shape. He has a flat stomach, muscular arms, and solid legs, despite spending most of his day behind a desk. I lift my gaze. We make eye contact. I shiver, even though the room isn't cold.

Sam steps toward me.

I retreat again, a subtle tease, until the backs of my legs bump into the bed.

"Jordan." Sam's voice is husky. Low. Desperate.

I've toyed with him enough. My hands go to the clasp of my bra. A quick twist and it comes free. I hold the bra against my chest for a moment longer, then drop my arms and let it fall to the floor.

Sam draws in another quick breath.

My nipples grow hard. The heat spreads from my cheeks, moving lower.

I slip my fingers under the waistband of my panties and slide them down.

The air-conditioning kicks on, sending a shaft of chilly air down from the ceiling vent and raising goose bumps on my naked flesh. Or maybe it isn't the AC.

"Jordan," Sam repeats, his eyes traveling the length of my body.

I step forward, take his hand, pull him toward the bed. We sink down together. He kisses my lips, my neck, goes lower. His mouth circles a nipple. I arch my back and gasp. His fingers brush the side of my breast, roam across my ribs to my belly, meander between my legs.

That's all it takes. I clutch at his hips and pull him down on top of me, let him inside. After that, it's all a magnificent blur.

13

The next morning, I linger in bed for an hour after Sam leaves for work. The previous evening is a pleasant buzz in my head that I don't want to let slip away. We are always good together, but last night was something else. Maybe it was the excitement of our new surroundings, or maybe it's because we're no longer stuck in my childhood bedroom.

But I can't lie in bed all day, so I get dressed, make a cup of coffee, then head into my new office, where I get to work on the project I'm in the middle of for my mother's friend Hillary.

I spend the next three hours scouring the web for the perfect fixtures and fittings. I compile swatches and find a gorgeous ceramic tile for the bathroom walls, and another equally fantastic one for the huge walk-in shower that's so big she could hold a party in it—assuming anyone would want to attend such an event. By the time I come up for air, it's lunchtime and my stomach is growling. The fridge is decidedly bare, so I grab a slice of leftover pizza and eat it at my desk.

That's when I notice it for the first time. The silence.

The Jamaica Plain apartment always had a faint background noise. The rumble of traffic or the beep of horns on the street outside. The occasional wail of sirens.

But not here at the Glendale. Even though we're in the heart of the city, I can barely hear the traffic outside. The AC is nothing but a faint whisper of air. If our neighbors are making a sound, there's no sign of it. The place is gloriously, magnificently quiet. If anything, it's a little *too* quiet, because I'm overcome by a sudden and inexplicable sense of unease. I ask Alexa to play white noise. The steady hum calms my nerves, which I put down to being in the still-unfamiliar apartment on my own for the first time.

I sit back and close my eyes, let out a contented sigh.

That's when I become aware of a sound rising over the hum of white noise. A crying baby. I push my chair away from the desk and stand, go to the window, and gaze out at the street below, expecting to see someone with a baby carriage. But the sidewalk is empty. Yet I can still hear the wailing child, and it's louder now. Maybe the Glendale's walls are not as thick as I originally thought. I wonder if one of our neighbors on this floor has a young child. I hope not. The harsh sound grates against the otherwise tranquil atmosphere. It also stirs within me a faint longing for what I've lost.

I sit back down and stare at my computer, determined to ignore the baby, which isn't easy. Thankfully, after a few minutes, the wailing stops, and I relax.

At least until I hear a thud from somewhere in the apartment beyond my office door, followed by a tinkle of breaking glass.

14

Him

Then

I've been watching you for three weeks, my dark-haired Raven. At first it was strange, focusing my attentions on someone else. I was with Jade for so long that it felt almost like cheating. Sometimes it still does. I have to remind myself that she is good with you taking her place. After all, she brought us together. I'm sure of it. She didn't want me to be lonely, which is why she put you in my path, showed me your tattoo. She knew I would understand what it meant.

Now I'm standing in the shadows opposite where you live, because you will be coming out soon. I've observed you at every opportunity since I trailed you from the coffee shop and onto the train that first day—followed you home to an apartment building that puts my own humble abode to shame.

Since then, I've gotten to know your routines pretty well. Every Tuesday, Thursday, and Friday you work at Cindy's Closet, a vintage clothing store on Newbury Street, from noon to 8:00 p.m. You don't need the job. It's more of a lifestyle thing, I'm sure. Because no one with a pad like yours in such a fancy building could afford to work so few hours in a place like that unless they were doing it for something other than the money. But it's okay. I like that you have a work ethic. It gives you character.

On Saturday evenings you go out for drinks with friends. A young woman with mousy blond hair and a nose too big for her face and a short, tubby one with a bad complexion. Last time you met them, I sat at the far end of the bar and watched the three of you drink martinis and gossip like a bunch of adolescent schoolgirls, tittering and leaning close when you spoke as if you were imparting wicked secrets to each other. Last weekend, you were laughing so hard that at one point I swear tears were running down your face. There was an open table right next to you, and I wanted to know what was so funny. I almost grabbed my drink, got up from my spot at the back of the bar, and took it, but I didn't dare. It was too soon. You might have noticed me, and I wasn't ready for that. Not then.

But now I think it's time we get better acquainted.

I follow when you come out of your building, hurry down the steps, and walk along the sidewalk. I cross the road and pick up the pace, anxious not to lose sight of you, even though I know your destination. You are a few steps ahead of me, oblivious to my presence, even though I've been close to you so many times over the past few weeks. If you were a more mindful person, you might have noticed me. But you live in that blissful world occupied by the innocent. You aren't looking at the faces of those around you, searching for the ones who might do you harm, because nothing awful has ever happened to you, and you don't believe that it ever will. Or maybe you just don't think about it at all. That's the beauty of innocence.

We've been walking for a quarter of an hour, and you're almost at work. I can see the store up ahead. It opens at noon, and you—the conscientious employee—are ten minutes early, as usual. I know what will happen next. You will duck into the alley between buildings and go to the rear door—the one marked Private—unlock it, and go inside. Then, at the stroke of noon, you will open the store. You will be alone, because whoever owns this place doesn't need two employees working at the same time. You're not *that* busy. Which is perfect, because today feels right, and I don't like witnesses. I don't like them one little bit.

15

JORDAN

Now

When I hear the glass breaking, my heart leaps into my throat, even as my thoughts fly back to the day I found the door of our Jamaica Plain apartment busted open. Is it happening all over again? I stand frozen for what feels like an eternity but in reality is no more than thirty seconds. Is someone in our home? The thought of venturing beyond my office, investigating the cause of the noise, fills me with dread. What should I do?

Then I remember: I can call Angelo! He's right downstairs in the lobby, and he has a key to our door. He has keys for *all* the doors in the Glendale. Even better, he can be up here in less than a minute.

I reach for my phone, but it isn't in my pocket. With a growing sense of panic, I glance toward the desk, hoping to see it lying there next to my computer. It isn't. Then I remember. It's still on the nightstand in the bedroom, which means I'll have to walk through the apartment if I want to summon help.

Crap.

I edge toward the door, which stands half open, and peer out into the living room beyond. Everything looks fine. The apartment is silent, the only sound coming from the white noise playing on the Echo. Suddenly, I want the silence, because that white noise might be hiding the movements of an intruder. I move close to the Echo, which is sitting on my desk, and whisper a terse voice command. Thankfully, the white noise shuts off as Alexa issues a cheery *Okay.* I cringe at the response, which is much too loud, even as I turn my attention back to the door.

Deathly silence descends upon the apartment.

I strain to listen, praying that I won't hear a stealthy footfall or a careless exhalation of breath from somewhere beyond the office that will confirm I'm not alone. Thankfully, I detect nothing out of the ordinary. Only a barely audible hum of traffic from the city beyond my window. But it means nothing. An intruder could still be here, lying in wait.

Get a grip, I mentally chide myself. *There's nothing to be afraid of in this apartment.*

It helps . . . a little. Even so, when I step toward the office door, push it wider to get a better view, my stomach is in knots. I ease the door all the way open to make sure no one is standing behind it, then venture out, glancing left and right. Nothing. The living room is empty. I hurry through it toward the bedroom, finding that to be empty, too. Then my gaze shifts to the walk-in closet. If this were a horror movie, a killer would be hiding inside, knife in hand. But it's not a slasher flick, and I can't let myself think like that. I stride over to the closet, fling the door open, and step inside before I can change my mind. I sweep the clothes back on the rail, even though I already know the closet is empty, because I would have seen an intruder's feet the moment I walked in.

After grabbing my phone, I return to the living room and check the kitchen.

At first, I see nothing out of place. No reason for the sound. But then my gaze drops to the upturned wineglasses sitting on the counter next to the sink. Last night, when I rinsed them out after my parents had left, there were four. Now I only see three. The reason soon becomes evident. There is broken glass in the sink. A stem and base. Pieces of tulip-shaped goblet and smaller shards. This was what I heard. A glass falling into the sink and smashing. Did I leave one too close to the edge? If so, why did it fall now, after so many hours? And what about the thud that preceded it?

I stare at the broken glass, trying to make sense of how it got there, but come up empty. The most obvious answer is that one of our neighbors slammed their front door—the thud—which caused a vibration that toppled the glass into the sink.

That must be it.

I slump and release a calming breath. I hadn't realized until now, but I've been clenching my jaw and gripping the phone so tight that my fingers are starting to ache. I put the phone down on the counter, relieved that I won't have to summon the doorman to rescue me. I'm about to reach down, pluck the broken pieces of glass from the sink, and dump them in the trash when another sound makes me jump.

Three sharp knocks on the apartment door.

16

I don't recognize the woman standing on the other side of the door. She's in her mid-thirties, tall and slender, with an exotic foreign beauty that I can't quite place. She has dusty-blue eyes and skin like silk.

"Hello," I say, still a little distracted by the broken wineglass. "Can I help you?"

The woman smiles, and somehow her face becomes even more exotic. "I'm Kalina. Your neighbor from across the hall."

"Oh." Other than the board and Angelo, I haven't met anyone else in the building. "I'm Jordan."

"Jordan. Such a lovely name," Kalina replies in a light accent that sounds vaguely Eastern European.

"Thank you."

"I brought you a housewarming gift." She holds out a plate upon which sits a delicious-looking cake with yellow frosting in a honeycomb pattern. "It's a chocolate honey cake. My grandmother's secret recipe. I make one whenever someone new moves into the building. What better way to welcome a new friend than with cake?"

What better way, indeed. I take the cake and invite Kalina in. After my scare, I'm happy to have someone around, even if it's only for a few minutes. "Can I get you something to drink? Tea, coffee?"

"I'm fine, thank you." Kalina looks around the living room. "This is a lovely apartment. So very well decorated."

"It's a mess right now," I reply, wishing I could take credit for the decor, which I can't, since pretty much everything came with the place.

"Catherine tells me that you're an interior designer."

"Fledgling interior designer," I reply, self-consciously. "I only have a few clients so far, mostly my mother's friends."

"Well, you live in the right building. Between you and me, some of the people around here could use a little help with their decor. Trust me." Kalina waves a hand in the air. "And you shouldn't be so modest. If you're being paid for your services, then you're a professional."

"I guess." I put the cake down on the kitchen counter. "How long have you lived at the Glendale?"

"Oh, about nine years. I moved in not long after they turned the building into a co-op. I love it here, and I'm sure you will, too."

"Honestly, I still can't believe we're actually here. It's like a dream come true. I keep expecting Catherine to knock on our door and tell us that the board made a mistake, and we aren't approved, after all."

Kalina laughs. "She'll do no such thing. You are a part of the Glendale family now, and we aren't letting go of you that easily." She takes a quick breath. "Speaking of which, there's a cocktail party in the library on Wednesday evening. We hold one every few months. There's always so much food and drink and good cheer. You and your husband must come. It will be a great way for you to meet the other residents."

I smile at her phrasing. *Good cheer.* There's something endearing about the way she talks, and the accent only adds to her charm.

"We'd love to come," I say.

"Wonderful."

"And Sam isn't my husband. He's my fiancé."

"My mistake." Kalina makes an apologetic face that quickly fades. "The party starts at seven. No jeans or T-shirts. Strictly formal attire."

"Really?" I suddenly feel like a slouch in my sweatpants and baggy sweatshirt. It doesn't help that Kalina looks like she just stepped off some fashion show runway in Milan or Paris in her black silk charmeuse funnel-neck top and matching pants that hug her hips and flare at the bottom. She already has a good six inches on me, but the outfit, along with her slender form, makes her appear even taller. I wonder if she baked the cake wearing those clothes and how she looks so effortlessly put together on a random Monday morning. "You mean like a little black dress?"

She clearly mistakes my quizzical look for one of panic because the apologetic face is back.

"You *do have* something to wear?" she asks, her gaze drifting toward the open bedroom door and the few boxes of clothes we haven't yet unpacked still sitting on the floor beyond. "Because I'll just die if I've made you feel uncomfortable."

"Of course I have something to wear," I stammer, wondering why the question bothers me so much. Am I so vain that I'm appalled at the thought of this woman thinking I don't own a cocktail dress? "Sam and I will be at the party."

"Wonderful." Kalina's eyes glint. Her gaze settles on a photograph in a silver frame sitting on the fireplace mantel. A picture of me and Sam at the Christmas bash his company threw last December. She walks over and picks it up. "Is this your fiancé?"

"Yes."

"He's very handsome." She studies the photograph. "You're a lucky woman."

"I think so." A faint heat touches my cheeks.

Kalina puts the picture back down and steps away from the fireplace. "I've taken up enough of your time. I'm sure that you have much to do."

"Honestly, I'm glad you came over." I walk her through the foyer to the door. "The apartment is so quiet; I was beginning to think we were the only people in the building."

"It *is* very quiet here, isn't it?" she agrees, stepping into the hallway and turning back to me. "It must be because the walls are so thick. They certainly knew what they were doing back when this place was built."

"It's almost a bit *too* quiet. Except for the baby." I look past her toward the door across the hall that stands open a crack. "Is it yours?"

"Baby? No, I don't have a baby. No one in the building does."

"Are you sure? It was so loud earlier, and when I looked outside, there was nobody on the street below."

"Quite sure." The corners of Kalina's lips lift in a slight smile. "I'll see you on Wednesday, yes?"

"Yes." I watch her cross the hall and disappear back into the apartment opposite. Then I go to the bedroom in search of that little black cocktail dress. The one I haven't worn in ages because I haven't had a reason to. For all I know, it doesn't even fit anymore. The same might be true of Sam's suit jacket. When was the last time he even put it on? His office has a relaxed dress code. He normally wears a pair of slacks and a polo shirt or sweater to work.

I search the closet first. The dress isn't hanging up. I turn my attention to the boxes we haven't unpacked yet and start pawing through them, pulling clothes out and flinging them on the bed. By the time I find it, the room looks like a rummage sale. But it doesn't matter, because the stuff needs to be put away anyway. Now all I have to do is make the dress look as good on me as Kalina's outfit looked on her . . . not that it's a competition. At least that's what I tell myself.

17

I put the dress on, praying it will fit, which it mostly does, although I'm a little disappointed with how it looks on me. The last time I wore this dress was over three years ago, and I'm still holding on to a bit of weight from the pregnancy, and the months of depression after the miscarriage. If we weren't so strapped for cash, I'd buy something more suitable. But that feels irresponsible, since my only rationale for doing so is borne from some unfounded inadequacy brought on by Kalina's own impeccable style. In the end, I decide that no one but me will notice the slightly outdated cut or that it's a little too tight around the hips. And it will look better with jewelry. Not *my* jewelry, of course, which is long gone thanks to whoever broke into our apartment back in Jamaica Plain, but jewelry I borrowed from my mother. Soon, once we have a bit more money, I'll replace the stuff that was stolen. Except for the silver Tiffany bracelet with the angel charm. That will never be replaceable. Thinking about it brings a lump to my throat, and I quickly look for a distraction. I change out of the dress and hang it up, then turn my attention to the rest of the scattered clothes. An hour later, I've put them all away and broken down the boxes. Next, I take care of the smashed glass in the sink and give the kitchen a quick tidying, even though it doesn't need one. Then I haul my ass back to the office and place a much-needed grocery order online, which I'm surprised to see will arrive within the hour.

◆ ◆ ◆

By the time Sam comes home that evening, I'm sitting on the couch reading a book.

"How was your day?" he asks after pulling me into a quick embrace that ends with a lingering kiss. "Not too weird being here all alone in a new place?"

"Not *too* weird," I tell him, even though that's not exactly true, given the incident with the wineglass and the phantom crying baby that apparently doesn't live in this building. I proceed to tell him about our fashionable visitor from across the hall, and the cocktail party on Wednesday evening.

"Huh." He raises an eyebrow, even as his gaze shifts to the cake, which I suspect he would happily eat instead of a real dinner if I allowed it. "A formal cocktail party. How fancy."

"We don't have to go," I say, "if you think it will be too stuffy."

"What? And start off on the wrong foot with the other residents when we haven't even been here for a week yet?"

"If you're sure." It looks like the cocktail dress will be getting an evening out, despite my reservations about how I look in it.

"I'm sure." Sam heads for the kitchen and opens the fridge, grabs a bottle of water. His gaze settles on the groceries I purchased. He almost sounds disappointed when he says, "We have food in the house."

"I figured it was better than starving."

He closes the door and twists the cap off the water. "You really feel like cooking tonight?"

"No." I admit this with a twinge of guilt.

"Good. It's been a long day. Neither do I." He saunters back into the living room. "Angelo told me about this great Chinese restaurant. Figure we could give it a try."

"Sure." Apparently the doorman doesn't just accept deliveries and keep the riffraff out. He's also our own personal Yelp.

Sam calls in an order. When it arrives, we devour the food in front of the TV. Afterward, we dig in to Kalina's chocolate-honey cake, which turns out to be as delicious as it looks. I resist the urge to have another slice—the little black dress isn't forgiving—and look on with envy as Sam helps himself to seconds. Then we snuggle on the couch watching a movie, although I doze off halfway through and don't wake up again until the credits are rolling.

"Come on, sleepyhead," he says, shutting off the TV and pulling me up off the couch. "Let's go to bed."

He leads me through the darkened living room and past the kitchen. As we go, my mind slips briefly back to the bump I heard earlier in the day and the broken wineglass, which is now in the trash. Was it really a slamming door that jogged the glass off the counter? I tell myself that it was—that my unease is nothing but a lingering effect of the unpleasant incident at our old apartment. After all, what other explanation could there be? But even as I undress and climb into bed, I'm not so sure. I try to push the doubt from my mind, because I'll be alone here when Sam is at work, and I can't afford to creep myself out. Yet even as I fall asleep, the thought persists, an unsettling footnote to the happiness I feel at finally having a place that is all our own.

18

The library is humming when we walk in a few minutes after seven on Wednesday evening. Judging by the number of people milling around with drinks in their hands and plates of canapés, it looks like pretty much the entire building has shown up. Soft music permeates the room. The lights are dimmed, bathing the library in a warm yellow glow.

We stand near the door, unsure of ourselves. The other attendees cluster in small, intimate groups, deep in conversation. I find the whole thing intimidating and wonder why I ever agreed to show up. It's not like I'm a wallflower, but I'm hardly the life of the party, either. Situations like this, social events full of strangers I need to schmooze with, practically give me hives.

I pull at my dress, smoothing an imaginary wrinkle.

Sam, who knows me almost as well as I know myself, leans in close. "We can sneak back out if you want. Go upstairs and make our own party."

"We're here now," I say, fighting the urge to take him up on the offer. I glance toward a bar set up on the other side of the room. "Might as well get a drink, at least."

"Fair enough." He snags a small, round pastry from a passing server clad in black pants and a white jacket, pops it into his mouth, and takes my hand. But before we can move, I sense a presence over my shoulder.

I turn to find a couple in their thirties standing by the door.

The woman smiles at me. "You look about as lost as we do."

"It's our first time at one of these things," I say, returning the smile.

"Us too." The woman steps deeper into the room. "My name's Belinda, and this is my husband, Craig."

Craig nods a greeting before his eyes rove the room.

"We've just moved in," I say. "It's so fancy. I keep pinching myself to make sure it's not a dream."

"*Fancy* is one word for it," mutters Craig. "Personally, I find this place a little bit creepy. I wouldn't be surprised if it's haunted."

Belinda nods. "I agree. I mean, look around. It's like something out of a gothic horror novel. If I had to pick one word to describe the Glendale, I'd choose *unsettling*."

"Why do you live here, then?" I ask, surprised.

"Oh, we don't live here," Belinda replies. "I work with Dr. Burgess at Mass General. He invited us. To be honest, I'm not sure why he did. I don't know him very well. But he's head of the department, so . . ."

A strained silence descends, because I'm not quite sure how to respond.

Instead, I let my gaze wander the room. Burgess is talking to Catherine's husband, Ron. They are both sipping drinks from tumblers. When he sees me observing him, he nods, his expression stony, then returns to his conversation.

At that moment a server walks past with a tray of champagne flutes and cuts off my view.

"Ooh. Champagne." Belinda quickly plucks two glasses from the tray and hands one to her husband, then looks at us when we don't do the same. "You might as well. It's free. And hey, it's not like you have to drive, right?" She gives a nervous laugh.

"I think I'd like something stronger," Sam says, eyeing the bar.

"Me too," I say.

The server moves off. Another uncomfortable moment of silence passes between us.

Belinda shuffles her feet, then says, "We should probably go say hello to Dr. Burgess since we're his guests."

"Okay." Deep down, I'm relieved. "It was nice meeting you."

"And you." Belinda takes her husband's hand, and they set off toward the doctor and Ron.

As I watch them walk away, a thought occurs to me. Why would the doctor invite a random coworker to a party that's meant for residents of our building? He's clearly not trying to date her, since Belinda arrived with her husband. It's weird, and I say as much to Sam. He shrugs. "Maybe he's just trying to be a good boss."

"By inviting them to a private party where they won't know anyone?" I reply. "You don't think that's a bit . . . odd?"

"I think you're overanalyzing," Sam says, his tone soft yet dismissive. "Want to get that drink?"

"Sure."

We weave through the throng to the bar, where I order an espresso martini. Sam goes for a Manhattan. I look around for somewhere inconspicuous to stand where we won't be in the way. I spot a vacant corner and nudge Sam, but before we can move, I hear my name being called.

It's Catherine. She strides toward us, drink in hand, with another familiar face a step behind. Kalina.

"Jordan. Samuel. I was hoping you would come." Catherine flashes a beaming smile. "How are you liking our little shindig so far?"

"We've only been here a few minutes," Sam replies. "Just enough time to get a drink."

"Well, I do hope that the two of you will mingle and take full advantage of the opportunity to meet your neighbors and their friends. That's why we throw these little soirees. To foster a sense of family within the building and the wider community."

"I'm sure that we will." Sam sips his drink a little too fast. It's half gone already, even though I haven't even touched mine yet.

Kalina steps forward, extends a hand toward Sam, and introduces herself.

"Ah. The architect of that delicious cake," he says.

"I'm so glad you liked it." She drops her eyes briefly. A demure gesture I find at odds with the confident woman who knocked on our apartment door. Not that her outfit is even close to demure. She's wearing a tight black dress that looks just as much like it came straight from the Paris runway as the outfit she was wearing the first time we met. It hugs her in all the right places and accentuates her figure, with a plunging neckline and a slit at the side almost to her waist. But that isn't what draws my eye. It's her gorgeous earrings and matching necklace. Each of them is made of yellow gold with a dangling stream of the most brilliant rough-hewn green gemstones I've ever seen. There are at least eight stones in each, falling like sparkling miniature waterfalls from her ears and neck.

"Your jewelry is stunning," I say, unable to contain my admiration. "Are the stones emeralds?"

"Thank you." Kalina lifts a hand and touches one of the earrings. "And no, not emeralds. The stones are tsavorite, which is actually a type of garnet despite the green coloration. The set is one of a kind, handmade by a talented artisan from a small village in the Carpathian Mountains."

"Romania," says Sam.

"Correct. It's my birth country, and most of my family still lives there."

"But not you."

"No. I came here to attend college many years ago, just like my brother before me." She looks at Sam. "The photograph on your mantel doesn't do you justice. You're much more handsome in person."

Sam smiles and glances at me, clearly uncomfortable. He clears his throat. "Thanks."

Catherine steps in, steering the conversation back into less delicate territory. "Samuel works for a nonprofit dedicated to saving and restoring historic buildings."

"Really? Then it appears we have something in common." Kalina's eyes are still locked on my fiancé's. "I have more than a passing interest in that subject myself. Tell me, what is it you do at this nonprofit?"

"I'm a lawyer. I stand up to developers when they want to demolish or otherwise destroy our heritage. In Boston alone, hundreds of historic structures have been lost over the years. The Arlington, the Old Howard Theatre, and the Madison Hotel, to name a few. I could go on—"

"But he won't," I say quickly. "This is a party, not a lecture on historic preservation."

"Actually," says Catherine, "I wanted to introduce Kalina to Sam specifically because of his work. She has something of a thorny problem herself when it comes to historic buildings."

"In particular, one historic building," Kalina says. "The Wainwright in Cambridge."

Sam's eyes light up. "I know the Wainwright." He looks at me. "It's been sitting empty for years. We've been keeping our eye on it in case some unscrupulous developer scoops it up and wants to demolish it. Every historic building that we lose strips away more of the city's cultural heritage."

"Which isn't going to happen," Kalina says. "I can assure you of that."

"I wish I had your confidence," Sam says. "But unfortunately, I've seen that exact scenario way too many times."

"In this case, Kalina is speaking from a position of authority," Catherine says. "The only way the Wainwright would suffer such an ignominious fate is if she agreed to sell it to one of those unscrupulous developers."

"Wait. Really?" I can tell that Sam's interest is now at a fever pitch. He has the look he always gets when he's excited. "You own the Wainwright?"

Kalina smiles demurely. "More like my family owns it. They bought the building as a project many years ago for my brother after he graduated college as an architect. They figured that breathing new life into the building would give him a good start in life, along with some practical experience. A place like that, with so much historic charm, would look great on his résumé."

"So what happened?"

Kalina looks away briefly. "Let's just say that it never came to pass. My brother, he . . . he . . ."

Catherine places a soothing hand on Kalina's shoulder. "I'm sorry. I shouldn't have brought this up."

Kalina shakes her head, wipes away a tear. "No. It's okay. It was a long time ago." She looks at us. "My brother passed away."

"That's awful. I'm so sorry." I wonder how he died, but I don't have the nerve to ask.

"Thank you, but like I said, it was a long time ago. We probably should have sold the building back then, but we just couldn't let it go. We still can't, which is why I convinced my parents that we should finally move forward with the project, as a tribute to my brother."

"That's such a wonderful gesture," Sam says.

"It would be," Kalina says. "Except that the city has bogged our plans down in red tape. They won't let us touch the building. To be honest, it's all been very frustrating."

"Maybe Sam can help you with that," Catherine says, looking between the two. "After all, he is a lawyer, and he does work for a nonprofit that saves buildings like yours."

"No." Kalina shakes her head. "That's too much to ask. It's too presumptuous, especially since we don't even know each other."

"Nonsense," Catherine says. "Jordan and Sam are part of the Glendale family now, and at the Glendale, we look after each other." She turns to Sam. "Isn't that right?"

"Sure. I guess," Sam says, his face lighting up. He lives for this stuff. "I'd love to help."

"Really?" Kalina's eyes grow wide.

"Really. I mean, it would have to be on an informal basis outside of work hours. Obviously I couldn't involve the nonprofit, since it isn't an official project, but sure."

"That would be such a relief," Kalina says. "And naturally I would compensate you for your time."

"We can talk about that later." Sam waves a hand. "For now, how about you tell me about this red tape."

I glance toward the bar, contemplating a second drink. I can tell we're going to be here for a while. But before I can follow through, Catherine intervenes.

"Jordan, my dear, perhaps we could discuss a small project of my own while your fiancé is otherwise occupied. I would love to tap your expertise if you're amenable."

"Sure." I remember Kalina telling me that some of the other residents could use some help with their decor. It would be nice to expand my clientele beyond my mother's friends, and a renovation in the Glendale would look great on my website. "What is it you need?"

"I think it would be better if I show you. It won't take very long. I'll have you back to the party in no time, I promise."

"Um, okay." Sam is deep in conversation with Kalina, who's hanging on his every word. He doesn't seem to notice when Catherine places a hand on my shoulder and steers me toward the door. As we exit the library, I glance back in time to see her step closer to him, run a hand through her lustrous dark hair, even as she laughs at something he says. And in that moment, I'm overcome by an irrational thought that leaving Sam alone in her company is a mistake. But Catherine is already whisking me out of the library and toward the lobby, chatting merrily as we go. I'm only half listening, though, because my thoughts are back in that room with Kalina and my fiancé, and whether his professional opinion is *all* that she's interested in.

19

Catherine leads me through the lobby to a corridor that runs behind the mailroom, and we arrive at a nondescript door. She removes a key from her pocket and unlocks it, then ushers me inside.

At first, we're surrounded by darkness, but when Catherine reaches out and flicks a light switch, I see that we're in a long, mostly empty space with dark herringbone floors, yellow plastered walls with white wainscoting, and a coffered ceiling. A counter occupies the wall to my right. A slab of dark oak, nicked and scuffed by the ravages of time. Wide shelves in front of a mirrored backsplash line the wall behind it.

Frosted glass wall sconces illuminate the room at intervals. Tall bay windows flank double doors set into the far wall. Although the glass is covered with paper, I can see the glow of a streetlight beyond. We're at the front of the building, which means that those doors lead directly out onto the street.

"What is this place?" I ask, my thoughts shifting from Kalina and her interest in my fiancé.

"Originally, it was a gymnasium for the tenants of the apartments above," Catherine says. "John Putnam, my great-grandfather, wanted to distinguish the Glendale from tenement buildings in areas like the North End, low-income apartments built in the eighteen hundreds, mostly to house immigrants. As such, he wanted to offer a luxury living experience. That's why the Glendale had a dining room, a library, and a telegraph office so the wealthy residents could conduct their business with ease. And, of course, the gymnasium, which was an unusual feature back then. Apart from the library, most of the other spaces have been converted into either storage or apartments."

"But not this room?" I ask, curious.

"No. The gymnasium didn't last long because it turned out that no one had much interest in using it. Go figure. After that, the road frontage was added, and the space was rented out as retail. It stayed that way until the 1980s, when my parents, who owned the Glendale at the time, decided that having a storefront here was more trouble than it was worth. In the years since, it's mostly been used for storage. There was talk about turning it into another apartment, but that never came to fruition because of its location, narrow footprint, and small square footage."

"And now?" I wonder why Catherine is showing me this room.

"Now we wish to use it again. Letting this room sit idle and unloved is a waste of resources, so the board has given approval to convert the space into a coffee shop and use the profits to supplement the maintenance fees of the building's tenants. What do you think?"

"I think it would make a great coffee shop." I step deeper into the room, run a hand along the counter, which is thick with dust. The wood beneath is smooth and varnished, a lustrous dark oak. When I glance back toward Catherine, I notice a faint line of dusty footprints across the floor. My footprints. Clearly, no one has been in here for a very long time.

Catherine is studying me with folded arms. "Care to elaborate?"

I study the room, take in its untapped potential. The interior designer within me takes over. "This counter is gorgeous. It would make it a great focal point. Clean it up, get some furniture in here to reflect the Glendale's historic charm—antique sofas and comfortable chairs, maybe some old café stools. Hang the walls with vintage metal signage and retro advertising mirrors. You could turn this into a really unique space."

"Or *you* could," Catherine says. "Want to give it a go?"

"Seriously?" Her offer takes me by surprise.

"Yes. It's a perfect arrangement. You live right upstairs, and we'd prefer to work with one of our own." Catherine joins me at the counter, leaving a second set of footprints in the dust covering the floor. "Unless you're too busy with other clients, of course."

"No. I'm not busy . . . I mean . . . I'd love to do it." The words practically tumble from my mouth in my haste to accept her offer. I've never designed a commercial space before, but there's no way I'm turning this down. An actual, real client who didn't find me through my parents.

"Wonderful. There's a board meeting tomorrow afternoon in the library. I know it's short notice, but perhaps you could come along, and we can talk about it. Maybe give us your thoughts on how we should proceed."

"I can do that," I tell her enthusiastically. Tomorrow afternoon is short notice, but it's not like I have much else to do. Hillary is my only other client, and I've gone about as far as I can with that project until she approves my suggestions for the fixtures in her bathroom. And I already have the germ of an idea forming from my first impressions of this room.

"Then it's settled. We'll see you at two p.m. We can discuss your fee then, too."

"Sure," I say, wondering how I'm ever going to figure out what to charge for this job. It's a commercial contract, which will probably have a bigger budget than the projects I've been doing for my mother's friends, but I'll also be working for the same people who approved our application to live at the Glendale, and they might expect a steep discount.

As if reading my thoughts, Catherine says, "We'd like to keep the renovation budget tight. Every dollar spent is a dollar we'll have to make back before we show a profit. But that shouldn't affect your design fee. We wish to create a welcoming, warm space for our patrons. As such, your expertise will be the most important factor in the success of this venture."

No pressure, then, I think to myself.

"And now, we should return to the party. Sam is probably wondering where you've gotten to." Catherine looks down at her empty glass. "And I believe another drink is in my future."

I follow her to the door, glancing back one more time at the empty room, imagining what it would look like with the changes I've suggested. At least, until my gaze settles back on our footprints—proof of how long this room has sat empty and unloved. And then it hits me. If the Glendale's board members are so keen to convert this space into a coffee shop, how come no one has ventured in here before today? Because if they had, there would be more sets of footprints on the dusty floor. I ponder this for a moment, almost ask Catherine about it, but then I realize how ridiculous that would sound. Instead, I turn and hurry to catch up with her, reminding myself that this is a huge opportunity, and not to blow it.

20

When we arrive back at the library, Sam is still talking to Kalina, but they've been joined by another couple in their late sixties or early seventies whom I don't recognize. The man has silver hair and a neatly trimmed beard, and he holds a cane that he grips with one hand and leans on. The woman is slim and attractive, wearing a silky red skirt paired with an elegant sleeveless ivory cashmere sweater that looks better on her than my little black dress does on me. Catherine volunteers to fetch us fresh drinks from the bar, while I weave through the thinning crowd to join them.

But before I get there, Dr. Burgess steps into my path, a cut glass tumbler full of what I assume to be whisky in his hand.

"Jordan."

"Dr. Burgess."

"I hope you don't mind me intruding upon your evening." His eyes roam my body as if he's judging my little black dress, which makes me more than a little self-conscious because the fit really is a bit too tight. The corner of his mouth lifts into a half smile. "I just had to come over and say hello when I spotted you."

"I was hoping to slip back in unnoticed."

"Not much chance of that." Burgess finishes inspecting my attire—at least I hope that's what he was inspecting—and locks eyes with me. The smile takes on the barest hint of a leer. "You're a hard woman to miss with that mane of fiery red hair. It's absolutely captivating, and so unique."

"Thank you." I squirm under his gaze.

"It reminds me of this waterfall in Yosemite. In February, when the sun catches the water just right, it glows like tumbling red lava."

"Uh, thanks," I say again. No one has ever compared my hair to lava before. It feels . . . creepy. I decide to put him in his place, ever so gently. "Whatever would Mrs. Burgess say if she caught you flirting with the neighbors?"

"You don't need to worry about that. There is no Mrs. Burgess. I've had a few loves in my life, but none of them have lasted." The doctor drops his gaze and the smirk fades, as if he realizes that he's overstepped. "Not that I was flirting. At least, not intentionally. If I made you uncomfortable, I apologize."

"You didn't make me uncomfortable," I lie, then glance past him toward Sam, eager to escape. "I should really join my fiancé."

"Of course." Burgess hesitates, then steps aside.

I hurry past him, relieved that the awkward encounter is over, and make my way across the room.

"Hey," Sam says at my approach. "I want you to meet Frank and Jennifer Barnes. They live on the same floor as us."

"We're your neighbors in 4D," Jennifer says with a wide smile.

"You've probably heard our TV," Frank adds. "Jen is getting a little hard of hearing and has a tendency to blast the sound out."

"I can't say that we have," I tell him, even as I remember the crying baby. I bet it was their TV I was hearing.

"Well, if we disturb you, just come over and bang on our door," Frank says. "I keep telling Jen to use the Bluetooth setting on her hearing aids, but she never listens to me, pardon the pun."

"Hush." Jennifer gives her husband a playful tap on the arm. "I'm sure these folks don't care about my hearing aids."

"It's fine. And we'll be sure to let you know if the television disturbs us," I say as Catherine comes back and hands me another drink. Sam's glass is almost empty, and he glances toward the bar. I wonder how many Manhattans he's had while we were gone.

"Frank and Jennifer were just telling me about a great brunch place," he says, turning his attention back to the group.

"We were," Frank says. "Kelly's Kitchen. It's only a couple of blocks from here, and the food is fantastic, especially the lobster eggs Benedict. It's to die for."

Sam downs the rest of his drink. "Sounds great, right? Might be worth trying this weekend."

"We'll see." My mind is still on Catherine's offer, and I'm not ready to make plans for the weekend just yet.

"We try to go at least once a month," Frank says. "You should join us this Sunday."

"Yes." Jennifer nods eagerly. "That's a fantastic idea."

I'm about to say that we'll let them know when Sam chimes in first.

"We'd love to join you." He glances at me. "Wouldn't we, hon?"

I force a smile. "Sure."

"Great." Frank looks pleased. "Shall we say nine a.m. at the restaurant? If you give me your phone number, I'll text you the address."

"Sure." Sam rattles off his phone number.

"Got it." Frank types it into his phone. "This is so exciting."

"My husband loves his brunch," Jennifer says. "And he likes it even better when he has someone new to go with. I think you've made his day."

"We're looking forward to it." Sam turns his attention to Kalina. "You should come, too. I'd love to talk some more about the Wainwright."

"I'd like nothing more, but unfortunately I have a prior engagement on Sunday." Her pale-blue eyes catch Sam's gaze and hold his attention as she speaks. "We could chat another time, though. With your experience, I believe you could help my cause immeasurably."

"It would be my pleasure." Sam shuffles his feet and looks down quickly, breaking eye contact. He drains the last, barely perceptible drop of liquor from his glass, then holds it up. "Time for a refill."

When he turns and heads toward the bar, I excuse myself and follow.

"She's something else, huh?" I say quietly, after he orders another Manhattan.

"Who?"

"Kalina. That dress left nothing to the imagination. And the way she was flirting with you?"

Sam shrugs. "Can't say that I noticed."

"Good answer." I pat his arm.

Sam is silent for a moment and then nods. "You want to mingle?"

"Nah. I've had about as much mingling as I'm good for. How about you finish your drink, and we'll go back up to the apartment instead." I flash a seductive smile. "I can think of better things to do."

Sam doesn't need to be told twice. He tips his glass back, drains it, and puts it down on the bar. "In that case, what are we waiting for? Let's go."

21

When we arrive back at the apartment, I lead Sam straight to the bedroom. There's no small talk. No flirting. We're naked on the bed and in each other's arms practically before the front door has time to close. We don't even bother turning on the light. Our lovemaking is frantic and full of need, at least on my part. It's almost like I'm trying to reclaim my fiancé from Kalina, or maybe I'm trying to prove to myself that I'm just as attractive. That Sam is lucky to have me.

Afterward, while we lie in the darkness, Sam asks, "What did Catherine want tonight at the cocktail party? You were gone for a while."

"She wants to hire me," I reply. "The board are thinking of opening a coffee shop, and they want me to do the interior design."

"Seriously? Jordan, that's fantastic!"

It *is* fantastic, and not just because we could use the money, now that we have the expense of living in the Glendale. "I'm excited to put a client on my résumé who doesn't go to lunch with my mother."

"The first of many." Sam slides across the bed and puts an arm around me. "I'm proud of you."

"Thanks." I rest my head on his shoulder and close my eyes as a weary silence descends upon us. Sam's body presses against mine, warm and firm.

That's how we fall asleep.

◆ ◆ ◆

The next morning, I'm woken early by movement from Sam's side of the bed. It's 6:45 a.m., and he's getting up for work. I watch with half-closed eyes as he pads through the bedroom toward the main bath. A moment later, I hear the shower running. Ten minutes after that, he steps back into the bedroom, his beautiful body still damp, dark skin shimmering in the soft light spilling out from the bathroom. He dresses quickly and then he's gone. I stay in bed for another hour, wrapped in the sheets, before I slide out reluctantly from under the covers and pull on a pair of sweats and an old T-shirt. I've been thinking about the coffee shop project ever since I woke up, and I have some great ideas. I'm eager to put them down on paper.

After making coffee and grabbing a bran muffin from the fridge, I go into the office and settle in front of my laptop. My meeting with Catherine and the board is at 2:00 p.m. It feels like a lot of time but ends up passing in a blur as I work feverishly to get my ideas for the coffee shop out of my head and into a presentation that will wow them. Eventually, I rise and go back into the bedroom to shower and change into something more professional than sweatpants. Then I grab my laptop and head down to the library.

When I walk in, the members of the board are already there. Dr. Burgess observes me with an unblinking stare. I briefly make eye contact, then quickly look away, a blush reddening my cheeks as I remember the awkward conversation in which he compared my hair to lava.

"Right on time," Catherine says, motioning for me to take a seat. "We can't wait to see what you've come up with."

"And I can't wait to show you," I say, overcome by a weird sense of déjà vu. This feels very much like the interview we attended after we applied to live at the Glendale. The same intense stares from the members of the board, which makes me wonder if any of them ever smile. I wish Sam were here now for moral support. Despite Catherine's assurances the previous evening that the board wants to hire me, I can't shake the notion that this is an audition.

"Whenever you're ready," she says, leaning back in her chair and fixing me with a deadpan stare.

The gesture does nothing to ease my raging nerves. Until now, my presentations have been mostly informal events, like chatting about faucets and floor coverings with one or the other of my mother's friends. I wriggle in my seat, then stand up, remembering the advice my father gave me about dominating a room. I force my arms to my sides, resisting the urge to cross them—which he claims is a defensive gesture. Then I launch into my spiel without allowing myself time to think.

My idea is simple. Create a warm and welcoming space where people will feel at home and want to linger. Like a sort of communal living room. I'd dispense with the usual hard chairs and tables and go with more comfortable love seats and plush chairs arranged around low tables. I want to use mismatched yet complementary furniture to invoke a sense of effortlessness, even though the style and placement of each individual piece will be meticulously curated. Every item of furniture should be unique and visually appealing. The same applies to the decor. I'm thinking repurposed objects carefully chosen to provide maximum interest. Best of all, this approach will lend itself to a tight budget. Lastly, I talk about my vision for the fixtures. I suggest mixed metals. Brushed brass and chrome with touches of oil-rubbed bronze. Ideally, I would love to go vintage with fixtures that have some age and patina.

When I'm done, there's a brief silence, and I start to think they hate my ideas and I've blown it, that I'll be right back to designing bathrooms for my mother's friends. But then Catherine finally smiles.

"Wow! Great job. This is exactly what we're looking for," she says. "I love it."

The other board members nod approvingly.

Her husband, Ron, clears his throat. "We would like to open the doors before summer next year. Do you think that's doable?"

That feels like a long time away, since it's only September. I tell him that it's doable.

"Wonderful." Ron smiles. "Now all we need to do is talk about your compensation."

"Did you give it any thought?" Catherine asks.

I have . . . sort of. My dad would push for an hourly rate, but I don't feel comfortable with that because it lends itself to overbilling, especially since there will be no quantifiable way for the board to figure out how many hours it will take to complete the project. A flat rate feels fairer. That way, I'll be motivated to get the job done without delay. The only problem is, I have no idea what that rate should be. It's not like I have much experience beyond my mother's social circle, and the internet wasn't much help, since every new piece of advice contradicted the last. It made me realize that in my zeal to become an interior designer, I've focused more on the fun side—like picking paint colors and fabrics—than the structure of my business. I should know what I'm worth, but I don't.

I take a deep breath, hoping I'm not going to price myself too high "I was thinking four thousand dollars?"

There's another uncomfortable silence. The members of the board exchange glances. Crap. I really *have* blown it. I'm about to speak up, tell them that it's negotiable, that I'll do the job for less, when Ron speaks again.

"That simply isn't acceptable." He leans forward, elbows resting on his knees, hands pressed together with interwoven fingers. "I'm afraid that your fee is way off."

"Oh." My heart falls.

"My husband is right," Catherine says. "You're undervaluing your services. We have fifteen thousand in the budget for consultation and design fees. I believe that to be a more equitable figure."

I stare at them in mute disbelief. Fifteen grand? That's a lot of money for a job that probably won't take more than a month.

When I don't reply, Catherine speaks up again. "I trust that amount will be acceptable?"

"Yes," I say before anyone can change their minds. "It's more than acceptable."

Catherine looks pleased. We spend the next hour discussing the project, including the total budget, which turns out to be a hundred thousand. That doesn't seem like a large amount for opening a coffee shop. I've done some research since she showed me the space, and apparently there's a lot of equipment to purchase, like espresso machines and coffee grinders and a water filtration system. Then there are the mugs, plates, silverware, and all the other sundry items that will quickly add up. Not to mention the cost of materials for the build-out. But thankfully, those things aren't my concern. All I need to worry about is making the space inviting. Finding the furnishings and decor. I have no idea where to get those items, especially since my design brief calls for using vintage pieces wherever possible. But Catherine is way ahead of me.

"I wonder if I could borrow you for just a little while longer," she says when the meeting ends. "There's something you need to see."

22

Whatever could Catherine need me to see? I've been stressed enough about the coffee shop project and my presentation, and now this? My confusion heightens when she leads me through the lobby to the elevator and presses the button for the basement. Surely she doesn't want a designer to fancy up the laundry room.

When we reach the bottom, Catherine steps out and turns on the lights. There's a laundry room to our left. On the right is a door marked Boiler Room. From within the laundry room, I can hear the thrum of a dryer. In front of me is a corridor with metal storage cages on both sides, many of which contain boxes, furniture, and other items. Some cages are empty, their dusty concrete floors testament to the owners' lack of clutter. One of these is the one that came with our apartment, although for the life of me, I can't remember the cage number.

Catherine leads me past the cages and into the gloomy recesses of the basement until we arrive at the door to a much larger cage that must take up a good chunk of the basement's floor area.

"This is our common storage," she says, pulling a set of keys from her pocket and removing the padlock that holds the door closed. "Everything we don't have room for upstairs goes in here. Cleaning supplies. Items that are too big for the resident cages. Old furniture from the common areas and stuff left behind by previous residents."

So this is where our leather couch would have ended up if we hadn't wanted it. I wonder why people would ever abandon good furniture.

True, we put a bunch of our stuff out on the curb when we moved out of the apartment in Jamaica Plain, but that was different. It was cheap, and mostly secondhand, and was ruined with graffiti. It just wasn't worth trying to rescue. The furniture in this cage, at least what I can see from the doorway, is nothing like that. Some of it even looks antique.

"I love your idea of using eclectic pieces in the coffee shop," Catherine says, holding the door open for me to enter. "It made me think of all the furniture we have in storage. I'm sure you can find some great items here."

"I'm sure." I look around at the jumble of furniture stacked in the cage. Immediately, I see a fantastic couch, as well as a table with metal legs and a distressed wood top. I wonder what other gems lie deeper back in the storage cage. I can't wait to explore.

"Feel free to stay here awhile and take a look around," Catherine says. She hands me the padlock. "Lock up when you're finished."

"You're not staying?"

"No." She glances at her watch. "I have a conference call in ten minutes. But there's no reason you shouldn't rummage through all this stuff and see if anything catches your eye."

"I will." The cage stretches before me like Aladdin's cave, brimming with potential. I step deeper inside, barely noticing when Catherine leaves. To my left and right are shelves brimming with cleaning supplies. Beyond that lies the good stuff. A narrow walkway leads to the back of the cage, flanked on both sides by all sorts of interesting items. My first stop is the couch that I noticed when we walked in. On closer inspection, it won't work for the coffee shop. The seat fabric is torn, and there's a large red stain that I'm sure won't come out. One of the legs is broken, and the couch wobbles precariously when I test it. I'm disappointed, but then I spot a red velvet love seat with polished wood arms.

A rolled-up rug is leaning against it, which I heave out of the way to get a better look. The love seat is old. The polish on the arms has worn away to expose the bare wood beneath, and the velvet's been rubbed smooth by countless bodies sitting on it. The love seat has an old-fashioned look that borders on tacky, but staged the right way, it just might work. I take out my phone and snap a photo, then wander deeper into the basement and photograph several more interesting items.

As I get farther back, the shadows grow deeper, and I end up turning on my phone's flashlight. I can still hear the rhythmic thrum of the dryer in the laundry room at the other end of the basement as a faint soundtrack to my search.

The flashlight beam plays across an old wooden dresser, its cherry-colored varnish flaking off. A tabletop with no legs is propped up against one side of it. I can just make out four dining room chairs, woefully outdated. A floor lamp that's missing its shade. Then my flashlight lands on a figure standing in the darkness watching me.

I whimper and jump back, my butt slamming into another piece of furniture, before I realize that it's not a figure, but rather an old dressmaker's mannequin. It doesn't even have a head or arms. Instead of legs, it has an iron stand.

My racing heart slows, and I almost laugh out loud. Until I turn around to see what I bumped into.

A baby's crib with a mattress still wrapped in plastic. Baby-size sheets, also still wrapped, and a lone plush toy in the shape of a bumblebee sitting at one end . . . and without warning, I'm right back in the worst moment of my life. My hand flies to my mouth. I blink away a tear. Why is this down here, crammed in with all this old furniture? Did some other young mother-to-be lose her baby like I did? Was this waiting in their nursery for a child who would never come?

Don't go there, I tell myself. *There are plenty of reasons why someone would put this down here.* A change of decor. Maybe they received one too many as a gift and couldn't return it. But it's too late. My heart has raced ahead of my mind, and I'm flailing for a lifeline. Something to pull me back from the brink.

Then I get my wish.

A squeal of unoiled hinges followed by a loud metallic clank reverberates through the basement.

I spin around, startled.

"Hello?" I call out. Has Catherine returned? If so, I don't see her anywhere.

But I see something else.

The cage door, which I'd left open, is now firmly closed. I race back through the piles of mismatched furniture to the door and push, but it doesn't budge. I try again, putting my shoulder against the door with all my weight at the same time, figuring it might be jammed, but it still won't move.

That's when I realize . . . I'm trapped in the basement.

23

Him

Then

I don't approach the store right away when you unlock the door and turn the sign in the window to OPEN. It would be too weird. Who goes into a place like that the moment it's open for business, like they've been hanging around just waiting for the opportunity? No one. That's who. I linger outside for another fifteen minutes, forcing myself to give it a suitable amount of time, even though I'm beyond eager to finally make your acquaintance. Because the past few weeks, watching from afar, have been unbearable. And I know you would feel the same, if only you were aware of me. But now, my sweet, beautiful Raven, I'm moving our relationship to the next level, and it's going to be perfect. The chemistry is undeniable. We'll be so good for each other. But I'm getting ahead of myself. Let's just take this moment as it comes.

I step off the sidewalk and cross the road. Cindy's Closet is one of those trendy, chic places that uses words like *vintage* and *repurposed* to fool its customers into thinking they're buying something other than old used clothes. That purchasing someone else's shabby castoffs makes them somehow more cool or interesting. It's not the kind of establishment I would frequent if you didn't work there—I find the thought of wearing another person's secondhand garments distinctly unappealing—but I'm willing to be open minded. Because relationships are all about personal growth, and you must think it's fine, and who knows, maybe you'll change my mind.

But not yet. Our meet-cute will have to wait a little longer. Because I'm only halfway to the front door when someone else beats me to it. A painfully undernourished young woman all dressed in black with a complexion so pale I'd think she was a vampire if it wasn't broad daylight. She's carrying a cloth bag over her shoulder that's bulging with clothes, which I'm sure she wants to sell because why else would she be taking clothes *into* the store?

I ease up and try to look casual, like I'm not going where she is, and let the vampire go ahead of me. I linger near the window, far enough away that I won't be noticed, and peer casually inside past the mannequins with their mismatched garments that do nothing to make me want to shop here. I hope you weren't responsible for this dreadful display of window dressing, Raven, but I don't think you are, because you dress yourself with flair and style, and whoever did this clearly has no talent in that department.

And if I need further proof of your good taste, you aren't buying what the vampire is selling. I watch you pull clothes out of the bag and go through them one by one, putting a single garment aside before giving the rest back to her. When she leaves, her bag is still bulging and there's a scowl on her face. I'm proud of you for not wasting your employer's money on threadbare garbage.

Now it's my turn. Butterflies are swarming in my stomach. This is the moment. *Our* moment, and I want it to be perfect.

When I open the door, you glance up. Our eyes meet. A faint smile touches your lips before it's over and I'm moving deeper into the store.

It's nicer inside than I expected, for a place that sells used clothing. Exposed brick walls offset a floor of deep polished oak. The lighting is bright but not harsh. Clothes hang on faux-antique iron racks, sorted by size and style. An old nineties song that I vaguely recognize is playing. I think it's the Cure. They appear to be obsessed with Fridays.

I make my way to the rear of the store and the men's section. I need a reason to be here, after all. I paw through the shirts, and I'm pleasantly surprised. The garments are not dreadful. I spot lots of designer labels, many of them clearly vintage. Now it makes sense why the vampire left with most of the clothes that she came in with. You only take the best pieces. And strangely, I actually find something I like. A gray cotton shirt with small brass buttons and a band collar. I don't recognize the brand, but I'm not exactly a fashionista. My aesthetic is more subtle. I like to blend into the background. I'm not sure this shirt will achieve that, but it will serve its purpose. I have to purchase something so it won't look strange that I came in here, even if I don't intend to ever wear it.

I browse the racks for a few minutes more, just for show, but nothing else catches my eye. Which is good, because one secondhand shirt is enough.

No one else has come in. We are still alone. It's you and me.

I take the shirt and approach the front of the store. You're focused on your phone, which you hold in one hand while tapping at the screen with the other. When I place the shirt on the counter, you look up, pretending that you've only now noticed me.

"Hi." The smile from when I walked in comes back.

"Hello."

"Just the one item?" you ask, as if you're surprised that I'm not buying an entire rack.

"Guess I didn't see anything else I liked." *Except you.*

"Too bad. Maybe next time." When you put the phone down—go to pick up the shirt—your sleeve rides up to offer a glimpse of the tattoo. The one that first caught my attention. You hold my shirt up and study it, then turn your attention back to me. "I like the color. Matches your eyes."

"Thank you." I look down at the counter and the phone. A casual glance. You've been texting. I see mention of drinks tomorrow night. A bar. The New Brew. Today is Friday, so that makes sense. I wonder who you're talking to. There's no way to tell. And even if there was, it's too late. The screen goes black. I lift my eyes again, my gaze roaming your shirt on the way up, hoping there's a name badge. There isn't. I could introduce myself, give you a name—false, of course—in the hope that you will reciprocate, but that is too much.

For now, you are still only Raven.

"I haven't seen you in here before." You ring up the shirt, take it off the hanger, and fold it, then slip the shirt into a brown paper bag.

I shrug. "First time, but hopefully not my last." Yeah, right. I'm not coming back in here again. Apart from the obvious—that I don't like to be seen in the same place too often—I'm still not sold on the concept of overpaying for used clothes just because they are nicely presented. I change the subject, nodding toward a sewing machine in a nook to the right of the counter. "You do alterations here, too?"

You look around at the sewing machine, then back to me. "Kind of, but not for customers. Sometimes the stuff we get in here needs repair, and I also upcycle some of our less interesting clothes. Kind of create my own Frankenstein fashions from them." She nods toward a garment hanging on a hook near the sewing machine. A multicolored shirt made from a patchwork of fabrics. "That used to be three different tops. I cut them up and put them back together as one piece."

"You're very talented," I say, and I mean it, because the top is actually pretty cool.

"Thanks." A faint blush touches your cheeks. "This is hardly what I had in mind after four years of college and a degree in fashion design. But hey, everyone has to start somewhere."

They do, indeed. I smile. "I see big things in your future."

"That's nice of you to say." Your blush deepens even as you push the bag containing my shirt across the counter. "That'll be $39.50."

"A bargain." I pull a wad of cash from my pocket, because I never put stuff like this on a credit card, and peel off four tens, which I hand over, then tell you to put the change in a charity box sitting on the counter.

I pick up the bag and go to leave, making for the exit.

"Hope to see you again sometime," you call after me.

I push the door open, then look back at you before I step outside. "You can count on it."

24

Jordan

Now

The padlock Catherine gave me—the one she removed when she let me in here—is heavy in my pocket, proof that the door should open easily. Yet it won't, no matter how many times I try.

I rattle the door, then tug on it, praying that I've been doing something wrong. When it still doesn't open, I pound on the cage with balled-up fists.

"Hello?" I call out, praying that somebody will hear me. The dryer is still running in the laundry room at the other end of the basement. Maybe someone is down here. "I'm stuck. Is anybody there?"

I don't get an answer, and no one comes running.

This is bad.

I squint past the cage wall toward the other end of the basement and the elevator but see no movement. I appear to be alone. How did the door even close like that, let alone jam? It doesn't make sense because I still have the padlock.

I call out again, even as the futility of doing so dawns upon me, because if anyone had heard my cries, they would have responded the first time. Despite this, my heart sinks when I get no response.

Then I remember my phone. I'm still clutching it in one hand, the flashlight beam playing on the floor. I turn the flashlight off and decide to call Angelo, the doorman, who will come down and free me. Except that he won't, because when I look at the screen, there isn't any service.

Hardly surprising, given my location.

A wave of claustrophobia threatens to topple me into full-blown hysteria, but somehow I maintain my composure. I fight back against the unreasoning fear. Losing it down here won't help anything. If I can't open the door, I'll need to find another way out. Maybe I can climb up and over the cage walls. But when I look up, I'm dismayed to see a ceiling of wire mesh that effectively cuts off that escape route.

The cage presses around me, feeling suddenly smaller than it did before.

I wonder how often people visit this end of the basement, even as a disturbing thought rattles through my mind. An image of Catherine or one of the other residents coming down here, days or even weeks from now, and finding my lifeless corpse, fingers raw and bloodied and nails ripped off from my final desperate attempts to claw my way out. How long can a person survive, stuck in a place like this, anyway? I have no idea, and I don't want to find out.

Stop it. You're being ridiculous, I chastise myself, because it's true. I'm not going to be down here anywhere near long enough for that to happen. At worst, Sam will come home and wonder where I am. When I don't show up, he will ask Catherine when she last saw me, because he knows that I had a meeting with the board today about the coffee shop. Then they will come down here and rescue me.

Except that I don't want to be stuck in here for several more hours. After rattling the door one more time, I turn and make my way deeper into the cage again. Maybe there's another way out, or even a service elevator. But after a thorough search, I come up empty. The cage is firmly attached to the back wall, and I can find no other doors or elevators.

I glance over my shoulder at the never-used crib, and the hair prickles on my arms, because I'm sure that the stuffed bumblebee was sitting on the left side, near the still-wrapped blankets, but now it's all the way at the other end.

No. That must be wrong. My mind is playing tricks on me. Toys don't move on their own. And obsessing over that crib and what it represents won't make the situation any better. Thinking about the baby I lost, tumbling into that particular pit of despair, is the last thing I need right now.

I tear my gaze away from the crib and rattle the door one more time in the vain hope that it will open now. It doesn't. I'm trapped. All I can do is wait for Catherine to return, or another resident to collect their laundry.

I turn and walk over to the velvet love seat that interested me earlier and sit down.

I close my eyes and lean back, trying to distract myself from thinking about the crib, and that toy. The faint rumble of the dryer in the laundry room is comforting. It reminds me that eventually, someone will come. I listen for a while, until the dryer finishes its cycle and a deathly silence descends, broken only by the occasional knock of a water pipe somewhere off in the darkness. Then I hear something else. A loud clunk that drowns out the knocking pipe. A sound that I recognize.

The elevator.

I jump back up and race back to the cage door in time to see Jennifer, the neighbor we met in the library at Catherine's cocktail party, step out carrying a laundry basket.

"Hey! I need help back here," I holler at the top of my voice. "I'm trapped. The door won't open."

To my utter dismay, she doesn't stop or turn to look in my direction. Instead, she vanishes into the laundry room.

That's when I remember that Jennifer is hard of hearing.

The panic surges back. I ball my hands into fists and slam them against the cage door, screaming at the top of my lungs. Again, my cries go unheeded, and soon the sound of a washing machine reverberates through the basement. Then, after a couple of minutes, Jennifer reemerges.

I redouble my efforts, yelling and pounding on the cage. But it's useless. She walks back to the elevator. Then, to my horror, she snaps off the lights, plunging me into pitch-black oblivion.

25

I'm overcome by a blind, stifling panic. The only illumination comes from the green glow of an emergency exit sign mounted somewhere near the laundry room door. My end of the basement and the cage that I'm currently trapped in is so dark that I can't even see my own hands.

I turn my phone's flashlight back on, which provides a small measure of relief. But it won't last for long, because the battery is below 10 percent. Shit.

I retreat to the velvet love seat and sit down. Common sense dictates that I should turn the phone's flashlight off to preserve what little juice it has left, but I can't bring myself to do it. Being stuck in the basement is bad enough without having to do so in almost total darkness. And I still cling to the hope that someone will find me before the worst happens. There's still that load in the dryer, and Jennifer will return for her washing at some point. But the longer I wait, watching the minutes tick by on the screen like a death row inmate counting down to the inevitable, the less sure I become. Then, with brutal indifference to my plight, the screen goes black, and the flashlight snaps off.

The darkness rushes in around me as if it's been waiting for the opportunity.

I've never been particularly fond of basements, even at the best of times, and now, trapped down here with no clue when I might be released, I feel my imagination churning like a runaway freight train barreling along out of control. I can't help thinking about that crib behind me in the dark. A crib that I'm increasingly certain was purchased for a baby just like mine, one who never got a chance at life. And in that moment, my mind makes a strange connection to the house my parents owned when I was a kid. Not the one they have now, which they purchased when I was twelve, but the old 1790 house they lived in when I was born. It had a cramped, dirt floor cellar that was infested with spiders, and I loathed it. I would do anything to avoid going down there. But the spiders weren't the source of my discomfort. It was the small gravestone standing in a dark corner—the final resting place of a four-year-old boy named Archie Hazen who died in the early 1800s. I can still remember the inscription on his gravestone: *Too sweet for this earth, God took him to be with him.* Why his parents chose to bury their son under the house instead of in a graveyard is anyone's guess, but it was unfortunate, because my bedroom was on the ground floor, directly above the gravestone. I would imagine that child lying down there, probably a victim of tuberculosis, smallpox, or some other terrible disease that practically nobody dies from anymore. I was terrified that he would come back, crawl out of his grave and up the cellar steps, then come looking for vengeance because I was alive, and he was dead.

I know this situation is different. There are no graves down here, and I'm not a kid anymore, but that doesn't help. Because I've made a connection between Archie Hazen and the loss of my own child. In this darkness that I can't escape, my mind betrays me.

Which is why, when I first hear the shuffling—a noise that sounds to my stressed mind just like that of an infant crawling along on all fours—I dismiss it as a trick of the darkness. Sensory deprivation has been known to cause hallucinations, both auditory and visual, and in my suddenly fragile state, who knows what my terrified mind might conjure up.

But soon, I can't ignore the obvious. There really is something moving in the dark basement. At first, I try to reason it away. Dismiss the noises as the furnace kicking on in the boiler room or the sound of someone moving about on the floor above and filtering down though the elevator shaft. But the sound isn't coming from that direction. It's behind me, and it's getting closer.

I shrink back on the love seat.

The hairs on the back of my arms stand on end.

I resist the urge to scream—I don't want to reveal my location to whatever is there. I strain to see, my eyes darting around uselessly in the darkness. If only the phone hadn't died . . . but it did, and now I wish I'd turned it off and saved some of that precious battery power for when I really needed it.

Then a new sound disturbs the still air, somehow worse than the shuffling. A scratching, scraping noise like tiny fingernails on concrete. An image flits through my mind, of Archie Hazen climbing out of the dirt and crawling across the floor toward me . . . pulling himself along with emaciated, bony fingers. I can almost feel his fetid presence. Except that it isn't Archie. Not quite. In my mind's eye I see something far worse. A young child with a face that resembles mine and eyes that look like Sam's. It crawls forward, reaches out, small hands grasping at my ankles.

I scoot backward on the love seat, pull my feet up off the floor, hug my knees to my chest, and pray that I won't hear a small voice utter a breathless word that should never be frightening, but down here in the darkness would be more terrifying than I could bear.

Mommy.

Instead, the basement falls silent.

Whatever was moving in the darkness has stopped.

Silence surrounds me like a cocoon.

Then, out of nowhere, something slams into the cage with a sharp, echoing bang.

Now my wits desert me, and I scream at the top of my lungs.

26

The scream is barely past my lips when the basement lights snap on, extinguishing the darkness. I lift a hand to shield my eyes, squinting against the sudden glare. When they adjust, I see Catherine standing at the other end of the basement. I don't know how she got there—I didn't hear the elevator—but it doesn't matter. I'm saved.

I jump off the love seat and rush to the cage door, shouting to get her attention in case she hasn't seen me.

But Catherine is already hurrying toward the cage.

"Please get me out of here," I beg as she draws close. "I'm locked in."

She grips the handle, and the door swings wide.

I stare at her, dumbfounded. "I swear, it wouldn't open."

"That's impossible. I gave you the padlock." Catherine observes me with narrowed eyes. "You must have been doing something wrong. And why were you sitting there in the dark like that?"

"Jennifer came down to do laundry. She didn't see me, and switched the lights off when she left," I tell her, hurrying out of the cage and turning to look at the offending door. "Maybe the latch jammed or something."

"I don't see how." Catherine closes the door, then opens it again. "See. Works fine."

I want to tell her that I'm not stupid. That the door really wouldn't open, but the look on her face tells me it's pointless. There's one thing that I can't ignore. The shuffling, scratching sounds. Now that the lights are back on and I'm safe, the idea of some phantom child crawling toward me feels absurd. Yet I heard *something*. It was real. And now that I think about it, there is one obvious culprit. "Have you ever had rats down here?"

"Rats?" Catherine pulls a face. "I hardly think so. Why?"

"I heard something moving around after the lights went off."

"I assure you we don't have vermin in this building," Catherine replies with conviction before her face softens. "Look, I'm sure it was very stressful when you thought the cage door wouldn't open, but it was probably just your mind playing tricks."

It was nothing of the sort, but I *really* want to get out of this basement. Like, right now. Which is why I nod and force a smile. "Maybe you're right."

"I'm sure that I am." Catherine holds out her hand.

I look at her blankly.

"The padlock? So that I can lock up . . . for real."

The way she phrases her request irritates me, but I hold my tongue, even as I fish the padlock from my pocket and give it to her.

"Thank you, my dear." Catherine secures the door, then leads me back toward the elevator.

Unable to help myself, I cast a quick glance back over my shoulder toward the cage, past the piles of old furniture to the crib, and the bumblebee toy that I was sure had moved from one side to the other. Except now the crib is empty. The toy is gone.

I come to a halt and turn around, walk back toward the cage.

That's when I see the bumblebee. It's sitting on the love seat and staring back at me. The same love seat that I was occupying only moments before.

Catherine follows me, places a hand on my shoulder. "Are you okay, my dear?"

"I'm fine," I reply, even though I'm not. I can't stop staring at that bee.

"Are you sure? You look like you've seen a ghost."

"I don't like basements, that's all," I tell her, because what else can I say? Toys don't move by themselves. So maybe it was a ghost . . . Or perhaps I'm losing my mind.

27

When I get back to the apartment, I head straight for the kitchen and pour myself a large glass of nerve-calming wine. I can't get the image of that bee toy out of my mind. I know what I saw. The toy was in the crib, then it wasn't.

By the time Sam comes home an hour later, I'm still no closer to an explanation for what I saw.

He takes his coat off and drapes it over a chair, then turns to me. His gaze drops to the empty wineglass. "Everything all right?"

"Uh-huh." My answer is not convincing. I try to sound cheery. Normal. "How was your day?"

"You know, busy as usual. Spent all morning in court and then had a meeting with the city's Office of Historic Preservation that dragged on for most of the afternoon." He takes a breath. "I also did some digging into that building Kalina told us about. The Wainwright."

"Oh."

Sam keeps going, oblivious to my mood. "I figure it can't hurt to earn a little goodwill with the neighbors."

And you love coming to the rescue, I think to myself. "Just don't get too carried away, okay?"

Sam grins. "When have I ever done that?"

"Uh . . ." I stare at him. My fiancé's passion for his work is admirable, but I've lost count of how often I've found him hunched over his laptop at midnight, bleary eyed and adding the finishing touches to an injunction, when it could have waited until the next day. If he's moonlighting on this project of Kalina's, he'll throw himself into it with the same gusto that he does at his day job.

"All right. Point taken." Sam pushes his hands into his pockets. "How was your meeting with the Glendale's board?"

"Great. They want to hire me," I say, then tell him everything they said, glad for the distraction.

When I get to the part about my huge fifteen-grand payday, his jaw drops. "That's fantastic."

"I know, right?" I can't help a swell of self-satisfaction. "I only charged Hilary $950."

"Which I told you was a ridiculously low amount for what she wanted. You always underestimate your worth."

I squirm. "That's not true. It's not easy, building a business, and I've only been doing this full time for a year and a half. And you're the one who told me to do it, and—"

"Hey. I wasn't criticizing. You'll get there," Sam says, taking a diplomatic tack as usual. "I know you weren't sure about starting your own business after what happened, but—"

"Okay, I get it." I don't want to think about that, especially after my experience in the basement today. Because after I lost the baby, I could hardly get out of bed, let alone go back to my job. I worked as a buyer for a college back then, procuring everything from desks and chairs to art installations for the public areas. It wasn't my dream job, but I loved working for the college. Then came the miscarriage. An event so unexpected and shocking that it threw me into a fit of despair. I was twenty weeks pregnant, way beyond the usual time frame for such an event. The doctors called it a "second trimester miscarriage." I had no symptoms. They discovered that our baby had no heartbeat during a routine ultrasound, and induced labor. After that came a funeral, which was dreadful in its own right, and weeks of recovery. Finally, the exhaustion and physical pain abated, but the emotional trauma remained.

I retreated into myself. Refused to talk about it, even to the therapist my father found for me. There were pills. Lots of them. They took the edge off my anguish but dulled the senses. Life turned gray and bland. Eventually, I refused to take the meds, tried to pull myself together. But I still couldn't face returning to my old job . . . my old life. That was when Sam said I should work for myself and become the interior designer I'd always wanted to be. Which is what I did, and it worked, giving me a reason to get up in the morning and keeping me occupied so I wouldn't dwell on all that we'd lost. Now, eighteen months later, here I am, and I should be looking to the future. But after what happened in the basement—after my reaction to the crib, and the strange incident with the bumblebee toy—I'm worried that my mind is turning on me again. That the depression is making a comeback.

"All I was going to say is that you're doing great. You haven't had an episode in almost two years, and now your career is taking off. I'm proud of you." Sam goes to the fridge and grabs a can of soda. He pops the tab and turns back to face me. "When does the board want you to start?"

"They never really said. Now, I suppose. Catherine took me down to the basement this afternoon. They have all this old furniture in storage, and . . ." I trail off as the memory of being locked in that cage rushes back.

The look on my face doesn't go unnoticed. "What?"

I shake my head. "It's nothing."

"Come on, Jordan. I know you better than that."

I hesitate to tell him because I know how it will sound, but I don't want to keep it to myself, either. "I got locked down there. I was in a storage cage at the back of the basement when the door closed on me, and it wouldn't open again."

"I thought you said that Catherine took you down there?"

"She did, but then she left, and I was on my own."

"And she locked you in?"

"No." I shake my head. "She gave me the padlock."

"Then how could the cage be locked?" There's a hint of skepticism in Sam's voice.

"I don't know! The door locked on its own. Which I know sounds nuts, but I swear, it happened. Then Jennifer came down to do laundry, and I thought she would let me out, but she left and turned the lights off instead." I shudder at the memory. "It was *so* dark."

"Maybe you panicked, and that's why the door wouldn't open."

"You're not listening. I was trapped in there *before* she came down. I had the padlock, so the door should have opened, but it didn't. I'm not making this up."

"I never said that you were."

"There's something else, too."

"Go on."

"I found a crib down there. It was new. Even the blankets were still wrapped in plastic, like they'd never been used."

"Oh, Jordan." The look on Sam's face says it all. He's worried that I'm having a relapse.

I'm not sure that he's wrong. But I need to get this off my chest. "There was a toy, too. A stuffed bumblebee. And—"

"And what?"

I hesitate to tell him the rest of it, because I realize how it will sound. But I've already started, so I don't have much choice. "The bee moved. It was at one end of the crib; then it was at the other. Then, after Catherine let me out, I looked back, and it was sitting on the opposite side of the love seat I'd been sitting on only a few minutes earlier."

"Toys don't move on their own, Jordan."

"Don't you think I know that?" My tone is so sharp that Sam flinches. I hang my head. "Sorry. It really freaked me out. All I could think of was—"

Now it's Sam who interrupts. "I know what you were thinking." He takes my hand and tugs me toward the door. "Come on."

"Where are we going?" I ask as he leads me toward the front door.

"To figure this out." He steps into the hallway, then makes for the elevator. "There's a logical explanation."

The terror from this afternoon surges back. I don't want to go back to the basement. Ever again. I want to argue, but what can I say that would not sound unhinged? I know that I'll have to go down when it's time to choose the furniture pieces for the coffee shop, but I sure as hell won't do it alone. And if I have to start wearing my dirty clothes inside out and order packs of new underwear online every week, I'll do that rather than go down there to do laundry on my own.

I dig my heels in and stop.

Sam turns back to look at me with concern.

"I can't do this," I say.

"Yes, you can, if only to prove to yourself that stuffed toys don't get up and wander around on their own."

"Please don't make me go back down there."

"Fine." Sam comes to a halt. "We'll call your dad and see what he has to say."

"There's no need for that."

"I disagree. You scared me after we lost the baby. I didn't think you were going to come back. I'm not sure we can survive going through that again."

"Okay. Fine." He has a point. I'm not happy about it, but I force my feet to move, because there's no way I'm going back into therapy, and I'm certainly not going back on the medication.

We take the elevator to the basement. When we reach the cage, Sam inspects the latch and rattles the door, noting how much give there is, even with the padlock in place. He checks the hinges to see if something might have caught and kept the door closed. When he can't find any reason that the door would refuse to open without the padlock on it, he declares that his first impression must have been correct. I simply panicked when the door slammed shut. Then he stares through the wire mesh and asks, “Where’s this bee toy that has you all freaked out?”

I don’t answer him because I can’t. I’m too busy staring at the red velvet love seat. The empty red velvet love seat.

28

I wake up the next morning to a shaft of sunlight that forces its way past the mostly closed bedroom curtains. Sam has left for work already, and I'm alone in bed. The sheets are cool and fresh on my skin. I stretch, relishing the luxury of space, and close my eyes again.

I must doze off, because the next thing I know, it's an hour later and the sunlight has crept even farther across the floor. If I didn't work for myself, I'd be super late for work.

After swinging my legs off the bed, I pull on yoga pants and a T-shirt, then head for the kitchen and my morning infusion of caffeine.

I'm excited to get started on my first commercial project, so I end up on the internet until late in the afternoon doing research. The apartment is so much quieter than our old place in JP that I lose all track of time. Only once do I notice that I'm in a building with other residents, when the faint sound of a crying baby breaks the silence. I stand up and pad through the apartment, then open the front door and poke my head out into the hallway.

And then I realize. The crying has stopped, and there's no TV noise coming from the apartment across the hall. In fact, it's so still and quiet that I wonder if the old adage about hearing a pin drop might actually be true.

Until my phone rings, the sudden jangle making me jump.

It's my mother.

I close the door and answer, my heart still racing.

She launches right in.

"Jordan! I was talking to Judy Abelman earlier today, and I think she could really use your services."

"I'm sorry, who?" I've never heard of Judy Abelman.

"She's a friend of Cynthia Goldstein's. I think they attend synagogue together. Anyway, I had a lunch date with Cynthia, and she brought Judy along. Nice woman but doesn't have very good taste. She was wearing this awful jacket that . . . well, that doesn't matter. I told her you can help her."

I don't know who Cynthia Goldstein is, either. "Mom, have you seen the way I dress most of the time? What makes you think I can give this woman fashion advice?"

"Oh, honey, that's so cute. I'm talking about her bathroom, not fashion. She showed me photographs, and it's really awful. All pink sinks and tacky brass fixtures."

"Oh." That makes more sense.

"She's leaving for Europe tomorrow—lucky thing. She'll be gone for two weeks, but I told her you'll go over there when she gets back and sort it out."

"What? You shouldn't have done that before speaking to me."

"Nonsense. You need the work, and you can't expect her to use that bathroom the way it is."

"Heaven forbid," I reply, not bothering to hide the sarcasm, although I doubt my mother will pick up on it.

She doesn't. "Wonderful. It's settled, then. She lives in Chestnut Hill. I'll text you the details."

"Wait. I never said that—" I stop myself, realizing that it's pointless. "Fine, I'll be there."

"Good." My mother sounds pleased. She likes to feel useful in my life, which I've come to realize over the years is partly out of a genuine desire to help, but also because she has a controlling streak and isn't self-aware enough to recognize it. This has caused us to clash more than once and is one of the reasons I like to assert my independence.

I also find her lack of awareness ironic, considering that my dad is a psychiatrist.

My phone vibrates as the text message comes through. I tell her that I've received it, wrap the conversation up, and get her off the phone.

Afterward, I go back to work on the coffee shop project, turning my attention to a task I've been avoiding all day because I don't want to be reminded of my ordeal the previous afternoon. The photos I took of the furniture in the basement. I AirDrop them to my laptop and go through the images, then sort them by color, shade, and style, to see which pieces of furniture will work best with my overall design concept. After that, I head down to the lobby, where I ask Angelo to let me into the future coffee shop.

I spend the next hour taking measurements with an app on my phone, which I'll use to make a 3D model of the space on my laptop. After that, I can build out the coffee shop in a virtual environment, play with color palettes and add furniture, then output a 3D walk-through—much like they do on the home reno shows—to give the Glendale's board a preview of my concept. I'm so engrossed in my work that I don't realize I'm no longer alone until a voice behind me says, "Hello, Jordan."

Startled, I whirl around, a scream building on my lips, even as I see him standing there, watching me from the doorway.

29

Him

Then

The New Brew is one of those pompous drinking establishments that thinks way too much of itself. Walking in, I spot a row of framed newspaper and magazine articles hanging on the walls near the door that gush about how great the place is, with its innovative chef-curated food selections and artisan cocktails. Not to mention the eponymous brews, which are made in a facility at the back of the building. I can see the silver fermentation tanks in a room separated from the taproom by a wall with a huge glass viewing window.

The place is jammed with a crowd of mostly under-thirties, many of whom I suspect are students. A band is playing on a stage at the far end of the room, doing their best to sound like Nirvana for some unfathomable reason, and failing miserably. Most of the people in this bar weren't even born when Cobain was singing about teen spirit.

I look around. You must be here somewhere because it's almost nine thirty, and you arranged to meet here at nine. But I don't see you, which makes me nervous. I wasn't watching your apartment today because I was working a shift at the hospital, but I wasn't worried, because I knew where you would be this evening. I can't be with you all the time, my beautiful Raven. But now I wonder if you changed your mind after we met at the store yesterday. I hope not, because I planned for us to spend the evening together.

But then I spot you standing at the bar in a tight little knee-length sleeveless red dress that I've never seen you wear before. Is it new to you, maybe something you found at the vintage clothes store, or is it just not part of your regular rotation? I circle around, hoping to get a better look and see who you are with, and at first, I think you must be alone, because I don't see your friends. Not the one with the bad complexion, nor the one with the big nose. I was certain that you'd be out with one or even both of them, because they're the only friends you've hung out with in all the time I've been seeing you. But then, I realize that you *aren't* alone.

You're on a date.

He stands there sipping a hazy IPA and staring like a teenager enraptured by his first crush while you talk a mile a minute, clutching your cocktail glass.

This is unexpected. No wonder you're wearing that dress that shows so much cleavage. I can tell that you're not wearing a bra. I wonder how you met this guy and how you could do this to me.

I want to listen, to hear what you're saying and see how serious this is between the two of you, but I dare not get too close. Not so soon after visiting the store. That would not be smart. You might still recognize me, even though I'm not wearing the shirt, the one with the brass buttons. Not that I would. Imagine if you spotted me here tonight wearing the shirt I bought from you yesterday while you were making plans to meet at this bar? That would unsettle you, Raven, and I'm no creep.

I make my way to the other end of the bar and order a beer—a hefeweizen with the ridiculous name of One Night Stand—not because I like beer all that much, but because I don't want to draw unwanted attention, and being in a brewpub without a drink looks . . . well, weird.

I watch you play with your hair and flirt and laugh. You stand too close and touch his arm once in a while, and you are trying too hard. It makes me think that yes, this is a first date. You don't know him well enough to be yourself yet. I wonder if this is how you would behave if we were on a first date, but I don't think so. The chemistry between us is undeniable, but the two of you . . . I don't see it lasting. In fact, I'm sure it won't last. Which is why I'm so surprised when, a short while later, you finish your drink and start toward the door, with your doe-eyed companion in tow.

Are you ending the date early? Is he walking you to the subway like a gentleman? Or is it something worse? I don't like to think about that last one. I don't want to go there. I slap a ten down on the bar to pay for the drink I've barely touched, slide off my stool, and follow.

You are heading toward the T station, just as I suspected. I'm disappointed to see that he's still at your side. In fact, he has slipped an arm around your waist. When you disappear underground, start down the steps toward the station, I pick up the pace because I can't lose the pair of you.

The platform is mostly empty, so I hang back near a post that blocks your view and wait for you to board the train. When you do, I choose the next car and stand near the door so that when you disembark, I can do the same. We go five stops, and then you get off and change trains, hopping on the Orange Line. I know where you're going because we've been here before. And I'm not wrong. Soon we're in the Back Bay and heading to your apartment, and that man is still with you. I want to believe that he's just seeing you safely home, that when we get there, he's going to give you a peck on the cheek, turn around, and walk back toward the train station. Instead, you let him into the building, and the door closes behind you. I'm left with nothing but my imagination for company. Which is not a good thing, Raven, because my mind is going to dark places, and I'm starting to think this could be a problem.

30

Jordan

Now

It's Dr. Burgess. I should feel relieved, but I don't. Something about the man makes me wary of being alone in a room with him, which is weird, given his profession. He should be a comforting presence, not a frightening one.

"I'm so sorry," he says, stepping out of the doorway and coming closer. "I didn't mean to scare you. I'm not in the habit of making young women scream."

"It's fine," I reply. My heart is still thudding so loud I'm sure he can hear it. "I didn't know you were there, that's all."

Burgess nods. "I was passing through the lobby and saw you in here. Thought I would poke my head in and say hello." He glances around the room. "Getting a feel for the place, huh?"

"Something like that." I push my phone into my pocket but keep a hand on it.

"Hard to believe that sometime in the not-too-distant future, this will be a coffee shop bustling with people, isn't it?" The doctor moves closer still. He observes me with brown eyes that should be soft and gentle but lack warmth, almost as if his friendliness is just for show. "It looks so empty and forlorn right now."

"That's why you hired me," I say, edging past him toward the door. "To make it warm and inviting."

"Indeed."

"Speaking of which, I should really go. I have a lot of work to do." It's an excuse. In reality, I have hardly any work to do, since the coffee shop is pretty much my only open project, and there's only so much I can accomplish until I show the board my ideas and they approve them.

If Burgess senses that I'm trying to escape his company, he doesn't show it. He just smiles and moves aside. "Better not keep you any longer, then."

That's my cue. I bid him farewell and make for the door, glancing back at the last moment. I expect him to be watching me, but he isn't. He's standing facing in the other direction, toward the large window that will soon entice thirsty Bostonians to come inside for a mug of joe, and gazing off into space, clearly lost in thought. I just hope those thoughts are not focused on me.

31

I hurry to the elevator and press the button, then wait anxiously, hoping the doctor won't follow me out into the lobby. He doesn't, and soon the elevator comes.

When I get to the fourth floor, I step out to see that our apartment door is open a crack.

Sam appears in the doorway. Jennifer and Frank are standing behind him in our foyer.

"Hey, hon. I was wondering where you'd gotten to," he says.

I step into the apartment. "I was downstairs measuring for the coffee shop."

"Ooh. We've heard about that," Jennifer says. "Such a good idea. I hope they don't go all modern and stark like those nasty chain coffee shops, with uncomfortable seats and no soft furnishings to dampen the noise."

"I can promise you that isn't going to happen," I tell her, with a note of pride. "I'm in charge of the design."

Sam steps close to me and puts his arm around my shoulders. "Jordan's an awesome interior designer. You should see some of her work. It's fantastic."

"Stop." My cheeks burn. "I've mostly done residential stuff until now. You know, bathrooms and kitchens and things like that. This will be my first real commercial job."

"Well, we can't wait to see what you're going to do," Jennifer says. "You'll have to tell us all about it on Sunday."

I look at her blankly.

"Brunch?" Frank says. "We made plans at the cocktail party."

"Oh. Right. Of course."

"That's why Frank and Jennifer came around," Sam says. "To make sure it hadn't slipped our minds."

It absolutely had slipped my mind, but I fake a smile and look like it hadn't. "We're looking forward to it."

"As are we." Frank pushes his hands into his pockets. "I have to say, we're so happy that you're here. It's not often that we get new blood at the Glendale."

"And right next door to us," Jennifer adds, her eyes sparkling under the recessed lights set into the foyer ceiling. "How lucky is that? I was beginning to think this apartment would sit empty forever."

"How long *has* it been empty?" I ask, confused. "Catherine told us the previous occupants only moved out a couple of months ago."

Jennifer looks flustered. "Oh, well, what I meant to say was—"

"What my wife meant to say was that sometimes the board can be picky about who they allow to move into the Glendale," Frank says quickly. "We were concerned they would take a long time finding new tenants, which would leave the apartment unoccupied for an extended period." He puts an arm around Jennifer. "Isn't that right, my dear?"

"Yes, of course. That's what I meant to say." She drops her gaze briefly toward the floor. "Sometimes I get a mite confused. Perils of old age."

"Did you know the previous occupants well?" I ask her.

Jennifer shakes her head. "Not really. Addison and Mark were—"

"A polite young couple," Frank cuts in, "but they mostly kept to themselves."

"How long did they live here?"

"Oh, I don't know, maybe six months. I guess their situation changed, and they moved back out. I believe it was something to do with a job offer in California, although don't quote me on that. Like I said, we really didn't know them very well."

"Their loss is our gain," Sam says. "You won't be getting rid of *us* so easily."

His comment reminds me of the paperwork we signed, and the rules about selling our shares back to the cooperative. "How were they able to move out so soon? Our contract says that we have to be here for five years before we can resell."

Frank stares at me for a moment. "I wouldn't know anything about that. I'm not a member of the board, but if I had to guess, there were extenuating circumstances, what with them having to move for work and all." He casts a glance toward the front door. "We should probably leave you to your evening. We've taken up enough of your time."

"Nonsense," Sam says. "It's nice to have friendly neighbors."

"It is," I agree. Our neighbors in Jamaica Plain barely spoke to us. We mostly just heard the Culvers next door when they were playing their music too loud or screaming at each other when they got into a fight. The only other neighbor on our floor was Mrs. Johnson, the old woman across the hall. She might as well have been a ghost. We only saw her occasionally, peeking out at us as we passed by on our way to the stairs through her cracked-open front door, which she would quickly shut if we so much as looked her way. "We're so happy to be making friends."

"That goes for us, too," Frank says, steering his wife toward the door. They step out into the hallway, then turn back to face us. "See you on Sunday."

"Nine o'clock sharp," Sam says. "Don't want that brunch line getting too long."

"We absolutely do not." Frank grins and starts toward their apartment.

I cross to the door and watch him go, with Jennifer trailing behind. They reach their apartment, and he disappears inside. But right before she steps across the threshold to follow, Jennifer hesitates and casts a furtive glance back toward me. Our eyes meet, and in that moment I sense something I hadn't noticed before. A coldness, almost as if her friendly demeanor is a mask. A facade that has briefly cracked to let me peek at the emptiness beyond. Then the look is gone and so is she, leaving me staring out into the empty hallway and wondering if it was just my imagination.

32

On Saturday I decide to work on a mood board, which is a standard tool of interior designers. It's basically a piece of foam board with samples of items I want to include in the design attached to it to give the client an idea of the overall style and feel I have in mind for the coffee shop. Ever since the incident in the basement, I've been avoiding thinking about the project, because the thought of having to go back down to that cage and pull furniture has my stomach in knots. But this opportunity is huge for me, so I need to get past whatever weirdness happened down there and focus on what I know I'm good at—comfortable and eclectic design.

Sam isn't home. He's been thinking about the Wainwright Building and was eager to do some more research before he talks to Kalina, so he headed into the office for a few hours. Which is fine with me as I retreat to my office.

I spread materials across the desk. A rainbow tapestry of snippets from magazines, color swatches, fabric samples, and printed photographs of the furniture in the storage cage. Then I pare them down, discarding what I don't like and adding the rest to a large square of white foam board. Each item is carefully chosen to reflect the atmosphere I wish to create. A warm, inviting space that ignites the senses. I push aside the image of that crib and the creepy magically moving stuffed bee as I pin a swatch of deep-crimson velvet next to a picture of the love seat that caught my eye when I was in the basement. I add an image of a brick wall cut out of a furniture catalog for some rustic charm. My fingers hover over a photo of a vintage chandelier, its smoky crystals dancing with amber light. I add a dried flower, an expression of my desire to work natural elements into the design, and attach several coffee beans with glue, not only for the visual, but also for their pleasant aroma.

On Sunday morning we rise, take turns showering, and are out the door for our brunch date with Frank and Jennifer a full ten minutes early. It's a fifteen-minute walk to the restaurant. When we arrive, the line is longer than I expected. It snakes down the block and around the corner. We wait for almost thirty minutes but still don't spot Frank and Jennifer. Then, as we're nearing the front of the line, Sam's phone dings.

After checking the message, he shoots me a sour look. "Frank and Jennifer aren't coming."

I fight a glimmer of disappointment. "Why?"

"Jennifer has a migraine. Looks like we're on our own."

"That's disappointing." I'm about to ask if he still wants to bother when the couple behind us speaks up.

"We couldn't help overhearing," says the woman. "Maybe we could join you and double up on a table. That way, we won't have to wait so long."

"I mean, if you're up for it," says the man. "We don't want to impose."

"Um, sure. I guess," I say, caught off guard by their forward manner.

"I think that's a great idea," says Sam enthusiastically. "Better than eating alone, right?"

"Wonderful." The man rubs his hands together. "I'm Jamie, and this is my wife, Dawn."

The couple are about our age. Dawn is of slight build, pretty, with dark hair drawn back into a ponytail that sits tight against her head. Her husband is tall and broad shouldered.

I introduce myself and Sam, even as the group in front of us is led away to a table. Then it's our turn. We end up at a table near the window, and the server takes our drink order—coffee for me and Sam, and Bloody Marys for Dawn and Jamie.

Dawn and Jamie live in an apartment building across the street from the Glendale, a coincidence that fills me with joy since we don't have many friends who stayed in the area after college, and I was hoping to meet some locals to expand our social circle. Dawn is a freelance writer and works from home, just like me. Jamie is a manager at an insurance company. By the time we've finished eating—all four of us go for the lobster eggs Benedict because it looks delicious—we've agreed to meet up for drinks the following Friday. We leave the restaurant and stroll back toward the Glendale, still deep in conversation. Even though our morning got off to a rocky start, it's turned out great, and despite my earlier annoyance, I'm glad that Frank and Jennifer canceled at the last minute, because if they hadn't, we would never have met Dawn and Jamie, and I just know we're going to be the best of friends.

33

Someone's at the door.

It's a Monday two weeks after we first went out with Dawn and Jamie, and we've met them each Sunday for brunch, and we've also gotten together a few times in the evenings. I've also been hanging out with Dawn on and off while Sam is at work, because I've been at a bit of a loose end. The renovation for my mother's friend Hillary is all but done, and I haven't heard anything else about the coffee shop. The few times I've crossed paths with Catherine, she's been too busy to talk about it, and the board hasn't held another meeting.

Thankfully, my appointment with Judy Abelman is today, and I'm looking forward to picking up another client. Then, just as I'm about to leave, there's that knock at the door. I put my jacket on, then grab my phone from the kitchen island and bag from a hook near the front door before answering.

It's Catherine.

"Jordan, my dear, I do hope I haven't caught you at a bad time," she says, even as she blocks me from leaving the apartment. "I was hoping to have a chat about the coffee shop."

"It is kind of a bad time. I have an appointment across town," I tell her. "Can we talk when I get back?"

"I'd rather talk now, if you have a minute. I'll try not to keep you very long."

"Catherine, I'd love to talk, but I have a meeting with a potential client."

"And what about *our* meeting?"

"I'm sorry, what?" I check the calendar app on my phone because I always enter my commitments and set an alarm so that I won't forget, but there's nothing. The only entry is for the appointment my mother made, and I'm not so busy that I would have double booked. "There must be a mistake. We don't have a meeting. It's not in my phone."

"It's *you* who must be mistaken, my dear. We talked about it last Thursday in the lobby, and you said it would be fine. Maybe it slipped your mind?"

"I don't think so." I did bump into Catherine in the lobby that afternoon while I was getting the mail, but our conversation was brief, because as usual, she was in a hurry. We barely talked, let alone made plans to meet.

"Are you calling me a liar?"

"What? Absolutely not. I just think there's been a misunderstanding." I glance at my phone to check the time. If I don't leave right now, I won't make it across town in time for my appointment. "Look, I've got to go. I'll be back in a couple of hours. Can we talk then?"

Catherine doesn't move out of my way. Instead, she pushes past me into the apartment. "Jordan, this is completely unacceptable. I haven't heard a thing from you in weeks, even though you promised to keep me informed of your progress. I'm not sure what you've been doing with your time, but you could at least tell the truth and admit that you forgot."

I'm not sure what's going on. It's Catherine who hasn't wanted to talk about the project, not me. "I'm happy to discuss the coffee shop anytime you want."

"Except for right now." Catherine shakes her head. "I went out on a limb to convince the board that we should hire you. They weren't totally convinced, given your lack of experience. You haven't ever designed a commercial space before. From what I understand, you've been doing odd jobs for your mother's friends, which is hardly the same. But I like to keep things in the Glendale family, which is why I fought so hard for you. I do hope that wasn't a mistake."

I stare at her, open mouthed. What the hell? "No. It wasn't a . . . I can do this . . . You didn't make a mistake," I stammer.

"Are you sure about that? Because you seem more concerned with racing out of here than honoring the commitment you made to your client. A well-paying client, I might add. And for what? The opportunity to chat about paint colors with yet another one of your mother's friends?"

"That isn't what I'm doing."

"Isn't it? Oh, Jordan, don't you see? Those people aren't hiring you because they want to. You didn't earn their business or wow them with your talent. They're only doing it as a favor to your mother, probably because they can't figure out how to say no."

"I don't think—" A lump rises in my throat, choking off my reply. This is a mean, vindictive side of Catherine that I haven't seen before.

"Look, I'm not saying this to upset you, my dear. Maybe you're right and those people really do value your talents, but you need to get your priorities straight. We're paying you a lot of money, and we're putting a lot of trust in you. I understand that mistakes happen, but now that you realize your error, a little humility would go a long way."

I drop my head, because she's correct. The board of the Glendale *is* paying me a lot of money, even if I haven't seen one red cent of it yet and don't know when I will. It would be foolish to risk my first commercial client—who also happens to be my landlord, in a roundabout way—just to go see a woman who probably *is* doing a favor for my mother. And that's what hurts the most, because Catherine has hit a nerve. It's not like I haven't had the same thought. I slip the bag off my shoulder, then hang it back on the coatrack next to the door before removing my jacket. "You're right, Catherine. I'm so sorry."

"That's better. Now if you don't mind, I would like to discuss the coffee shop. Make sure we're both on the same page."

"Sure." I don't want to leave Judy Abelman waiting for me. "Would you mind if I make a quick call?"

"If you must." There is a tone of weary frustration in Catherine's voice, as if even making a two-minute phone call is somehow a sign of my lax priorities.

I retreat to my office and make the call, rescheduling for the following week. Judy isn't in a hurry, despite how my mother made it sound, so she's happy to put it off.

When I step back out of the office, Catherine is waiting with folded arms. "All set?"

I nod. "Yes."

"Good. Then perhaps we can get back to more important business." She reaches into her pocket and takes out a folded wad of papers. "I have a contract for you to sign."

"There's a contract?"

"Of course there's a contract. This is exactly what I was talking about, my dear. But if you'd rather continue taking scraps from your mother's friends because they feel sorry for you, we can find someone else who will appreciate this opportunity."

"No. Don't do that." I had thought our agreement was more casual, especially after all that talk of the *Glendale family* and keeping it in-house. Apparently I was wrong. But I know enough not to sign something I haven't read. "Would you mind if Sam looks it over?"

She hands me the contract. "Be my guest. But don't take too long, or we might be forced to look elsewhere." She fixes me with a hard stare. "And that would make things very awkward, given your residency at the Glendale. Very awkward indeed."

34

Catherine's thinly veiled threat does not escape my attention. I want to protest further, since none of this is my fault. But I suspect that it wouldn't be a good idea. And my instinct is right, because the mean-spirited woman who appeared at my door quickly evaporates, to be replaced by the Catherine of my previous encounters. I expect her to ask about my progress on the coffee shop design, but instead she takes up the next two hours of my time, chatting about all manner of things that have nothing to do with it, despite my best efforts to steer the conversation back to work. She tells me about the history of the building, and how her family built a Boston real estate empire before selling most of it off during the Great Depression. When she rises to leave and we haven't even touched on the coffee shop, I ask if she'd like to see the mood board I've put together, but she declines, saying it would be better if we waited until the next executive board meeting so I could present my ideas to everyone. When that meeting will be, she doesn't say.

After she leaves, I sit on the couch, lost in thought and wondering what the hell just happened.

Is Catherine right? Did Judy only agree to meet with me because she didn't know how to turn my mother down without upsetting her? I've never suffered from a lack of confidence before, but Catherine's words have gotten under my skin. I briefly consider calling Judy back and canceling altogether, telling her that I'm too busy, but then

I would just hear about it from my mother, who would surely find out, so I don't. I turn the TV on instead and find a documentary on Amazon Prime. Not one of those endless shows about people remodeling their home, which I would usually choose—that feels a bit too ironic—but the other staple of reality television. Violent crime. Specifically, a program about a pretty young grad student who went missing eight years ago and hasn't been seen since. It's dark and disturbing. It fits my mood, even if I'm barely paying attention.

At six o'clock, I'm still sitting there, watching as yet another young woman goes missing on the idiot box, and expecting my fiancé to walk in at any moment. Two hours later, it's Sam who is missing. He always calls or texts to let me know if he's held up at work, and he's done neither.

At one point, I think that I hear his voice out in the hallway. I expect him to come walking in at any moment. When he doesn't appear, I go to the door and look out, but the hallway is empty. I return to the couch and wait. When he still hasn't come home forty-five minutes later, my concern boils over. Grabbing my phone, I tap out a worried text.

Where are you?

He doesn't reply right away. I stare at the screen, waiting for a response. Then, just as I'm about to call him, he replies.

Sorry. Ran into Kalina in the elevator.
Talking about the Wainwright Building. Be right over.

Several more minutes pass. I resist the urge to text him again. *Nagging girlfriend* isn't a good look. But after another quarter of an hour, he's still absent. I go to the front door and press my eye against the peephole.

Kalina's apartment is directly across from ours. The hallway is empty, and her door is closed. But then it opens, and Sam appears with Kalina right behind him. He steps out and turns to her. She leans in, slips her arms around him, and they hug, her cheek pressing briefly against his. When she pulls away, the barest hint of a smile touches her lips. She says something that I can't make out, delivered with a look that borders on sultry. Then she vanishes back inside her apartment and closes the door. My stomach clenches.

Sam turns toward our apartment.

I don't want to get caught spying, so I scurry back into the living room and plunk myself onto the sofa, just as Sam opens the door.

His voice drifts from the foyer. "Hey, honey, I'm home."

I don't reply, because I'm not sure that I trust myself to answer. What have I just witnessed? Sam's been looking into the Wainwright for a couple of weeks now, spending hours on the computer after he comes home, because he can't do it at work. He's also been spending time with Kalina. They've even met for lunch a couple of times. Which is fine. At least it was when I thought they were just talking about some moldy old building. Now I'm not so sure.

"Sorry I'm late. I should have called. But Kalina was in the elevator, and I wanted to share what I've found out about the Wainwright." He's still talking when he walks into the living room. "We were still chatting when we got up here, and she invited me in. I guess I lost track of time. You know what it's like." He stops in his tracks, seeing the look on my face. "Everything okay?"

I nod.

He stares at me for a long moment. "You're being very quiet."

And now I have no choice but to answer. I think happy thoughts and fake a smile. "Just pleased that you're home . . . finally. How's Kalina?"

"She's good." He settles next to me on the sofa and kicks his shoes off. "And so grateful for my help with the Wainwright. I really think we can get through the red tape so she can finally finish that conversion. I've already convinced the city to take another look at rezoning the building as residential, and I'm hoping to hear back about the interior changes at any time. Honestly, it's a lot more work than I imagined, but hey, that's why I got into this line of work. To save our heritage for future generations."

"Doesn't she want to gut the place and turn it into high-priced lofts?" I ask. It seems to me that what Kalina intends for the Wainwright is exactly the opposite. "How is that saving our heritage?"

Sam laughs. "You make it sound like I've gone over to the dark side. It's nothing like that. The building is in appalling condition. It's sat empty for decades. Ripping out the interior and modernizing is the only way to save the facade."

"I suppose." I still don't see why the interior can't be renovated without destroying it. But I don't argue the point. "Just don't disappear into Kalina's apartment too often, okay? Remember, you have a fiancée sitting across the hall waiting for you."

"Point taken," Sam says. "Anyway, I can update her on Friday night if I hear back from the zoning board."

An icy cold envelops me. "What do you mean?"

"I invited Kalina over for dinner."

"You did what?"

"She pointed out that the two of you haven't really hung out together, so I thought it would be nice."

"Oh."

"We can make it a full-fledged dinner party. Ask Dawn and Jamie if they would like to come. Maybe invite some of the other neighbors, too."

"Sure," I say, even as an image of Kalina wrapping her arms around Sam and pressing her cheek against his forces its way into my head.

35

My mood is subdued for the rest of the evening. I don't want to be, but I'm irked at Sam for inviting Kalina to dinner on Friday without discussing it with me first. We've been together long enough that I'm sure he senses my displeasure, but he lets it be, which is probably wise.

In bed that night, I lie awake and analyze my feelings, even as Sam sleeps with his back to me and snores. I like to think that I'm self-aware enough not to let unfounded fears get the better of me. But when it comes to Kalina, I'm not so sure. I keep seeing that hug in my mind's eye. The way she leaned in and pressed her cheek against his. The faintly seductive smile that played on her lips as she bade him farewell. It haunts me when I close my eyes, and when I finally fall asleep, Kalina follows me there, too.

Over the next few days, I do my best to purge the suspicious thoughts from my mind. I trust Sam, and Kalina is our neighbor. Would she really be so brazen as to make a play for him when her apartment is less than twenty feet from ours? And even if she did, Sam would never reciprocate. He loves me, and I'm secure in that.

On Wednesday evening I show Sam the contract. He looks it over and tells me that it's fine. In fact, he's relieved that our agreement is now in writing, including when I'll get paid—a quarter of my fee after I sign, then a further 25 percent once the design is approved, and the remainder upon completion. He also sounds happy that we'll be seeing some of the money right away, because we're hardly flush with cash.

Buying into the Glendale was a strain on our finances. It took every penny we'd saved, leaving us with no financial safety net.

On Friday morning, I go shopping. What started as a small and informal dinner has since turned into a full-blown formal affair. On Thursday evening Sam ran into Frank and Dr. Burgess at the mailboxes in the lobby and extended an invitation to them, which they happily accepted. The thought of spending a whole evening with the doctor, and in my own apartment at that, fills me with dread. The man gives me the creeps. But that's not Sam's fault. He has no idea how I feel about Burgess. Maybe if I'd told him, I wouldn't be in this situation. But it's too late. I now have six people coming for dinner, including the odious Dr. Burgess, and nowhere near enough food or drinks in the house.

To make matters worse, this is the first real dinner party we've ever thrown. None of our previous apartments were suitable for such events. Not that it mattered. The few people we counted as friends were more comfortable meeting in a bar than sitting around a candlelit table sipping a fine Bordeaux. *No pressure there, then,* I think to myself, *hosting a bunch of neighbors who are also practically strangers.*

I grab my keys and purse and leave the apartment. There's an organic market and deli on Newbury Street that I've been meaning to check out, anyway. In the elevator, I go over the shopping list on my phone. I've spent days fretting about what to serve, especially since Sam informed me that Kalina is vegan. Which is why, after a lengthy conversation with my mother—who wasn't a whole lot of help since her idea of a dinner party is not the same as mine—and a couple of hours of searching online, I settled on a menu that covers every eventuality. A salad of baby greens with pear and a lemon-mint vinaigrette. Two types of pasta—regular fettuccine and zucchini noodles—in a vegan pesto sauce and paired with arugula, roasted cherry tomatoes, and chickpeas. Shaved Parmesan and grilled shrimp, both on the side. I also pick up a couple of crusty French bread loaves. I haven't decided on dessert yet, but I'll find something.

Satisfied, I slip the phone back into my pocket as the elevator reaches the ground floor. When I step out, I'm surprised to find the lobby empty. The doorman, Angelo, is not at his desk, and there's a small plastic sign sitting on the counter: I'M HELPING ANOTHER TENANT, BUT I'LL BE RIGHT BACK.

I'm halfway across the lobby, heading for the exit, when I hear a door close. I glance toward the noise, expecting Angelo. But instead, I see Catherine, who's coming out of the only apartment on the ground floor. She turns toward the elevator, face flushed.

"Catherine, is everything all right?" I ask, starting toward her.

Her eyes dart in my direction, but she doesn't answer. Instead, she picks up the pace and steps into the elevator, walking right past me like I'm not even there.

36

At the store, I gather everything on my shopping list. I also pick up rosemary sea salt crackers, a roasted garlic hummus, vegetarian stuffed grape leaves, and an awesome cheese plate that sets me back a whopping sixty-five bucks. For dessert, I find a vegan apple and ginger galette in the bakery section. I should be enjoying myself, but I'm distracted. My thoughts keep returning to Catherine when she was coming out of that apartment, and how she looked right through me. She was acting so odd.

When I return to the Glendale, Angelo is back. He hurries over to relieve me of the bags. I almost decline his assistance, but then I remind myself that we are not living in Jamaica Plain anymore in some grungy apartment. This is another world, and I need to get used to it. But there's another reason why I'm willing to hand my bags over. It provides me with an opportunity to ask about Catherine and the apartment.

"What do you know about the ground floor apartment?" I ask as Angelo pushes the button to call the elevator.

He gives me a quick sideways glance. "What do you mean?"

"Who lives there?"

"There's no one living there, miss. Hasn't been for a very long time."

"Are you sure?"

"Might I inquire why you're asking?"

"Just curious. I saw Catherine in the lobby earlier. She was leaving the ground floor apartment, and she didn't look like herself."

Angelo says nothing for the longest while, even as the elevator arrives with a jarring clank. He pulls the gate open and motions for me to enter, then follows me inside. It isn't until the elevator starts to ascend that he finally speaks again. "I know that you're new to the building, and unfamiliarity breeds curiosity, but you would be wise not to concern yourself with such matters."

"Oh." The tone of Angelo's voice suggests that I may have inadvertently crossed a line. "I'm not being nosy. Catherine just looked . . . off. I was worried about her."

"I appreciate that, miss. But you have to understand . . . The tenants of the Glendale value their privacy, and that includes Catherine. Even if I knew why she was in that vacant apartment, I would not be at liberty to divulge the information."

Okay. I get that. Discretion is a part of Angelo's job, so no more questions about Catherine. But still . . .

"How come the apartment is empty? There didn't seem to be any shortage of people wanting to live here when Sam and I submitted our application. At least, that's what the board told us at our interview."

"The unit is not in a rentable condition."

Now my thoughts shift to a more opportunistic line of questioning. "Do you think the board might consider renovating it at some point? They've already hired me to do the coffee shop, so . . ."

Angelo shakes his head. "I sincerely doubt that will happen."

"Why?"

"The board have their reasons."

Now I'm beyond curious. I stare at Angelo, desperate to ask him exactly what that means, but the stoic expression on his face tells me he isn't going to divulge any further information, no matter how much I press him. And there's no time anyway, because the elevator has arrived at the fourth floor. Angelo picks up my shopping bags, steps out, and carries them into my apartment. Once he's gone, I unpack the groceries. But I'm distracted, because all I can think about is that empty ground floor apartment. What was Catherine doing in there, why isn't it occupied, and why was Angelo being so evasive?

37

At six o'clock, Sam arrives home and dives straight into helping me prepare the meal for our guests. He lays out the cheese board and the crackers on the kitchen island and puts hummus into a dish. Meanwhile, I prepare the pasta, sauce, and shrimp. We're almost finished when the doorbell rings. Of course, it's Kalina, who greets both Sam and me with a warm hug after she steps into the foyer, although I notice that she lingers a bit longer with her embrace of Sam. She also comes bearing gifts. A bottle of wine. Although I'm far from a connoisseur, the bottle looks expensive. It's from a fancy-sounding French vineyard. One side is also coated in a thin layer of dust, suggesting that it's been laid up for quite some time. Another clue to its pedigree, because she has clearly been letting the bottle age.

Sam takes it from her, then leads Kalina into the living room. She's wearing a green lace and silk wrap dress that shows enough leg and cleavage to make me wonder if she chose it because she thinks it looks sophisticated, or if she's advertising. If it's the latter, then she's achieved her goal, because Sam can't help a quick, furtive look. When he sees me watching, he clears his throat and heads toward the kitchen island, still clutching the bottle, which he proceeds to open, leaving me to make small talk. I notice that she's wearing the same earrings she wore at the cocktail party, the green stones matching the shade of her dress perfectly. She toys with one of them absently as we talk. When there's another knock at the door, I excuse myself and answer. It's Dr. Burgess. He's standing in the hallway with a bottle of whisky clutched in his hand.

"Ah. The Glendale's very own Aphrodite," he says, his eyes lighting up.

"I'm sorry?" The same feeling of unease that's come upon me during our previous encounters now returns. I should have let Sam answer the door.

"Aphrodite? Greek goddess of love, pleasure, and beauty. A famously beguiling redhead, as depicted in Sandro Botticelli's masterful painting *The Birth of Venus*, although of course, he was referencing her Roman counterpart. It's hard not to compare you, given the obvious similarities."

"Thank you," I say, unenthusiastically. I'm familiar with that painting, and the subject is rendered in the nude. Is the doctor merely noting my hair as he claims, or do his thoughts run to more lurid comparisons? Ick. I move aside to let him enter. The quicker this encounter is over, the better.

Instead, he offers me the whisky. "A little housewarming gift to wet our whistles. Eighteen-year double-cask single malt."

I accept the bottle. It looks expensive and I say as much.

Burgess nods. "I picked it up from a quaint little distillery on a trip to the Scottish Highlands several years ago."

"You shouldn't have."

"Nonsense." Now Burgess steps past me into the apartment and heads toward Kalina, raising his hand in greeting.

I breathe a sigh of relief, even though I fear it will be a long night, and nothing like the intimate affair I originally anticipated with just ourselves, Kalina, and Dawn and Jamie. Which reminds me that they're not yet here.

But then, before I have a chance to close the door, they step out of the elevator at the same moment that Frank and Jennifer leave their apartment next door, as if they somehow timed their arrivals. Both couples have brought wine, which I add to our growing stock of libations.

For the next hour, we chat, munch on appetizers, and make light work of the alcohol. I do my best to avoid Burgess, and I'm grateful when he latches on to Dawn and Jamie, with whom he engages in a lively discussion. Sam refrains from focusing all his attention on Kalina and talking about the Wainwright. Instead, he stands with his arm around me and plays the role of host, steering the conversation and keeping everyone engaged with artful aplomb. My heart skips a beat when I glance sideways at him. He catches my eye and winks. He knows that I get nervous in social situations, and he's really stepped up the charm tonight. Finally, I excuse myself and go into the kitchen to heat up the pasta and sauce and grill the shrimp. I'm surprised when Kalina follows and offers her services, which I politely decline. Instead of returning to the living room, she lingers, wineglass in hand.

"I just wanted to say that I appreciate you letting me take up so much of Sam's time," she says. "I know that the two of you have just moved in and must have a million things to do, but he really has been a godsend. Your husband is such a sweetheart."

"Fiancé," I correct her sharply.

"Of course. I forgot that the two of you aren't yet married." A light smile lifts the corner of her mouth. "I wouldn't wait too long to seal the deal. He is adorable. I'd snap him up in a heartbeat given half a chance."

I bet you would, I think to myself. Then another thought rattles through my mind. Maybe that is exactly what she's trying to do with her ridiculously tight green dress, which is struggling to contain her breasts.

"Anyway, I just wanted to let you know how I feel," Kalina says.

She runs a finger slowly around the rim of her wineglass, which makes her appear even more seductive. The way she speaks with that Eastern European lilt doesn't hurt, either. I find myself wondering how I can ever compete with this woman, until I remember that I don't have to. Sam already chose me long before Kalina was on the scene, and he's not going to be swayed by a flash of cleavage and a sultry accent. Even so, I hurry to finish preparing the meal after Kalina makes her way back into the living room.

Fifteen minutes later, we're seated around the dining room table. Frank and Jennifer sit on one side with Kalina, while Dawn, Jamie, and Dr. Burgess take the other. Sam and I sit on opposite ends of the table facing each other. My meal is a hit and garners enthusiastic compliments. The wine flows freely, and the conversation is easy. My reservations about Kalina soon fade, but not my curiosity about the apartment on the ground floor. Which is why I take advantage of a lull in the conversation to mention it.

"What's the deal with the apartment on the ground floor?" I ask in a light, casual tone, directing the question at Dr. Burgess, who sits on the Glendale's board.

"Not sure what you mean," Burgess replies.

"Angelo told me that no one lives there. That it's been empty for ages."

"There was a water leak some time ago. The unit needs a lot of work."

"But it must be worth a fortune. I'm surprised the board would want to let it sit like that."

Jennifer puts her fork down. She glances at Frank. I think she's going to speak, but instead she picks the fork up again and goes back to her meal.

Burgess clears his throat. "It's not ideally situated, being right next to the lobby."

"That's right," Frank says as he spears a forkful of pasta, pops it into his mouth, and chews. "I can't imagine anyone would want to live there, with the other residents coming and going at all hours of day and night."

"Really?" I've lived in plenty of noisy apartment buildings, and real estate is at a premium in Boston. It seems like a petty reason to leave it unoccupied. "There must be more—"

"Jordan, why are you so worried about the ground floor apartment?" Sam asks, shooting me a sideways look. "There must be better things to talk about."

"I agree." Frank looks at Sam. "For example, your work. It must be so rewarding. People are so eager to tear down our historic buildings these days and replace them with ghastly steel and glass monstrosities."

And that's all it takes. Giving Sam an opening to talk about his work is like pouring gasoline on a fire. He happily regales everyone with stories of heartless developers and lost history for the next forty minutes.

Once the main course is finished, I clear away the plates and return to the table with the apple and ginger galette. Afterward, we sit and chat for another hour and sip wine, although thankfully the conversation has moved on from Sam's work to other topics that I find more interesting. At one point, he gets up and slides open the balcony door, and a cool, whispering breeze flows through the apartment. It's a perfect end to the evening. At least until Kalina rises and declares that she needs to use the restroom, because when she walks past Sam, her hand drops to the back of his chair and trails along it, the touch light and seductive. At the same time, her eyes meet mine, and the edges of her mouth curl into a smirk. And in that moment, I realize that I have a problem . . .

38

Him

Then

It's 5:00 a.m. and my feet hurt. My nose is frozen despite the hoodie that's drawn tight around my face. Can't you feel my devotion to you . . . to us? I've been here all night, mere steps from you, Raven. Standing outside your window, thinking about putting my fist through the glass to get to you. I am not a happy man right now. I don't know how much longer I can wait. The urge is starting to overwhelm me.

I hear a noise around the corner, and I move to the edge of the building to see what the disturbance is. There he is—the man you spent the night with—hurrying down the steps away from the building, looking at his watch as he turns in the opposite direction to me. The glass door is slowly closing behind him, and I have a decision to make. Do I slip into the lobby, your apartment, and express my displeasure at your infidelity, or do I take care of this clown for coming between us?

I move toward the door, my desire to see you raging white hot. But I'm not ready to consummate our relationship yet. We've only just begun.

Instead, I pull the hoodie tighter around my face, turn, and tag along behind your overnight visitor. We head down into the subway, which is empty at this time on a Sunday morning. Perfect. I'm not thrilled about what I have to do next, but my devotion to you is steadfast, my darling Raven, so I will fix this situation. For you, for me, for our future.

39

Jordan

Now

The next morning, I meet Dawn. There's a fantastic market every Saturday on the bank of the Charles River with local farmers and bakers selling their produce, and all sorts of arts and crafts. It's a glorious, crisp fall day with cloudless blue skies and a hint of chill in the air. We stop for coffee as we stroll toward the market, then drink it as we walk, our hands clasped around the cups for warmth. She was smarter than me and is wearing a thick wool sweater in addition to her jacket.

"Can I ask you something?" she says at one point. "What do you think about Kalina?"

"I'm not sure that I like her very much," I reply, thinking back to the look she gave me at the dinner party, and the unspoken message she was sending.

"I don't like her, either. The way she was acting around Sam . . . honestly, if a woman like her was showing that sort of interest in Jamie, I'd be a bit worried."

"I trust Sam," I tell her, but there's a sick feeling in my stomach, because if Dawn noticed it, too, then it wasn't my imagination.

"But can you trust *her*? From what she was saying last night, they've been spending an awful lot of time together."

"He's helping her navigate some red tape with a building her family owns. It's just work stuff." Even as I blow it off, I realize how naive I sound.

"On his own, in her apartment, without you there?"

"Okay. It's not good. I'm worried after last night." Admitting my fears makes them feel all the more real.

"You should be. Even if you trust Sam, he's still a man. And Kalina is—"

"Stunning." I almost choke on the word.

"Which is why you need to lay some ground rules. Tell Sam how you feel, before things get out of hand." Dawn stops and grabs my arm. "Trust will only get you so far. Believe me, I know. Been there, done that."

"You mean Jamie—"

"No. Jamie would never. What we have goes beyond trust. I'm just saying, it would be in your best interest to stop this thing between them before it goes somewhere you won't like . . . assuming it hasn't already."

"I told you: Sam wouldn't do that." I pull my arm away.

"Hey, I'm sorry. I didn't mean to upset you, okay? I just don't want you to get hurt, that's all." She looks at me, wide eyed. "Friends?"

"Friends." I force a smile and swallow my indignation. Because after all, she's just voicing what I was already thinking, even if I don't want to acknowledge it.

We wander through the market, going in and out of the tents, and I try to be upbeat, even though all I'm thinking about now is Kalina and Sam and the time he's been spending with her in that apartment across the hall. I want to be angry at Dawn for insinuating that Sam would ever cheat, but I can't, because if I truly believed my own words, then Kalina wouldn't bother me.

When we come across a booth brimming with what looks like vintage clothing, she goes to walk past. But I stop, because there's a gorgeous black sleeveless V-neck dress with a gold beaded neckline on a rack near the entrance. A dress that's just my style. It would look great on me at the next Glendale cocktail party. Much better than my current little black dress, which bulges in all the wrong places. Ordinarily, I'd put on a brave face and walk right past, since Sam and I are hardly flush with cash, but this dress is calling to me. And it might actually be affordable, because a sign affixed to the tent reads: CINDY'S CLOSET. CAREFULLY CURATED VINTAGE AND UPCYCLED ATTIRE.

"What are you doing?" Dawn turns and walks back to me.

"I want to go in here," I tell her, surprised that she's passing it by, because we've been in pretty much every other tent. I point to the dress. "Look at that."

"Seriously?" Dawn doesn't look convinced. "It's used clothing."

"Vintage and upcycled," I retort. "That's not the same thing."

"If you say so."

"Come on." I take her hand and practically drag her over to the tent. "You might find something you like."

"I doubt it." Dawn pulls a face, but she doesn't resist when I lift the dress off the rack.

It's gorgeous and in great condition, given that it's clearly old. There are no rips or frays anywhere. The dress is made from a jacquard-woven black silk and pulls in at the waist with an asymmetrical peplum. I reach out and touch the fabric. The silk is smooth under my fingers. I check the price tag and grimace. A hundred dollars. Pricier than I would ever have imagined and a bit rich, considering our finances. But then I tell myself that I need to look good in front of Catherine and the rest of the board at the next cocktail party. I'm supposed to be a designer, after all. Okay, it's interior design, not clothes, but that doesn't matter. What message am I sending when I wear a threadbare outfit that doesn't fit? And I can expense it to the business. This relieves my guilt. I hold the dress up against myself and turn to Dawn. "What do you think?"

"It's nice," Dawn admits.

"It's perfect." I glance around and spot a makeshift dressing room—really just a curtain strung across the back of the tent. "I love it."

"Great, try it on and let's get out of here. There's a jewelry tent across the way that I want to go into."

"Don't worry, they won't run out of earrings," I say to her, then step toward the dressing room.

Out of nowhere, an older woman with long, silver hair appears. "You have good taste. That's one of our more unusual finds. It's vintage. From the 1940s."

"That's incredible." I would never have believed that such an old dress could still look so chic. I can't help thinking of all the parties its previous owners must have attended in it. The balls and dinners it has seen over the years. If this dress could speak, it would have so many stories. "It's in such good condition."

"It wasn't that way when we got it," the woman says. "I have a store on Newbury Street. My assistant repairs stuff like this and upcycles whatever is too far gone to give it a second life. She's a miracle worker. I swear, she resurrects garments that I would have consigned to the rags bin."

"She did a great job on this one," I say as the woman pulls the curtain back for me to step into the makeshift dressing room.

With the curtain closed again, I slip out of my coat, quickly shed my clothes, then climb carefully into the dress.

I step back out and look at myself in a full-length mirror attached to one of the tent poles. The dress looks even better on me than I expected. It falls just past the knee and pulls in at the waist, making me look slimmer than I actually am. Even the bust fits, lifting my breasts and hugging them to reveal a seductive flash of cleavage. In this dress, I could give Kalina a run for her money any day. I turn back around to show Dawn, but she's still lingering near the front of the tent, half hidden behind a rack of clothes that she's pawing through slowly, head bowed.

I call to her. She looks up, then reluctantly saunters toward me.

"What do you think now?" I ask.

Before she can answer, the store owner pipes up. "Dawn? My goodness. I don't believe it. I haven't seen you for ages. Ever since the—"

"It's been a long time," Dawn says quickly. "How have you been, Roxanne?"

"Oh, can't complain." Roxanne steps close and pulls Dawn into a tight hug. "How about you?"

"I'm doing fine." Dawn glances back toward the front of the tent. "Married now."

"Wow. Congratulations."

"Thanks."

"And your parents?"

"They're good." Dawn looks at me. "So what do you think, is the dress going home with you?"

It is, because it's beyond fantastic. I hurry back behind the sheet and change. When I come out, Dawn is gone. I pay for the dress and wait while Roxanne folds my new favorite garment and slips it into a large twist-handle brown paper bag with the Cindy's Closet logo stenciled on the side. Then I go in search of my friend, whom I eventually find three booths away, inspecting a display of handmade scented candles.

"Sorry," she says at my approach. "Didn't mean to abandon you back there."

"No problem." I watch her pick up a candle marked Autumn Delights. "What's the deal with you and that woman? Sounds like you were old friends. Did something happen?"

"Not really." Dawn shrugs. "People drift apart. You know how it is." She sniffs the candle, then reaches for her purse. "I think I'm going to get this."

Dawn turns and walks to the register without a second glance in my direction. Did I do something wrong by wanting to buy that dress in the other booth? She's usually so relaxed and open. Friendly. Something is off with her, but I have no idea what, because she's clearly not in the mood to share her feelings. At least, not with me.

40

It's three in the afternoon when I arrive back at the Glendale with the cocktail dress and two brown paper bags full of organic veggies, jars of local marmalade and honey, a couple of cheeses, and a crusty sourdough loaf. I say goodbye to Dawn and lug my haul up the steps and into the lobby. As always seems to be the case, Angelo isn't there and the sign is back on his desk. The door to apartment 1A—the same apartment I saw Catherine leaving—is open a crack. Is that where Angelo has gone, or has someone left the door open by accident?

I can't help myself.

I leave my bags on the floor near the elevator, then approach the apartment, overcome with a burning curiosity. But when I'm almost there, just as I catch a glimpse of the interior through the narrow vertical gap—the edge of a sofa, one corner of an ornate metal end table, a tantalizing patch of wall painted light blue—the door swings closed and clicks shut.

"Angelo?" I knock on the door. "Hello?"

I receive no response. If Angelo is on the other side of the door, he isn't answering.

I almost grab the handle and check to see if the door is locked, but I don't. The door didn't close on its own, which means that someone is in there, and they clearly don't want me around.

Reluctantly, I walk back to the elevator, pick up my bags, and head upstairs.

When I enter our apartment, Sam appears and follows me to the kitchen, then paws through the bags with the unbridled excitement of a kid tearing the wrapping off their presents on Christmas morning. My fiancé is a foodie and practically squeals with delight when he discovers the cheeses, bread, and jars of marmalade and honey. He has a fondness for all things organic, and if it's also local, even better. I almost expect him to demand that we dig in to it all right away, but when he turns around, the tasty treats laid out on the kitchen island are quickly forgotten. Because I've unpacked the last bag and pulled out the cocktail dress, which I'm holding up for him to see.

"Holy smoke, that's hot," he says, wide eyed.

"I hope you don't mind that I splurged on this," I say, hoping to head off what I suspect will be the next question—how much the dress cost. "I know our expenses are higher since we moved in here, but—"

"Don't worry about it," he says, still ogling the dress. "You just landed a fifteen-thousand-dollar commercial client. Hopefully, the first of many. You're allowed to treat yourself." He steps closer and reaches out, touches the dress. "I mean, assuming it didn't cost like four grand or something."

"It was a hundred bucks," I tell him. "It's vintage and I love it. Figured I'd wear it to the next cocktail party."

"You'll be the best-dressed woman in the room," he replies. "No one else will hold a candle to you, not even Kali—" He stops himself before the entire name tumbles from his mouth. A look flashes across his face. "Sorry. I didn't mean that."

"It's fine." It's not really. Dawn's words echo in my head, and I'm overcome with a sudden desire to prove that Kalina isn't the only one who can turn heads. Draping the dress over my arm, I turn toward the bedroom. "Stay right there."

"Where are you going?"

"Just wait. You'll see." I hurry to the bedroom and close the door. It only takes me a moment to climb out of my clothes and slip the dress on. When I look at myself in the full-length mirror, I almost gasp. The dress looked good when I tried it on in the booth at the market, but looking at it now in the comfort of my bedroom, at the way it hugs my curves and accentuates my breasts, I'm floored. It's truly dazzling. A chic, sophisticated piece of fashion from another era that somehow feels as relevant and fresh in the twenty-first century as it must have done eight decades ago. I tear my gaze away from the mirror and go to the door, walk out of the bedroom with a flourish. "What do you think?"

"Wow." Sam's eyes are practically bugging out of his head. "You look like a million dollars."

I give him a twirl, and I'm delighted at how the hem of the dress swirls and flows as I turn. My imagination conjures up a ballroom in another era, with Glenn Miller and his band playing "Chattanooga Choo Choo" or "Pennsylvania 6-5000," as I glide across a packed dance floor.

Sam can't stop looking. "We should go out tonight, and you should wear that dress."

"Go out where?"

"Remember that quaint tapas restaurant we went to for your birthday a couple of years ago?" Sam wraps his arms around my waist. A hand roves up to the bare skin of my back.

"Of course." It would be hard to forget. The food was beyond delicious, and authentic, too. It conjured memories of a trip to Spain we took when we were first together. "Dali, right?"

"Right. That's the place. It's upscale, and that dress would be perfect. What do you think?"

"I thought you were excited about the bread and cheese and all the other stuff I brought home from the market."

"I am, but it's Saturday evening. Remember when we were first together? Our weekly date nights? We haven't done that in ages, and I think we should."

"We stopped going out because we were saving for a house, remember?"

"Right. And now we have one, so . . ."

I slip my arms around his neck and peck him on the lips. “Fine. We’ll go out. But if I’m wearing this dress, you’ll need to change into something a bit smarter than jeans and a sweater.”

“On it.” Sam kisses me, then extricates himself and starts for the bedroom. When he reaches the doorway, he stops and glances back over his shoulder. “You really do look hot!”

“Thanks.” I flash him a demure smile. And for the first time since Kalina gave me that look, I don’t feel like I’m playing second fiddle to our neighbor.

41

The restaurant is charming, and just like I remember. For a moment, as we're led to our table, I'm right back in Barcelona. The deeply textured stucco walls are painted a soft gold. Pendant lights hang from the ceiling. Candles flicker in glass jars. Flamenco music fills the air, its swift and bright notes mixing with the clink of glasses and hum of conversation. I'm delighted to see a guitarist sitting on a stool near the bar.

After we sit down, Sam orders us a couple of sangrias, which we sip while we wait for the food to arrive. It really does feel like our date nights of old, but there's a cloud hanging over me, and until I dispel it, I won't be able to relax.

"Can we talk?" I ask finally.

"Sure." He gives me a sideways look. "Everything all right?"

"No. Not really." I take a deep breath. "You've been spending a lot of time with Kalina over the last couple of weeks. She seemed to enjoy your company just a little too much at the party last night, and I'm worried that she might have gotten the wrong idea."

"Are you serious?" Sam stares at me across the table. "I'm helping her with the Wainwright. You said we should be friendly with the neighbors."

"Not *that* friendly. Even Dawn noticed it. She's so beautiful, and she has that accent, and the way she dresses, and—" A tremble creeps into my voice as I'm overcome by an unexpected flood of emotion.

"Hey." Sam leans across the table and takes my hand. He speaks in a low voice, his eyes fixed on mine. "You've got nothing to worry about. I don't have an ounce of interest in that woman. You're more beautiful than she could ever be."

"No, I'm not."

"Yes, you are. Not only that, but you're smart and sophisticated, and you don't need to wear some tiny dress that shows off way too much cleavage just to prove a point." He squeezes my hand before releasing it. "And also, I love you."

"I love you, too." Sam's words should sooth my fears, but I still can't get Kalina out my mind, and the look she gave me, like she was claiming my fiancé for herself. There's only one way that I'll feel better about all of this. "I don't want you to help her anymore."

Sam stares at me as if he wants to say something but doesn't quite know how to word it without making the situation worse.

I take the opportunity to press my point. "Look, I trust you, but I can't say the same for Kalina. I know you won't understand, but I can see what she's doing. Call it women's intuition, or whatever you want, but if we let her get too close, it's going to end badly."

"Jordan, I don't think that—"

"I'm serious, Sam. It's a big ask. I get that. But she's trouble. I can sense it. We need to protect ourselves."

"Protect ourselves from a neighbor?"

"I know it sounds paranoid, but when have I ever made a request like this before? I got a really strong vibe from her at the party, and it wasn't a friendly one, at least not toward me. I'm afraid that if we don't distance ourselves from Kalina, she's going to drive a wedge between us. Please, Sam, just do this for me?" I squeeze his hand. "For us?"

"You're that sure?"

"I am." This isn't a request I'm making lightly. I've given it a lot of thought.

"Okay. If that's really how you feel. I'll tell her I'm too busy at work. I know a couple of other lawyers who might be able to help her out. They won't be free, of course, but . . ."

"Thank you." I don't give a damn about that, just so long as she stays the hell away from my fiancé. I withdraw my hand and take another sip of sangria. It feels like a weight has been lifted, and I can finally relax.

We eat and chat and laugh at all sorts of silly things for the next two hours. After the meal is over, we linger, talking and laughing. We're lost in each other's company and only notice that we're the last ones left in the restaurant when the staff drop a not-so-subtle hint by breaking out the vacuum cleaner and tidying up around us.

When we get back to the Glendale—more than a little tipsy—the lobby is empty and silent. Even the doorman's desk is unattended. A sign on the counter reads BACK AT 6 A.M. Surprised, I glance at the time on my phone and realize it's almost midnight, which explains why no one is around. The lobby isn't staffed between 11:00 p.m. and 6:00 a.m., and the front doors are locked, accessible only with a key card.

When we reach the elevator, I glance sideways toward the empty apartment, remembering how the door was ajar earlier in the day and how someone closed it from the inside upon my approach. I don't know why I look. I'm not expecting to see anything out of the ordinary so late at night, but then I notice a thin sliver of pale light under the door. Leaving Sam at the elevator, I approach the apartment.

"Hey, where are you going?" he asks in a quiet voice.

"I just want to check this out," I reply, stopping in front of the door and reaching for the knob with alcohol-fueled boldness. But when I turn it, the door doesn't open.

"Jordan." Sam hisses my name as he comes up behind me. "What are you doing?"

"I want to see inside." I stare at the door as if it will fly open by the force of my will alone. "Aren't you curious why they would leave a perfectly good apartment empty like this?"

"Not really. It's none of our business, and you're pretty drunk."

"I'm fine," I protest, even as a hiccup escapes my mouth. "I only had two drinks."

"You had three." Sam places a hand on my shoulder and tries to steer me back toward the elevator. "Which is clearly more than you can handle."

"Maybe there's another way in." I ignore his comment and shrug off his hand. "Like a window or something."

"We're not climbing through any windows," Sam says calmly, as if talking me out of breaking and entering is the most normal thing in the world. "They aren't going to leave a window unlocked any more than the door. And in case you hadn't noticed, trespassing is a crime."

I rattle the door handle again. "We're not really trespassing. We bought shares in this building, so we kind of own this apartment, or at least a part of it."

"That isn't how it works. We bought shares in the building so that we could live in *our* apartment on the fourth floor. We don't have a right to go into this apartment any more than we could wander into Frank and Jennifer's uninvited."

"Aw, come on. Aren't you a little bit curious why there's a light on at midnight in a unit that isn't occupied?" I'm slurring my words. "And why was Catherine in there yesterday?"

"Don't know. Don't care. All I want to do is go to bed. I'm tired, and we've both had too much to drink. And in case you forgot, we have to be up early in the morning for our weekly brunch date with Dawn and Jamie."

"I didn't forget."

"Good, let's go. You clearly aren't making the best decisions right now."

"But—"

"No *buts*." Sam wrangles me back to the elevator and presses the call button.

From somewhere above us, I hear the clanking, torturous groan of the old elevator car as it descends toward the lobby. When it arrives, Sam pulls the gate open and bundles me inside, but at the last second I glance back toward the apartment, just in time to see the light under the door snap off.

42

Him

Then

The cops are at your door. It's been five days since I took care of him for you, and honestly, I was expecting this sooner. After all, you were the last person to see him alive. Well, except for me, but there are only two people in the world who know the truth of that, and one of them isn't breathing.

I wonder what you're thinking right now, what is going through your mind. I hope you won't be too upset, because I'm sure this is the first you've heard of his death. A brief report on the local news mentioned a body being found, but they didn't name him—something about not releasing his identity until they had informed his next of kin. Apart from that, there was nothing. No newspaper articles. No follow-up reports on the news. It's a sad commentary on the state of modern society that a person can be brutally murdered while walking back to his car in a parking lot, dumped in the trunk, and left there, and it isn't worth more than a few minutes of late-night airtime on a local station. Of course, it didn't help that another poor schmuck went and got themself stabbed to death the next day, stealing his limelight.

I wish I could be there to let you know that everything will be okay, to comfort you in your time of need, but we don't have that kind of relationship. Not yet. Besides, I don't have much love for cops. They make me nervous. Honestly, it's a testament to my devotion that I didn't abandon our relationship the moment I saw them. But I would never do that. Not to you, my darling Raven. I've been waiting across the road for the last forty minutes, watching your apartment building, because you leave for work around this time of day, and I like to make sure you arrive there safely. There are a lot of bad people in the city who might not have the best intentions toward an attractive young woman such as yourself. You see, that's the kind of guy that I am. Considerate. Loving.

But you didn't leave for work. Instead, the cops showed up. At first, I was tempted to follow them and slip into the lobby for a better look, but that would have been foolhardy. Kind of hard not to notice a guy hanging around like that for no reason. Even standing over here on the sidewalk opposite is a risk. Which is why I turn and saunter casually down the street when I see the lobby doors open and the cops come back out.

Not that I'm doing anything wrong by being here, and it's not like I've done that dumb criminal cliché thing of returning to the scene of the crime. Unless the crime was what that man did to you after you brought him home—after you let him stay the night, which makes you the real victim and me your savior. But the cops won't see it like that, even though we want the same thing: to protect the innocent.

I step off the sidewalk and make my way past the iron railings that mark the boundary between public land and the small garden at the back of your apartment building. I walk across a swath of grass between neatly planted flower beds to a gravel path, which I follow until I arrive at a large oak tree growing near your bedroom window. The curtains are not drawn this time. I stand with one shoulder leaning on the trunk of the tree and take my phone out, pretend I'm looking at it just in case you glance my way, even though there's only one true object of my attention. But I don't see you. The bedroom is empty. There's only one other window on this side of the building with a view inside your apartment, but the angle is wrong from where I'm standing. I move a little farther down the path, and now I can see into your living room and kitchen beyond.

There you are.

Sitting on the couch and staring toward the TV mounted on the wall above the fireplace, even though it's not turned on. You look like crap, and I know right away that you've been crying. If I got closer, if I walked right up to that window—which I have no intention of doing—your eyes would be red, and there would be tears on your cheeks.

My heart aches. I can't stand to see you like this. What did that guy do to cause you such upset at his demise? You should be happy that someone loves you enough to stand up to him, because I know about men like that and what they want from a woman, and if you think it hurts now, he would have hurt you even more down the road.

If I had let him live.

But I don't expect you to understand. Not yet, but soon enough, my darling Raven. When the time is right, you'll come to realize that there was only ever one guy in this world for you. One man who could truly fulfill your needs. And when that day comes, you'll thank me for providing a release from your pain.

43

Jordan

Now

I dream about shadowy figures hiding behind locked doors and endless dark and gloomy rooms with peeling, mottled wallpaper, rotten floorboards, and plaster flaking off the ceiling like snow. When I wake up, the nightmare refuses to dissipate, and for a second, the world of sleep overlaps the landscape of reality. I'm convinced the walls are stained with mold and that dark shadows are pressing in around me until the illusion evaporates to reveal my bright and airy bedroom, and a rapid beeping that I soon realize is my phone alarm. I reach out and swat at the screen to silence the alarm.

Sam stirs and rolls over, even as he rubs the sleep from his eyes. "Good morning, sleepyhead," he says with a grin.

"What time is it?"

"Seven thirty. You should remember that, since you set the alarm."

My head hurts, a lingering gift courtesy of the previous evening. I might not remember setting the alarm, but I do remember that we're meeting Dawn and Jamie for brunch. I'm not ready to move yet, though. I nudge Sam. "You can shower first."

"That bad, huh?"

"Little bit." I watch him climb from the bed and head for the en suite. A moment later I hear the sound of running water. I close my eyes and sink back down under the covers and start to drift back off. Until I hear something else that jolts me back awake. A wailing that cuts through the sound of the shower—the unmistakable cry of a baby.

I throw the covers back, jump out of bed, and race into the bathroom.

"Do you hear that?" I say, pulling the glass shower door open.

"Hear what?" Sam rinses shampoo from his hair.

"The baby. There's a baby crying somewhere in the building."

"So?"

"I've heard it before, but when I asked Kalina, she said there were no children living at the Glendale."

Sam turns the shower off and listens. "I don't hear anything."

Neither do I anymore. "There was a baby crying just now. I heard it."

"Jordan." Sam gives me a look. The worried look.

I know immediately where he's going with this. "This has nothing to do with what happened to me. I'm better now."

He says nothing in response. Just reaches for a towel.

The tense silence is as good as words. "I'm better," I say again, more forcefully this time.

Sam rubs his hair. "Are you? Because after what happened with the basement . . . you claimed a toy was moving on its own."

I glare at him, the man I love, drying himself in the stall because I'm blocking the shower door. Then I spin around and stomp back into the bedroom.

The next hour is uncomfortable. I wait for Sam to leave the en suite before pushing past him and turning the shower back on. By the time

I'm done, he's dressed and waiting in the living room, sitting on the sofa and reading on his phone.

"Sorry about just now," he says, looking up. "I'm worried about you, that's all."

"Sure." I want to reiterate that there *is* a baby, but it's not worth getting into it with him again right now, when we have to meet Dawn and Jamie. "You ready to go?"

"Yep." He jumps up.

Ten minutes later, we're in the lobby and heading for the door. We're barely halfway there when a familiar voice rings out through the lobby.

"Jordan, my dear. I've been meaning to stop by and see you." I turn to see Catherine hurrying toward us from the direction of the main staircase. "There's a meeting of the Glendale's executive board on Thursday afternoon, and I'm hoping that you can come along. We're all so excited to hear your ideas for the coffee shop."

"Oh. Sure. I can be there."

"Fantastic. One p.m. in the library?"

I nod. "Sounds good."

"Wonderful." She starts past us in the direction of the mailboxes.

I see an opportunity. "Catherine, can I ask you something?"

"Of course." She turns back toward us.

"Does anyone in the building have a young child?"

"Jordan—" Sam rolls his eyes.

"I'm serious. I keep hearing a baby crying, but Kalina said there aren't any children living at the Glendale."

"And she would be right," Catherine replies. "I can't remember the last time anyone with a baby lived here, but it was before the renovation."

"Oh." I can feel Sam's eyes heavy on me like a pair of lead weights, and I know what he's thinking. I don't give him time to voice his concerns. When Catherine continues on her way, I do the same and head for the door, changing the subject and telling him that we'll be late if we don't get a move on. But it's a temporary reprieve, because I know that sooner or later, Sam is going to say something. At least it won't be this morning.

44

When we arrive at the restaurant, Dawn and Jamie are waiting. I've come to look forward to our weekend brunches over the last few weeks, and the mysterious crying baby that no one believes is real takes a back seat. Sam perks up, too, and soon we're all deep in conversation, laughing and joking as we sip cranberry-flavored "poinsettia" mimosas, which are a specialty of the establishment, according to our server.

Afterward, the four of us take a stroll through the Public Gardens and Boston Common, then head toward the waterfront, finally ending up at Faneuil Hall, a well-known marketplace in the city popular with locals and tourists alike. We stroll the promenade and wander in and out of stores. That evening, as a brilliant sunset sets the sky ablaze in hues of yellow and orange, we make our way back home, leaving Dawn and Jamie with a promise that we will get together again soon.

We finish the evening out on our balcony overlooking the Boston skyline while sipping hot cocoa. It's the perfect end to a wonderful afternoon. As I sit there, watching the lights of the city twinkle and glow, I wonder what's going through his mind. I'm afraid he'll ruin the moment, bring up the baby and the mysterious disappearing toy in the basement, suggest I return to the therapist or go back on the meds, but he doesn't. He seems content to let it be. Then, around eleven, he takes me by the hand and leads me into the bedroom. It's obvious how he wants to end the night, and I don't protest. At least, not too much.

As usual, Sam has already left for work when I get up the next morning. I have a meeting with Judy Abelman today that I rescheduled after Catherine showed up and waylaid me last Monday. I've never met Judy—she isn't one of my mother's usual social circle, but rather a friend of a friend—so I don't know much about her. I also want to make a good impression, especially after canceling our previous appointment on such short notice. I finish my coffee, slip my laptop into its case, and leave for her house in Chestnut Hill with plenty of time to spare.

Or at least, so I thought, because it takes forever to get across town thanks to a broken-down train on the Green Line. In the end, the train gets to Chestnut Hill a full ten minutes after I should have been at my meeting, and I'm second-guessing myself for not spending the extra money and taking an Uber. By the time I arrive at Judy Abelman's house, I'm twenty-five minutes late and breathless from practically jogging all the way from the Chestnut Hill T station.

Judy lives in a large pastel-blue classic Colonial surrounded by manicured gardens with well-tended flower beds and a sprawling oak tree out front. Four steps lead up to the front door. I race up them and ring the bell, then suck in several deep breaths in an effort to make myself look less winded.

At first, no one answers, and I reach out to ring the bell again, but then the door opens to reveal a slender woman of about sixty years of age with short dark hair and thick glasses.

She studies me with a perplexed expression. "Yes? Can I help you?"

"Jordan Hollister. I'm the interior designer my mother referred to you. We have an appointment today."

Judy shakes her head. "No, we don't."

"Are you sure?" I say, taken aback. "We spoke on the phone last Monday. I couldn't make the original appointment, and we rescheduled. Maybe I misunderstood, but I thought you said this morning would be fine."

"And then you called me again on Wednesday and canceled. Something about a large commercial project and not having time for any new clients."

"What?" I would remember making a call like that. Apart from anything else, it's just not true. I need all the clients I can get right now. "The last time we spoke was a week ago. You must be mistaken."

"I can assure you that I'm not mistaken." Judy folds her arms. "You were very clear about your lack of time. I'm sorry that you came all the way out here for no reason, but perhaps you should have called first if you had a change of heart."

"I didn't cancel our appointment, and I didn't call you last Wednesday."

Judy observes me with stern indifference. "I'm not sure that I like your tone, young lady, and I don't appreciate being called a liar."

"I'm sorry. I wasn't trying to offend you. It's just that—"

"Let me stop you right there, because it's moot. I've already hired someone else."

"You did?" It's only been a few days. I'm surprised she could find another interior designer so quickly.

"Yes. Which is what I probably should have done in the first place."

A lump rises in my throat. "Who?"

"An experienced professional with a proven track record who won't let me down." Judy takes a step back into the house, her hand on the door. "Now, if you don't mind, I have better things to do than stand here listening to your excuses." Then she closes the door before I can utter another word, leaving me standing alone and mystified on her stoop.

45

What the hell just happened? I almost expect her to open the door again, say that she mixed me up with a plumber or an electrician or some other tradesperson and that everything is fine. But she doesn't. The door remains stubbornly closed. For whatever reason, Judy Abelman thinks I called her last Wednesday and that I'm too busy to work for her, which is ridiculous. But it doesn't matter, because she's hired someone else.

I make my way back down the steps and onto the sidewalk. I don't understand how a mix-up like this could have occurred. I didn't call her last Wednesday to cancel. And if I want proof, my phone provides it. The log clearly shows one call to Judy's number on the same day Catherine caused me to miss our original appointment. There are no other calls, and certainly not last Wednesday. Which leads me to an inescapable conclusion: Either Judy is lying because she doesn't want to hire me anymore, or someone else canceled the appointment. There is only one person I can think of.

I stop and make the call.

My mother answers quickly, sounding way too chirpy for someone who's just sabotaged her daughter's client.

"Did you cancel my appointment with Judy Abelman and tell her I was too busy to work for her?" I ask before she can say much.

"Why would I do that?"

"I don't know. That's why I'm calling." Then I explain to her what's just happened with Judy.

When I'm finished, my mother tuts. "You think I'm responsible for that?"

"Well, she says someone called and canceled, and I know it wasn't me."

"Then it must have been Sam."

"It wasn't Sam," I say with conviction. "He wouldn't do something like that."

"But you think that *I* would? I'm the one who got you the job, and I have a standing in this community. The last thing I want is people saying that my daughter can't live up to her commitments." There's a brief silence. "Have you considered that she might have misunderstood when you called to reschedule the appointment from last week?"

I let the comment about commitments go, because it just isn't worth it. "There was no misunderstanding. I called her last Monday afternoon and made a new appointment for today. I never said I was too busy, or that I didn't want to work for her."

"Then I have no idea. Did you say that you didn't cancel?"

"What do you think?"

"There's no need to be snippy," my mother retorts in an equally snippy voice. "Are you still at the house? Maybe I can talk to her."

"I already left. I'm on my way back to the subway. And before you ask, no, I'm not going back. She made it quite clear that she's already hired someone else and doesn't need me."

"That was fast."

"Tell me about it."

"There will be other opportunities, honey. To be honest, I've heard that Judy Abelman is a bear to work for, anyway. You're probably better off this way."

"Yeah." I appreciate that my mother is trying to make me feel better, but I could have done without a wasted slog across town. But there's no point in dwelling on it. "We should get together for dinner sometime soon. We haven't seen you and Dad since we moved into the Glendale."

"I'd love that, but it will have to wait," my mother says. "Your dad is up to his neck in work. He's getting home at nine or ten at night, and on the evenings when he does come home earlier, he makes a sandwich, then goes straight to his study and locks himself in."

"What has he gotten himself into this time?" I ask. My father would work twenty-four hours a day if only his clients were willing to have a session at 3:00 a.m. He fills his extra billable hours with all sorts of side work, like writing articles for psychiatric journals, evaluating patients at mental health facilities, and providing expert testimony in court cases.

"He's working with the district attorney's office. Something about a woman who shot her husband after claiming she had a mental break. Her lawyers are going for an insanity defense."

"Sounds about right." It's not the first time my father has worked with the courts. He's consulted for both the prosecution and the defense in numerous trials over the years and is in high demand thanks to his meticulous research and deep understanding of complex psychiatric issues. "Maybe we can get together next weekend."

"I wouldn't hold your breath." There's a note of resignation in my mother's voice. "You know how these things go."

"Yeah." I know exactly what my father is like when he gets lost in his work. When I was in eighth grade, I scored the lead in the school production of *Romeo and Juliet*. My father never saw the play because he was too busy. I later found out that he'd been consulting on a murder case. Things haven't gotten any better in the years since then. In fact, as his reputation has grown, he's found himself in even higher demand. I'm sure that my mother is looking forward to the day when he retires—although, given his single-minded devotion to his craft, that might never happen. At least not voluntarily.

"Maybe we can go out on Friday," my mother suggests. "Just the two of us. We can make an afternoon of it and go shopping."

"I'm not sure I can afford to go out. Not after what just happened," I say, a bit overdramatically.

"Nonsense. We're going out. My treat. We'll go to Stetski's. I know how much you like it."

"Sure." Stetski's Deli is my mother's favorite place, not mine, but I don't protest.

"Wonderful. I'll meet you there at noon." My mother sounds pleased.

"Okay." I'm at the subway station now. I tell my mother that I love her and that we'll speak again later in the week, then hang up. But not before she tells me one more time that Judy Abelman is not worth worrying about, that there are bigger and better things in my future. I appreciate her optimism and her attempt to lift my spirits, but as I wait for the train, my thoughts turn once more to Judy's claim that I called and canceled the appointment, and I find it as confusing now as when she first told me. It also raises a disturbing question: If my mother didn't call her, and it wasn't Sam, then who could it have been?

46

I hop back on the T, but instead of disembarking at the Back Bay, I ride the train over to the South End, to a wonderful fabric store where I can look at options for the coffee shop and pick up samples to add to the mood board.

The Sewfisticated Thread has been a staple in Boston for over fifty years, drawing a mix of hobbyists, students, and the increasing number of professional fashion designers who have made the city their home. And, of course, people like me.

The store occupies an entire building, with three floors of fabrics ranging in price from a couple of bucks a yard to fine silks and linens that come in at an eye-watering $2,000 or more per yard. I'm pretty sure that Catherine doesn't want to blow the entire budget on ridiculously overpriced fabric, so I head to the third floor, where they keep the discount and clearance stuff. With any luck, I can find a decent upholstery fabric at a great price, and since I intend to finish each item of furniture in a different pattern, there might be some interesting remnants that will work for my needs. After two hours, my cart is stuffed with fabric. I head to the register and purchase a quarter yard of everything.

When I arrive back at the Glendale, I go straight to my office. I'm still there, working on the mood board with my new fabrics, when Sam comes home. He pokes his head in the door to say hello and tells me he's heading down to the basement to put laundry on. I'm having so much fun that forty-five minutes pass before I realize he hasn't returned. I grab my phone and call him, but he doesn't answer. Instead, I hear his ringtone in the other room. When I step out of the office, his phone is lying on the kitchen island.

I hang up and go looking for him.

Sam is still in the laundry room, and he isn't alone.

Kalina is perched, cross-legged, on one of the dryers. She's wearing a tight white tank top and just as tight high-waisted gray leggings. The woman doesn't have an ounce of fat on her body. Sam is standing nearby, leaning against the wall. The two of them are deep in conversation. When I enter the laundry room, they look around and fall silent. Sam takes a step back. Kalina meets my gaze with smug self-confidence.

"Checking up on your man?" she asks.

I ignore her and focus my attention on Sam. "You've been gone a long time."

"He was talking to me," Kalina says before Sam can reply. "I was just saying how much I enjoyed dinner the other night. We should do it again soon. Maybe you can come over to my place this time." Her eyes shift to Sam. She uncrosses her legs. "I can be very entertaining."

"I bet you can," I snap, overcome by a sudden desire to take the woman by the throat and throttle the life out of her.

"Jordan?" Sam looks shocked. "What's gotten into you?"

"I could ask you the same thing," I say over the rumble of the washing machine. Our empty laundry basket is sitting on the floor next to it. But there's another, smaller laundry basket there, too, and this one is still filled with clothes. A lacy white sheer demi bra sits atop the pile, almost as if it had been placed there deliberately. I wonder if it was.

"I don't know what's going on here, but I think the two of you need some privacy," Kalina says, sliding down off the dryer. "I'll come back later."

She picks up her laundry, then heads for the door, stepping around me. I watch her go, waiting until she gets into the elevator before turning my attention back to Sam.

"I thought you weren't going to see her anymore."

"She came down while I was loading the washing machine. What was I supposed to do, ignore her?"

"That would be a good start." Even as I say this, I realize that I sound like a totally unreasonable bitch, but I can't stop myself. Because the last thing I expected was to find the pair of them together down here looking so friendly after I told Sam how I felt about her, and it hurts.

"Jordan, this is ridiculous. She's our neighbor. We're going to cross paths. Regardless of what you think of her, we still have to be polite."

"You don't need to be polite for three-quarters of an hour. What were you even talking about, anyway?"

"I told her that I'm too busy to help with the Wainwright Building, like you wanted. I said I'd text her the names of some other lawyers."

"Okay. That accounts for ten minutes, tops. What else?"

"I don't know. Just stuff. I could hardly say that I'm not going to help her anymore, then leave without saying another word. It would be rude, and we don't need to go around starting feuds with the neighbors."

"Still seems like a long time."

Sam frowns. "I was giving her some advice. Figured I owe her that much for agreeing to help, then going back on my word."

"You don't owe her anything."

"I'm just trying to do the right thing here, Jordan." The washing machine finishes its cycle. Sam turns to open the door, then looks back at me. "I don't understand why you're being so weird about this."

"Are you serious? I come down here and find the pair of you huddled as if . . ." I trail off, not sure I want to voice what's going through my head.

"As if what, Jordan?"

"If you can't figure it out, I'm not telling you." I spin on my heel and stomp toward the elevator. I might be overreacting—I'm positive that's how Sam sees it—but my gut is telling me otherwise. "Are you coming back up, or did you want to wait for that woman to return?"

Sam doesn't reply. Instead, I hear the dryer lid being lifted and then the sound of clothes dropping into it. When the elevator comes, I step in without looking back at him. On the fourth floor, I head toward our apartment, passing Kalina's door on the way. I hesitate, tempted to knock and tell her to stay the fuck away from my fiancé. But deep down, I know that Sam is right. We don't need to start a feud with the neighbors. Which is why I keep going, but as I enter our apartment and close the door, I'm overcome by a sudden feeling that we're not done with Kalina yet. Not in the slightest.

47

Him

Then

Today I'm at a funeral. Well, sort of. I'm standing alone under a sheltering copse of trees several hundred feet from the gravesite, dressed all in black—it *is* standard garb for the occasion, after all—and observing the proceedings. A minister is droning on, imparting the usual mumbo jumbo that comforts the grieving in their darkest hours. He's taking his sweet time, and I wish he would finish already, because I have other places to be. Like the hospital. I'm scheduled for a twelve-hour shift this afternoon, even though I've already worked fifty hours this week. Between that and my time with you, my sweet Raven, I've hardly gotten a wink of sleep. I would really love to go home, lay my head on a pillow for a while before my shift. But you need me right now.

And there you are, dabbing your eyes with a tissue and looking suitably sad, even though deep down you are happy that I saved you from what would have been a disastrous entanglement. I could tell he wasn't good for you from the moment I walked up behind him. He would have used you, then tossed you aside like so much trash, because that's what men do. At least, most of them. Not me. I'm in it with you until the end.

Honestly, realizing what he would have done if I had left him alive made killing the guy that much easier, even if I didn't particularly enjoy doing it. But I'll say this for him—your suitor was popular. There must be at least thirty people clustered around the grave. I shift my gaze from you to his parents. They are easy to spot. Next to them is a young man who looks positively distraught. A brother, perhaps? And there's a sister, too. A slender long-haired girl of maybe eighteen years, who stands looking down at the coffin as it is lowered into the ground. I watch with fascination, wondering how my actions will shape her life yet to come. One day, a few years from now, I might check in on her, just to find out. And who knows, maybe I'll see in her some nuance of character, some small detail that sucks me in, just like the tattoo that drew me to you. And wouldn't that be ironic, if killing that guy to save you becomes the catalyst for a new love in the future?

But I'm getting ahead of myself. I need to focus, because the minister has finished up, and the casket has slipped from view. The mourners are turning to each other and talking in hushed tones as they file away from the grave. I watch them go and watch you go, too, walking next to his parents and sister, and I can see that you are commiserating with them.

I should leave as well. The sky is overcast, and it looks like rain—a fittingly somber day—and I only came here for you. But I don't leave. I stay in the shadow of the trees and watch the cemetery crew fill the grave using a small backhoe. There is something weirdly fascinating about the process, like peeking behind the curtain at a theater and seeing the wings and the lights and the rigging and all the mundane stuff that creates the illusion. Because once the mourners have departed, the pretense of somber respect gives way to the reality of sticking a person down in a hole. The men who do this job wear hard hats and fluorescent jackets. They use noisy, dirty machinery. They might as well be repairing a broken water main or filling a ditch. There isn't even a headstone yet. That won't come for at least six months. In the meantime, they might put a temporary plaque on the grave, but he doesn't even have that yet. Just a bunch of sodden dirt and fading memories.

Yet once the workers are done, I'm compelled to visit that small mound of earth. I step out from beneath the trees and make my way across the grass. I don't know what I'm doing, or even why I'm doing it. I never visit the graves of those I have helped from this world. I want to remember them as they were in life . . . as they were on that last special night we spent together. Memories that will stay with me forever.

But this one is different. I have no attachment to him. Quite the opposite. I look down at his grave and wish he had possessed the good sense to stay away from you, because then I wouldn't have been forced to put him here.

A phrase rattles through my mind. Slightly misquoted, but a fitting eulogy to my actions.

Ashes to ashes, dust to dust, from whence you came, so I have returned you.

And I would do it again, although I hope it won't be necessary. In fact, I know that it won't, because—

"I didn't think anyone would still be here."

The voice startles me, and for a moment, panic sets in until I pull it under control and turn to face you, standing there with a stuffed toy in your arms. A pink fluffy . . . something. My gaze drops briefly to the raven tattoo peeking out from under the cuff of your black dress. "Me either."

You hold up the toy. "I meant to bring this to the funeral, but I forgot. He gave it to me for my birthday a couple of years ago. It was a joke, but I don't know . . . It kind of summed up our relationship in a weird way. I went back home and got it because I couldn't stand the thought of him being down there all alone. I wanted a piece of me to be here with him."

"That's so thoughtful."

"Thanks." You lean down and place the stuffed fluffy pink thing among the flowers and wreaths that the workers put over the grave once they were done filling it in. "You look familiar. I'm sure we've met before." A moment of uneasy silence. "Wait. I've got it. You came into the store."

I nod, my mind going a mile a minute.

"I figured you might come in again, but you didn't."

"It wasn't my cup of tea."

"And now you're here. It's so weird."

I shrug. "Just paying my respects."

"I didn't see you at the funeral."

"I'm a private person." This much is true.

You look into my eyes, and it's like you are searching for some hidden truth. "How did you know Alex?"

Stop. Think. This could turn into a trap, and I haven't prepared a suitable story. I wasn't intending for us to meet like this, at the grave of the person I killed for you, but now that we have, I'm backed into a corner.

I need to say something, anything, or it's going to look weird. I take a gamble. "College."

You nod thoughtfully and I breathe a sigh of relief. But you aren't done yet. "You must have known Lucas, then."

I stare at her, hoping she will be more forthcoming about who Lucas might be, because this really could trip me up. When she does not say anything else, I shake my head, hoping it will put an end to the conversation.

"Really? That surprises me. They met in college, and they've been together ever since. At least until a couple of weeks ago, when they broke up."

Wait. What the actual fuck? The guy I killed had a *boyfriend*? How could I have gotten this all so wrong? He wasn't interested in you, at least not like that, because he wasn't interested in any woman. I think back to the funeral and the brother who looked so distraught, except that it probably wasn't his brother, and I've messed up big-time.

I need to say something and salvage this mess. "Oh. Right. Lucas. I must have misheard you."

You wipe away a tear. "I still can't believe what happened. I was the last person to see Alex alive. He was murdered right after he left my place. Like, that very morning. At least that's what the police tell me."

"The police?" Finally, something useful. "Do they have any leads?"

"I don't think so. At least not yet. They asked a lot of questions about Lucas and why Alex was at my apartment."

"Why was he at your apartment?" I might as well find out, since I killed him for it.

"He was upset. He texted me and asked if we could meet up. I guess he needed a shoulder to cry on. We went out for drinks, and then I took him back to my place, because I didn't think he should be alone. God, if I had known this would happen, I wouldn't have suggested it. Or I would have stopped him from leaving so early. Or . . ." Your bottom lip is trembling. "They think someone followed him off the train. That he was targeted. It might even have been a hate crime."

Shit. So much for the cops not knowing anything, even if they did jump to conclusions on the motive. But it's fine. I was smart. Careful. And honestly, it was to be expected. But I'm pushing my luck staying here. The more we talk, the more chance I have of slipping up. This has gone on long enough.

I glance at my watch. "Well, it was really great meeting you, but I have places to be."

"Oh, okay." You nod, and I get the sense that you would rather be alone, anyway. Then you say, "See you again sometime?"

"It's a distinct possibility." Wow! Are you flirting with me at the grave of your dead friend?

"Good. You know where to find me."

"Sure do." I turn to leave, but you call after me.

"Wait. I don't know your name."

And you never will. At least, not my real one. "It's Jarod."

"Jarod. I like that." It's a lie, because no one likes the name Jarod, but you pull it off. "I'm Luna."

48

Jordan

Now

Things are tense between Sam and me for the rest of the evening. I make dinner and we eat in silence; then I leave him watching TV in the living room and return to my office to work on the coffee shop presentation for the Glendale's board. But I'm distracted. I can't focus on anything except Kalina. I don't know what to do, or if I'm even being rational. I keep telling myself that Sam is trustworthy, but after finding the two of them huddled in the laundry room, deep in conversation like that, I'm rattled. She appears intent upon becoming my rival for Sam's affections, even if I don't have any proof that he's reciprocated. And that's part of the problem. He's such a nice guy that he never wants to cause trouble or offense. He goes out of his way to be helpful. It's an admirable trait, but one that a woman like Kalina can use to her advantage. Eventually, after an hour staring at the mood board and getting nowhere, I throw in the towel and rise from my desk. When I enter the living room, Sam isn't there and the TV is off.

The room is dark except for a lamp in the corner that's been dimmed to its lowest setting. The only other light comes from the bedroom, which is where I assume Sam has gone, since it's past ten o'clock and he has to be up early for work. I go into the kitchen and make a cup of decaffeinated tea, then drink it at the island before heading into the bedroom.

Sam is sitting up with a pillow propped behind his back, reading a book. He doesn't look up, and I can tell that he's still miffed because he has a habit of becoming noncommunicative when he feels aggrieved. I ignore him and go into the bathroom to wash my face and brush my teeth, then undress, put on my warmest nightshirt, and climb into bed next to him.

Now he decides to speak up. "I'm sorry," he says in a stiff voice.

As usual, his big brown eyes and puppy dog expression melt my icy demeanor. "I'm sorry, too."

Sam lowers the book. "I shouldn't have stayed down there talking to Kalina for so long. It's just that I don't like letting people down. I didn't know what to say, how to tell her that I couldn't help with the Wainwright Building anymore, so I sort of danced around it."

"But you did tell her, right?"

He gives me a *What do you think?* look.

"Okay. I believe you."

"Then we're good?"

"We're good." I can tell that Sam wants to go to sleep—he's already yawned twice—so I give him a kiss, say that I love him, and slip down under the covers.

Sam does the same, setting his book aside on the nightstand before turning off the light. A few minutes later, he's snoring. But not me. Now that we've made up, my thoughts drift back to the mood board and the presentation I need to put together before Thursday. I do my best to shut my mind off, but it simply won't obey. All the inspiration that wouldn't come earlier in the evening now tumbles forth as if it had been trapped behind a dam that's suddenly burst. I feel the weight of creativity pressing down upon me. If I don't do something about it right now, my ideas will slip back into the ether by morning, leaving me with only faint, tantalizing impressions. With a groan, I swing my legs off the bed and quietly pad out of the room.

The apartment is silent and brooding. The light from the lamp in the corner of the living room, which I'd left on when I went to bed, seems dimmer than it did before. The shadows feel longer. I scurry past the kitchen and living room to my office and sit down at the desk, turning the light on. Outside my window, the city is sleeping.

I grab the rectangle of foam board and start rearranging the samples on it like I'm solving an abstract jigsaw puzzle. On my computer, I start writing, jotting down my ideas and crafting them into a presentation to go along with the mood board, and the digital walk-through I've been putting together.

After an hour, the inspiration that came to me while I was trying to sleep is out of my head and taking shape. Now I'm overcome by a deep weariness. I yawn and rise to my feet, turn the office light off. Then I make my way back to the bedroom, ignoring the weird sense of unease that grips me as I cross the living room. A strange sensation that I'm not alone, even though common sense tells me there's no one here except me and Sam, who's still asleep. When I reach the bedroom, I climb back into bed, thankful to be near him again, and try not to think about the darkness beyond.

49

I spend the next two days fine-tuning the 3D digital walk-through of the coffee shop on my computer. Since Judy Abelman essentially fired me before I even got started, this is now my fledgling company's only source of income. Which is why I can't afford to make a mistake, because new clients are hardly beating my door down. I'm not sure that my mother even has any other friends she can guilt into using me, so I need to pad my portfolio and hope that the coffee shop design is enough to generate buzz.

By six o'clock on Wednesday evening, I've had enough. My eyes are sore and my back hurts from spending so much time sitting in a cheap office chair. I step into the living room and close the office door—a symbolic gesture that helps me compartmentalize between my work and home lives—then go into the bedroom and change out of my sweatpants and T-shirt. I'm exhausted, and rather than waiting for Sam to come home and cooking, it just feels easier to go out for dinner. There's a cute and inexpensive taco place we've have been wanting to try ever since we moved in. I'm about to text him and suggest that we meet at the restaurant when there's a knock at the door.

It's Jennifer. She has an envelope in one hand and a bottle of wine in the other.

She holds out the envelope. "This found its way into our mailbox by mistake. I've been meaning to bring it around for a couple of days."

I take the mail and look at it. A credit card bill. "You shouldn't have bothered."

"I know, right?" Jennifer laughs nervously. She holds up the bottle. "I brought a gift to say thank you for your wonderful dinner party the other night. Frank and I had such a good time."

"That's so thoughtful," I say, reaching for the bottle, but Jennifer doesn't seem willing to part with it.

"It's petite sirah. My favorite. I thought maybe we could pop the cork and have a glass," she suggests with a mischievous glint in her eyes. "Get to know each other a little better, girl to girl."

"I'd love to," I reply. "But I was just going out—"

At that moment, my phone dings. It's a text message from Sam.

Stuck in a meeting at work. Looks like it will be a late one. Sorry.

I choke back my disappointment. I was looking forward to getting out of the apartment and trying somewhere new to eat, but it appears that it won't happen. At least not tonight. Which sucks, because Sam hardly ever works late.

"Everything okay, my dear?" Jennifer asks.

"Uh-huh." I slip the phone into my pocket, and my gaze falls to the bottle of wine. What the hell . . . I might as well make the best of a bad situation. I open the door wider and motion for her to enter. "Please, come on in."

Jennifer grins. "You sure I'm not intruding? You looked uncertain a few moments ago."

"Yeah. I thought we were going out to dinner, but Sam got held up at work."

"Well, his loss is my gain." Jennifer walks through the foyer and into the living room. She holds up the bottle. "Yours, too. This is one of my favorites. It's from a wonderful little boutique winery in Napa Valley that my husband and I discovered many years ago on our travels."

"Really?" I grab a couple of wineglasses and hand a corkscrew to Jennifer. "Sam and I got engaged in Napa Valley."

"Ooh. How romantic." Jennifer pulls the cork and pours two ample glasses.

"It really was," I say, remembering how Sam arranged a surprise vacation and wouldn't reveal our destination until we arrived at the airport. After we landed in San Francisco, he drove us to a guesthouse surrounded by quaint family-owned wineries. That evening, when we went out to dinner at a fancy restaurant more expensive than our meager budget would normally allow, I knew something was afoot. I was right. He asked me to marry him on a terrace overlooking a tranquil landscape dotted with vineyards as far as the eye could see, with the sun slipping down behind the distant Mayacamas Mountains and setting the sky ablaze in shades of fiery red and orange. Naturally, I said yes. That was twelve months ago.

Jennifer listens to my tale of Sam's proposal as we settle on the couch and sip our wine. Then she asks the obvious question. "When are you planning to get married?"

"We were originally thinking the fall of next year," I tell her. "At least until the house we were purchasing fell through, which put our plans on hold." I glance around the living room. "But then we found this place, so we might be able to get married next year, after all."

"That all sounds so romantic. Your parents must be overjoyed."

"They are. My mother was in full-blown wedding-planning mode until the hiccup with our home purchase. I'm sure that she'll be right back to it at any time, now that we're settled."

"As she should be." A wistful expression passes across Jennifer's face. "I always looked forward to the day my own daughter would get married, but sadly, it wasn't meant to be."

There's a moment of uneasy silence because I'm not quite sure what to say. Clearly, something happened to Jennifer's daughter, but I'm not sure how to ask what it was.

In the end, she answers my unspoken question on her own. "I'm so sorry. I didn't mean to make you uncomfortable. Frank and I had a daughter. Amanda. She died in her twenties."

Now it's my turn to say I'm sorry.

"It's quite all right. It happened a long time ago. Almost fifteen years." A wistful look crosses Jennifer's face. "Goodness, it still feels like it was only yesterday. I have such fond memories of us all out in Napa. Those long evenings at the vineyards, soaking up the atmosphere. I would do anything to get those moments back."

"Your daughter loved wine, too?" I ask, even though the real question I want to ask is how she died at such a young age. But that would be crass. If Jennifer doesn't want to tell me, then that's her prerogative.

"It was a shared passion." Jennifer looks up with a wan smile. "I'm sure you have a similar connection with your mother. Something the two of you bond over."

I really don't. My mother and I have gone down different paths. She has become more materialistic, judging everyone by the car they drive and the size of their house, while striving to outdo them at every turn. I have learned to look for joy in the small things and not hang my happiness upon the size of my bank account or how much better I'm doing than the neighbors. I don't say that, though. Instead, I jump to my feet and grab the wine bottle from the kitchen. "How about I top us up?"

"That sounds like a fine idea." Jennifer holds her glass out while I refill it, then takes a hearty gulp before asking me about the coffee shop project and how it's coming along.

I'm more than happy to talk about something that doesn't involve dead daughters, and we spend the next two hours discussing everything from my work to the fine selection of restaurants in the Back Bay and how much the area has changed in the decade since they moved into the Glendale. We polish off the first bottle and open a second, which I grab from the drink fridge under the island. It isn't anywhere near as expensive as the one that Jennifer brought around, and it's not a petite sirah, but she doesn't seem to notice. We sit and talk for another half hour before her phone makes a small sound.

"It's Frank. He's getting worried. Wants to know if I've been kidnapped." She checks the time, then stands up. "Goodness. It's after nine. I should go before he sends out a search party."

I follow her to the door. "I'm so pleased you came around. This has been fun."

"It has. We'll have to do it again sometime." She steps out into the hallway, then turns back toward me. "A word of advice, my dear. Don't let life get in the way of marrying Sam. You seem like such a loving couple, so good together. I do hope it stays that way."

"What do you mean?"

"It's just that . . . well . . . this apartment has . . ." Jennifer glances around the empty hallway.

"What about our apartment?" I ask.

"It's not important. Forget I said anything." Then she turns and hurries away, leaving me staring after her.

50

I close the door and stand there, letting Jennifer's parting words sink in. Whatever she wanted to tell me didn't sound good, like she knew some awful secret about this apartment but couldn't bring herself to impart it. I almost go to her door and knock, press her to tell me if there's something wrong with our home. But something in her tone gives me pause. Maybe I'm misreading it, but she looked nervous. There's another way I can find out if anything awful ever happened in our apartment. The internet. I turn and start toward the office. But I don't get that far, because at that moment, Sam arrives home.

He steps into the apartment looking weary, but when he sees me, his eyes light up.

There's a white plastic bag in his hand, which he holds up. "Hope you haven't eaten yet. I stopped for Thai food."

"I haven't eaten," I say, my eyes shifting briefly toward the glasses sitting on the coffee table. "I'm starving."

Sam follows my gaze. "Looks like you had company. Anyone I know?"

"Jennifer, from next door. We cracked open a bottle of wine."

"Ah. I see." Sam takes off his coat and drapes it over a stool. He goes into the kitchen and grabs a couple of forks and plates, then puts the bag down and opens it. "Did you have fun?"

"Uh-huh." I clear away the wine bottles. "Frank and Jennifer had a daughter who died."

"Really?" Sam raises an eyebrow. "How?"

"Don't know. She never said, but it was a long time ago. Like fifteen years. From the way she spoke, I got the impression she was their only child."

"That's sad." Sam brings the food over and sits down. He scoops out generous servings of pad thai, then plucks two spring rolls from the container, one for each of us.

"How did your meeting go?" I ask.

"Good." A faint odor of whisky wafts on his breath. "Happy to be home."

I pause halfway through lifting a mouthful of food. "Where did you have this meeting, at a bar?"

"What? No. Well . . . sort of." There is an uncharacteristic hesitancy to Sam's reply. He picks up his fork, pushes it into the pile of rice noodles on his plate, and twists. "We went out for a drink afterward."

"Oh."

"I should have called and let you know. Sorry."

I shake my head and tell him that it's fine, despite the flicker of irritation that courses through me. But I can hardly complain, since I spent the evening drinking wine with Jennifer. Of course, that was only because Sam was working late. For all he knew, I was sitting here alone, waiting for him.

"I get the feeling that it's not fine," he says.

"I was thinking we'd try that taco place this evening, that's all."

Sam puts an arm around me and kisses my cheek. "You should have let me know. I'd pick you over a boring meeting, any day of the week."

I appreciate the sentiment, and if I'm being honest, Sam going out for drinks after a long day at the office is really not a big deal. "Don't be silly. I'm sure your meeting was important."

"Yes." Sam looks down. He's still winding rice noodles onto his fork as if it's a competition to see how much he can get on there. If he keeps going much longer, the entire plate will be stuck to it. "How about we do the taco place over the weekend instead?"

"Sure."

"Maybe Dawn and Jamie would like to come with us. We could make it a night out."

"Why not?" I dig in to my food. If it wasn't for the wine, I'd be ravenous, but as it is, I eat about half, then push the plate away. I stifle a yawn. "I'm about ready for bed."

Sam has finished all of his. He picks up the plates and takes them into the kitchen, then turns toward the bedroom. "Coming?"

I nod and follow him, switching off the lights as I go. But then I pause, because that uneasy feeling is back. The feeling that we are not alone. I turn and scan the darkness, my eyes roaming through the living room toward my closed office door.

"Hey. What are you doing?" Sam asks from the bedroom.

"Nothing." I glance toward the kitchen, which is bathed in cool white light from the hood above the stove. The apartment is silent and still. Common sense tells me it's just us here, yet the feeling persists.

"Jordan." Sam pokes his head back out of the bedroom. "Is there a problem?"

"No. I'm coming." I turn back around and enter the bedroom, closing the door behind me, then engage the privacy lock. It's a practically useless gesture. The flimsy lock is meant to deter relatives and friends from barging into the bedroom at an inopportune moment, not keep a determined intruder at bay. But it makes me feel better. Yet after I climb into bed, I end up lying awake despite my weariness while Sam snores softly at my side.

That's when I hear it. The soft, barely perceptible cry of a baby floating in the darkness. A baby that everyone claims is not in the building. Now is my chance to prove that I'm not hearing things. But by the time I roll over to shake Sam awake and prove that it's real, the crying has faded yet again, and silence fills the void.

51

I don't sleep well, and when Sam gets up for work, I open my eyes and sit up.

"Hey, sleepyhead, didn't mean to disturb you," he says, pulling on a white polo shirt.

"You didn't. I was half awake anyway. Bad night."

"Nervous about the meeting today?"

"No. Well, a little, but that isn't it. I heard the baby again."

Sam stops what he's doing. "Jordan, there is no baby. You know that."

"And I know what I heard."

Sam falls silent for a moment. "I never heard anything."

"You were asleep."

The look he gives me says *That's convenient*. "I have to go. We'll talk about this when I get home tonight, okay?"

"Sure." Great. He thinks I'm losing my mind.

"Will you be all right on your own here today?"

Now it's my turn to give him a look.

"Hey, just asking. I'm worried about you."

"Just go." I slide back down under the covers and roll over. I can hear him moving around the bedroom as he finishes getting dressed. The door opens, then shuts softly. Silence wraps around me. I close my eyes, try not to think about where this might be leading. I shouldn't have said anything. Sam has been on alert ever since the miscarriage, looking for signs that I'm slipping back into the depression that almost tore us apart. I'm not sure how to convince him that I'm not losing my shit again. But I can see how it must look, and I don't blame him for being worried, because I'm scared of ending up in that headspace again. It was dreadful. But I know how I felt back then, and this isn't it.

I stifle a yawn and slide deeper under the covers, wrapping them around my body like a soothing cocoon.

The next thing I know, it's ten o'clock. Shit, I fell back asleep, and on the worst possible day. My meeting with the Glendale's executive board is at 1:00 p.m. I take a quick shower, dress, and make a cup of coffee before heading to my office . . . only to make a discovery that sends me into a panic.

The mood board is missing.

I stare at the desk, and at first I think I'm just not seeing it; then I launch into a frantic search. I check beside the desk on both sides to see if it's leaning there, even though I know it won't be. I pull my chair out and look under the desk. I even open the drawers and rifle through them, which is ridiculous, because the mood board couldn't even fit into a drawer. Finally, I go back into the living room and search there, too, but there's no sign of the mood board. Which is impossible because it should be right there, in my office, where I left it yesterday.

Except that it's not.

I go through the rest of the apartment like a whirlwind. Bedroom. Bathroom. Kitchen. Even the walk-in closet. Nowhere is spared from my scrutiny. Defeated, I return to the living room, sit down on the sofa, and cast my mind back to the previous night. Is there something that I'm forgetting? Did I go back into the office after Sam came home and put it somewhere weird? No. I might have been a little tipsy thanks to my evening of drinking wine with Jennifer, but I wasn't *that* drunk. Which leaves only one possibility. Someone else moved it. And the list of suspects is short.

There's Jennifer, but I can't think of any way that it could have been her. She never went near the office. And why would she even bother?

Which leaves Sam. But he is the most supportive person in my life and would never sabotage me like that. Plus, we need the money from the coffee shop project, which makes it even less likely that he'd do anything to risk it. And I'm pretty sure that he never even went near the office after he came home. Unless he went in there this morning.

I'm clutching at straws, but it's all I've got, so I call him.

The phone rings several times, and I expect to get his voicemail, but then Sam answers.

"Jordan?" He sounds concerned—hardly surprising, under the circumstances. "Is everything all right?"

"It's fine," I tell him. "Well, sort of. I can't find the mood board for the coffee shop, and I have a meeting this afternoon. Have you seen it?"

"No."

My heart sinks. "Are you sure? It was on my desk last night, and now it's gone."

"Of course I'm sure. How could you lose something that big?"

"I don't know." I'm starting to freak out. "That's why I'm calling you."

"Okay. Calm down. It has to be there somewhere."

"It's not. I've looked."

"Are you sure you didn't move it last night and forgot? You and Jennifer polished off a bottle and a half of wine." There's no recrimination in his voice, only worry. "You were pretty buzzed."

"Don't be ridiculous."

"I was just asking. What about Jennifer?"

"She never went near the office." I rub my temples with my free hand. "This is bad. Like, really bad. What am I going to do? I don't have anything to show the board."

"I'm sure it's there somewhere." Sam pauses, and I hear him talking to someone. His voice is muffled, as if he's holding a hand over the phone's mic. After a few seconds, he comes back on. "Look, I've got to go. We're knee deep in it here."

"Oh. Okay."

"Just try to stay calm. You'll figure it out. I love you and I'll see you tonight."

I'm about to say that I love him, too, when the line goes dead.

I sit on the sofa, racking my brain to remember if I did something weird with it after drinking all that wine, like Sam suggested, but I come up empty. I don't know why it's not in my office, but I know one thing . . . It wasn't me who moved it. Right now, that doesn't matter. The mood board is missing. Which means I'll have to pull together all the scraps and leftovers I can find and make another one. And quickly, because my presentation is in less than two hours.

52

I find an old mood board I made for a past client in the office closet and peel off the samples, photographs, and notes as carefully as I can, trying to preserve the integrity of the foam board beneath, since I don't have time to run out and buy a new one. Then I re-create the missing layout as best I can with the leftover scraps of fabric, photos, and paint chips that I didn't use on the original board. I stare at my hasty replacement with dismay. After ninety minutes of frenetic activity, all I've managed is a pale comparison to the original. Which is hardly surprising, because I poured my heart and soul into the missing board, and this one looks like a school art project thrown together by a disinterested student.

In the end, I accept that it's what I have to work with. I gather together my laptop and phone, grab the mood board, and head for the door. Ten minutes later, I arrive at the library on the ground floor to find the executive board already seated and waiting.

The presentation takes about an hour. I show them my less-than-perfect mood board, then go over my vision for the coffee shop, explaining how I'll use mixed metals for the fixtures alongside reupholstered and refinished vintage furniture to create a cozy, inviting space where patrons can relax and enjoy their favorite beverage. The board members sit in silence and listen with blank expressions on their faces, then subject me to a barrage of questions at the end. It's hardly the enthusiastic response I was hoping for, but I don't expect much else under the circumstances. The missing mood board has left me unsure of myself, and my presentation is discombobulated and rambling. Instead of projecting an aura of confidence, I come across as nervous and unprepared. The crying baby from last night and my exchange with Sam this morning aren't helping.

At one point, Dr. Burgess clears his throat and asks if I'm just having an off day, or if my work is always this shoddy. He fixes me with an unnerving stare as he speaks, and when my gaze briefly meets his, there's a coldness in his eyes. I give him a stuttering, clumsy answer, even as I wonder where the compassion normally associated with people in his profession has gone, or if it was ever there in the first place.

When the executive board finally dismisses me, I can't wait to get out of there. The weird vibe I'm getting from Dr. Burgess, and the general mood of everyone else in the room, only adds to my discomfort. I slink from the library and head toward the elevator. But I don't get far. I'm halfway across the lobby when Catherine catches up with me.

"Jordan, my dear," she says in a stern tone that foreshadows what's about to come. "I assume that you have a good explanation for the uninspired nature of your performance just now."

"I'm sorry," I tell her, trying to sound calm and collected when in reality I'm anything but. "I had some issues with the original mood board and had to make a new one. I guess it threw me off."

"Issues?" Catherine raises an eyebrow. "You've had weeks to prepare your presentation. Perhaps you shouldn't have waited until the last minute."

"You don't understand. It wasn't like that. I had it made ready, but then—"

"I'm not interested in excuses." Catherine cuts me off and folds her arms. "Your presentation was sloppy and unprofessional. That mood board looked like some sort of dreadful kindergarten art project."

"I know." The strap of my laptop bag is starting to slide from my shoulder. I hike it higher and in the process almost drop the offending board, which is tucked under my other arm. "I'll do better next time, I promise."

"Assuming there is a next time."

My heart sinks. After all my hard work, I'm on the brink of losing this job. After what happened with Judy Abelman, it feels like fate is kicking me while I'm down. "Please, don't fire me."

Catherine studies me with narrowed eyes. I shuffle my feet, uncomfortable under her gaze.

At last, she sighs and shakes her head. "I suppose we can give you one more chance, but fair warning, we were not impressed with your work. Honestly, if you weren't a part of the Glendale family, we would probably just cancel the contract right now for noncompliance."

What is she talking about? I might have been a little off my game today, but noncompliance? The replacement mood board wasn't *that* bad. My first instinct is to argue back, but it would just make things worse, so instead, I try to look contrite. "Thank you, Catherine. I won't let you down."

"Make sure you don't, because if there's a repeat of this debacle, we're done. Understand?"

"Yes."

"I hope so, for your sake." Somehow, Catherine manages to look even more stern than before. "Because the contract you signed has a performance clause that clearly states you must return any advanced payments if you cannot fulfill your end of the bargain due to incompetence, and I'm pretty sure that you can't afford to do that."

Incompetence? What a nerve this woman has. I might not have been in top form today, but I was far from incompetent. Still, she's not wrong about the money. I've already been paid a quarter of my fee, which was due upon signing the contract and amounts to $3,750. Half of it has already been spent on living expenses like the Glendale's monthly maintenance charge. If the board decides to fire me and demand the money back, I don't know what I would do. How would we survive with only Sam's wage coming in? Because I don't have any other clients right now. I was hoping that the coffee shop would be a springboard for my future. The catalyst for picking up more commercial clients. Now it's all crumbling around me.

Catherine fixes her gaze upon me, as if she expects me to say something else. When I don't, she tuts, then pivots and strides back toward the library, leaving me staring after her.

I watch her go, stunned and dismayed, then turn back to the elevator and press the call button. Five minutes later, I'm back in the apartment and heading for my office. After stepping into the room, I let the laptop bag slip from my shoulder and place it on the floor near the door; then I start toward the desk, intending to put the mood board down.

Then I notice something that stops me in my tracks.

The original board is back, leaning against the wall under the window, as if it was there all along.

53

Him

Then

I've given you time to grieve, my darling, but now the game must begin. I've been waiting for you to notice me, but you've been distracted. Not paying attention to the subtle clues that I am here, waiting for you. My former loves began to feel me watching, turned to look when they felt the weight of my eyes on those long, dark walks home. Noticed an item or two moved in their apartment.

I'll not lie, it's been a bit of a disappointment, your lack of attention to my gestures of courtship. But that ends now, my beautiful Raven. Today our courtship begins.

I watch through the window as you pick up the pajamas you always lay at the bottom of your bed in the morning. And now you notice that those cute little bottoms are missing. I see you look down and discover the small black jewelry box I've left in their place. Confusion. Curiosity. Panic. I watch the emotions run across your face and feel my excitement growing. I duck back as your head swings around, an uneasy glance to check that you are alone.

After a few moments, I peek back through the window, and now you've picked up the box. Your hand trembles when you open the lid to reveal a silver crescent moon on a black leather cord with a silver clasp. Yes, I know your name. I know where you live. And I shall enjoy the scent of you tonight as I sleep with your pajamas beside me. I can't help but smile as you toss the trinket across the room like you've been burned. Welcome to our courtship, my Raven.

54

Jordan

Now

The mood board was missing, and now it's back, leaning against the wall under the window in plain view. It's enough to make me wonder if I really am losing my mind. But who cares, because it's a chance to redeem myself. I snatch it up and dash back through the apartment, ride the elevator down to the lobby, and all but run to the library, only to find that the lights are off, the chairs have been rearranged in a circle around the table, and there's no sign of Catherine, her husband, or Dr. Burgess.

I rush back through the lobby and to the room they want to turn into a coffee shop, hoping they'll be there, but the door is locked. When I return to the lobby, it's empty. Angelo is missing, and the sign is out on his desk. Considering how quiet this building is, he sure does spend a lot of time helping other residents, most of whom I've never even seen. When I step back into the elevator, I'm tempted to go up to the penthouse to show the magically reappeared mood board to Catherine and Ron. But I don't, because I'm afraid it would only make things worse if I showed up out of breath and flustered, banging on their door in a frantic attempt to redeem myself. Instead, I press the button for the fourth floor. Maybe I'll text Catherine once I get back to the apartment, ask her to stop by whenever she has a minute. That way, I won't look quite so desperate.

But I don't get that far.

Because when I step out of the elevator, I notice the painting hanging on the wall opposite. It should be an impressionist rendering of the Glendale, which Catherine claimed her great-grandfather had brought back from Paris in the late 1800s after meeting Édouard Manet at the Folies-Bergère and providing him with a photo.

But it isn't.

The painting that now confronts me is about the most grotesque piece of art I've ever seen: a woman wearing a pale-blue dress, tears streaming down her face as she tries to hold on to an infant, arms lifted toward the sky as the back half of the child disintegrates into a swarm of bees that spiral up into a dark and angry sky.

I recoil. Who would put such a dreadful piece of art here, and more to the point, why? I'm overcome by a flash of memory from my trip to the basement. Of the stuffed toy in the shape of a bee. Surely this must be coincidence. Horrified, I can't stand to look at this dreadful painting a moment longer. I tear my gaze away and hurry into the apartment. Only then can I breathe again, because the painting has stirred in me a deep sense of loss. The woman trying desperately to keep her baby even as the dream of motherhood crumbles through her fingers. If whoever replaced the previous artwork knew anything of my history, they would never have put such an awful canvas right outside my door.

I spend what's left of the afternoon in a funk. The day's events hang over me like a dark cloud. The *missing, then not missing mood board* and my discovery of that hideous painting. I have a feeling there's an uncomfortable conversation with Catherine in my future, because I have no intention of letting that painting stay there.

I read for a while, but it's hard to concentrate. After several chapters, when I realize that I haven't absorbed a single word, I give up. At one point I pick up the phone and call Dawn, hoping she'll come over and keep me company, but she doesn't answer. Disappointed, I turn on the

TV, then sit on the couch with a cup of herbal tea and a pack of cookies I find in the pantry.

That evening, when Sam arrives home from work, I'm expecting him to mention the new painting in the hallway, but he doesn't. Instead, he saunters into the living room as if nothing is wrong and throws his coat over the back of a chair. "I hear your presentation went well."

I look up, confused. "Where did you hear that?"

"Catherine. I ran into her in the lobby, and she told me how pleased everyone was with your work and how excited they are to have you on the team. She said your concept was 'fresh and unique.' Those were her exact words. It'll make a great quote for your website. I guess you found the mood board, huh?"

"No, I didn't. I had to make a new one at the last minute using leftover scraps, and it was awful. I completely screwed up. Regardless of what Catherine told you, no one was impressed. She made her disappointment abundantly clear."

"That's weird. But hey, sounds like she's changed her mind, so it's all good."

"Yeah. Especially since the original mood board was right here when I got back."

Sam looks at me, and I can tell what he's thinking. That I somehow missed it and freaked out. I lay those suspicions to rest before he can even voice the thought.

"Whoa. Easy there," he exclaims once I'm finished. "I wasn't going to say that."

"But you were thinking it."

"No, I wasn't. And you should be happy. Catherine and the board liked your ideas. Even if you did misplace the original mood board, there's no harm done."

"I guess." I struggle to inject even an ounce of enthusiasm into my reply.

"What's wrong?"

"What do you think? That painting opposite the elevator. Why would someone put a thing like that on the wall?"

"What painting? The one of the Glendale?"

"No." I can't believe he didn't notice it. "The one that replaced it of the woman holding the disintegrating child. It's creepy and gross and in poor taste, and I understand that no one here knows about my miscarriage, but—"

"Jordan, what are you talking about? The painting in the hallway is the same one that's always been there."

"No, it's not. I'll show you." I jump up and head toward the foyer.

I pull the door open and step into the hallway, then come to a halt. Because he's right. The painting of the Glendale hangs on the wall as if it never went anywhere.

"Well?" Sam is standing in the doorway.

"I swear, it was a different painting earlier."

"Or you saw what you wanted to see."

"Why would I want to see *that*?"

"You tell me." Sam turns and goes back inside.

"Sam, wait." I hurry after him. "Please, listen to me."

"No." He shakes his head. "This can't go on. You're hearing babies in a building where there are none. You somehow got locked in a storage cage, even though you had the padlock in your pocket. A storage cage that contained an unused crib, I might add. You lost that job with your mother's friend Judy because you told her you were too busy, and you don't remember doing it. You're seeing paintings that aren't there of disintegrating babies. I'm worried, Jordan. I know how much it hurt when we lost the baby. We went through hell—both of us. But I thought we'd come out the other side. That you were ready to accept what happened and move on. Now I'm not so sure."

"This has nothing to do with the miscarriage," I snap at him. "That was awful, and it almost tore us apart, but I'm better now."

"Yet you're hearing phantom babies and hallucinating moving toys," Sam says. "Oh, and let's not forget the mysterious disappearing mood board. This isn't normal, Jordan. Maybe you need to start taking your meds again."

"I'm not going back on those antidepressants. You know how they made me feel."

"Then at least talk to your dad. He'll know what to do."

"I'm not doing that, either. This isn't in my head, Sam. It's real. Why won't you believe me?"

"Because it doesn't make sense. I'm right here in the apartment with you, and I haven't seen or heard a thing." Sam reaches out like he wants to comfort me.

I take a step back. "Don't touch me. If you won't listen to what I have to say, then I don't want your pity."

"You're being ridiculous."

"And you're being an asshole." I know that he's not, but my frustration gets the better of me. Because if the tables were turned and he was experiencing stuff like this, I'd like to think that I would believe him. Instead, he doubts me and my mental stability, even though he's supposed to be the one person who will always support me, through thick or thin.

Sam's face is thunder. "I can't deal with you right now." He turns toward the bedroom. "I'm going to take a shower. Maybe when I'm done, you'll be more reasonable."

"I wouldn't count on it." My teacup is still on the coffee table. I resist the urge to pick it up and throw it as Sam stalks off into the bedroom and slams the door. After all, the cup hasn't done anything wrong. Instead, I pick it up and go to the kitchen, rinse it, then put it in the dishwasher, mostly because the alternative is to stand there stewing.

I hear Sam moving around in the bedroom, and then the shower running.

There's a ding from Sam's phone, which is sitting on the island.

I glance down in time to see a text message flash up on the lock screen, then disappear. But not before I've read it. And what it says sends a chill running through me.

Last night was fun. We should do it again soon.

55

“What the hell is this?” I demand, holding the phone up when Sam steps out of the bedroom, his hair still damp.

He stares at the phone. There’s a stiffness to his voice when he says, “You’ll need to be more specific.”

“‘Last night was fun,’” I say, reciting the text message. “‘We should do it again soon.’ Care to explain?”

Sam furrows his brow. He takes the phone from me, then looks down at the screen, which is unlocked because I know his passcode. “I have no idea what this is.”

“That’s convenient.” It’s a local number that isn’t in Sam’s contacts, and I don’t recognize it. “You came in last night really late and smelling of liquor. Who were you with?”

“You know very well who I was with because I told you already. My meeting ran over, and then I went for drinks with the guys from the office. It’s probably from one of them.”

It doesn’t sound like the sort of text that one man would send to another, especially a coworker. It feels too . . . intimate . . . even though there isn’t any overt display of emotion in the message. I say as much.

Sam shrugs, anger dancing in his eyes. “I can’t help that.”

“Don’t you have the phone numbers of everyone you work with in your contacts?”

“I don’t know. Probably.” He looks down at the phone and types a quick message, then turns the screen toward me so that I can see what he wrote.

Don't recognize the number. Who is this?

For a moment, nothing happens. Then a new message appears.

Sorry. Wrong number.

"Satisfied?"

I nod, because what else can I do? Of course, if the text was from our neighbor, or some other woman he was having a dalliance with, she would probably read between the lines and reply exactly like that.

"Good. How about next time, you don't jump to conclusions. What did you think? That I was out screwing around?"

"I never said that." It's a weak attempt to backpedal, especially since that was exactly what I was thinking. I mean, who wouldn't?

"Yeah, right." Sam sees right through my protestations. "There's nothing going on between me and Kalina, and I don't appreciate the insinuation that there is." He shakes his head. "I don't know, maybe this is all just another manifestation of whatever the hell is going on with you, but pushing me away, accusing me of stuff I haven't done, isn't going to bring our child back."

"That's a horrible thing to say." I glare at him, tears welling in my eyes. How dare he go there. It's heartless. "None of this is about our baby."

"No, it's about you thinking I fucked the woman across the hall," Sam rages. He turns and stomps toward the front door, throwing one last dig over his shoulder as he goes. "This isn't normal. You need help, Jordan. Like serious, professional help."

"What?" I can sense the threads of our relationship falling away. I want to catch them, put everything back the way it should be. I just don't know how. "Where are you going?"

"Out. I need some time alone. Don't wait up."

56

Sam doesn't come home for hours. I sit on the couch staring at the door, my stomach in knots, until eventually I call him, but he doesn't answer. I call twice more during the next hour, then finally send him a text message around eleven asking if he's okay. Now I get a response. A curt yes, followed by go to bed.

So that's what I do. If Sam wants space, there's nothing I can do about it. I climb between the covers and turn the TV on, mostly because the silent apartment is unnerving.

Then, at midnight, Sam comes back.

I hear the front door open, then close. A moment later, he appears at the bedroom door. I think he's going to try to make up. He's right there. I can see it in his face. But instead, he grabs his pillow and stomps off to the living room and the couch, slamming the bedroom door closed as if to punctuate his exit. I don't sleep for a long while, lying and waiting for him to return. Hoping his anger will thaw. It doesn't, and eventually I drift off into a fitful sleep.

I'm awakened early the next morning by the sound of Sam moving around the bedroom. I pretend I'm still asleep, watching him through mostly closed eyes, as he showers and dresses. When he's gone, I lie there a while longer, then get up, make coffee, and sit at the island wallowing in a pool of misery. I'm not feeling much better by the time I meet my mother for the lunch date we'd arranged over the phone several days before.

Stetski's Deli is everything the name suggests. They even declare their pastrami on rye to be better than anything found on New York's Lower East Side, which is a dubious claim at best. It wouldn't be my first choice, but it is the safe one, since my mother doesn't exactly have adventurous taste in food. A couple of years ago, Sam and I met my parents at an Indian restaurant. She refused to partake of anything except the naan bread and even complained about that. She has no such problem today and demolishes a corned beef sandwich while talking a mile a minute between mouthfuls about Dad, and how he's working himself into an early grave.

When she asks about Sam—more out of duty than genuine interest—and how we're liking it at the Glendale, I say what's expected of me. He's fine. I'm fine. The apartment is fine. Everything in my life is a bed of roses! I tell her nothing of our conversation the night before, or what I've been experiencing, because I don't want her to think I've relapsed. And I certainly don't want my father to hear about it, or he'll be trying to book a session to crack open my head and rummage through my perceived psychosis.

Afterward, we make our way to Chestnut Hill and spend a couple of hours wandering in and out of stores. It's three thirty by the time I arrive back at the Glendale with a couple of shopping bags in each hand. I take the elevator to the fourth floor and reach the apartment. I drop the bags on the floor and rummage in my pocket for the door key. But before I can use it, the door opens, and Sam is standing there. He looks surprised to see me.

I'm even more surprised, because it's three thirty on a Friday afternoon, and he should be at work.

"Jordan. I didn't think you would be home so soon." His tone is flat and tense—no surprise, under the circumstances. He looks past me as if he was expecting someone else. "You're always gone for so long when you go out with your mother. I figured you'd be at least a couple more hours."

"Trust me, three hours is long enough." I glance around, wondering who Sam is looking for, but I don't see anyone. But I do notice Kalina's door, which is slightly open. A thin sliver of apartment is visible through the gap. A wood floor, a slice of dark-green-painted wall, and part of a swirling abstract painting. "Why are *you* home so early?"

"Catherine." Sam looks over my shoulder one more time, his eyes roaming the hallway, then steps aside to let me into the apartment. "She called me at work. Apparently, there's some sort of problem with the pipes in a bathroom above us on the fifth floor. She wanted to make sure water wasn't leaking into our apartment. She said you weren't home and didn't pick up when she called you."

"You knew I was having lunch with my mom today." I take my phone out and check the call log—not that I'm in any way suspicious. There is nothing from Catherine or anyone else. "I didn't get a call."

"Just telling you what she told me."

"Why didn't Angelo take care of it?" The whole point of having a doorman is that he has access to the apartment if there's a problem.

"How would I know." There's a weary *Here we go again* tone in his voice.

Sam's explanation is perfectly reasonable, but I can't help thinking that something is off with his reaction. How his gaze kept shifting past me into the hallway. A knot twists in my stomach as an image forces its way into my head of how I found Sam and Kalina down in the laundry room, huddled like conspirators. "How long have you been home?"

"Since about two thirty."

It feels a little too convenient that the plumbing issue happened on the *one* day I'm not at home and working in my office. I'm tempted to turn around and go upstairs, find Catherine, and ask her if Sam is telling the truth. But I don't, because that would only solidify his conviction that I need counseling. And anyway, would he really be stupid enough to tell such an easily disprovable lie?

57

We spend another evening barely talking to each other, but at least we keep things civil enough to avoid an all-out argument. Sam doesn't even try to follow me into the bedroom when I rise from the couch at ten and declare that I'm getting an early night. He eventually slinks in two hours later and climbs quietly into bed, then lies facing away from me. Apparently, one night on the couch was enough.

I sleep late on Saturday morning. When I wake up, the bed is empty and there's a text message on my phone. Sam has gone into the office to finish up some work he couldn't complete before the weekend.

Weak sunlight filters in through the shades. A faint breeze stirs the air when the heating unit kicks on. In our old place back in Jamaica Plain, I would almost certainly have heard our neighbors having one of their regular weekend fights, bleating car horns on the street outside, and the distant wail of sirens from the firehouse on Centre Street. Here, though, there is nothing. The Glendale's construction is so sturdy that I doubt a twenty-one-gun salute would penetrate its walls. At least if I ignore the crying baby I've been hearing. The one Sam thinks is all in my head. Thankfully, it isn't crying right now.

I linger in bed for another half hour—it's the weekend, right?—then reluctantly decide that I need to get moving. But when I swing my legs off the bed and stand up, a sharp, piercing pain shoots up my leg from my foot. I let out a startled yelp and sit back down on the bed, then pull my foot up and examine the sole. A small glob of blood oozes from a pinprick on my heel. Confused, I look down, searching for the cause of my injury.

And there, on the floor next to the bed, I see a delicate gold earring.

But not just any earring. Because when I reach down and snatch it up, I recognize the cascade of shimmering rough green gemstones that dangle between my thumb and index finger as part of a one-of-a-kind, handmade set that Kalina was wearing at the Glendale's monthly cocktail party and our dinner party.

58

I stare at the earring and try to convince myself that the dreadful realization of what this means isn't true. That Sam didn't cheat on me with *that* woman right here in our bed. That he didn't lie about it right to my face. But no matter how I try to rationalize my discovery, I can't, because how else could the earring have gotten there? It all makes sense now. Sam might have started out helping our neighbor navigate her issues with the Wainwright Building, but it didn't stay that way. That's why he was reluctant to distance himself from her. It also explains the dinner party. I wasn't just imagining that look she gave me. It really was a message.

And what about yesterday? He claimed that Catherine had called him to come home early because of a leak in the apartment above, but now I know the truth. He left work early because he knew I wouldn't be home, and it gave him an opportunity to spend the afternoon with Kalina. But what really makes me see red is that he didn't even have the decency to screw the woman somewhere else, like the apartment across the hall. Instead, he did it right there in our bed. Was it somehow more exciting to fuck our neighbor right there in the same bed we've made love in so many times?

I want to shout, and cry, and scream at the top of my lungs, and break something. I want to grab a pair of scissors and cut up his shirts, stab the pillow where he lays his head every night, and throw his stuff off the balcony and into the street below. But most of all, I want to turn the clock back and make sure that we never move into this building. I want to erase the weeks since we met Kalina and continue along a different, happier path, blissfully unaware of the dire consequences that one seemingly innocent decision can have. But I can't rewind time, and even if I could, it wouldn't change the underlying flaw in our relationship—the flaw in him—that I hadn't seen clearly until this moment.

I'm still holding the earring. I let it drop into the palm of my hand. It's such a small object to cause such a large rift. To rip a person's life apart with cold indifference. I close my fingers over it and make a fist, squeeze until the rough stones and sharp metal dig into my skin. The pain is cathartic. It sweeps away the fog of disbelief. But it can't erase the dark sense of loss that gnaws at me from within.

I open my hand and stare down at Kalina's earring lying in my palm, and in that moment, I decide. I need to know for sure, and I need to know right now. I stand and get dressed, pulling on a pair of jeans and a T-shirt, then hurry through the apartment to the front door. Catherine lives two floors above us in the penthouse suite, which occupies the entire top level of the building, and this is where I go. I step into the elevator and press the button for the sixth floor. It's only when the elevator starts to rise that I realize I'm still clutching the earring. I'd put it down on the nightstand while I got dressed and must have picked it up again without realizing. I push it into my pocket as the elevator arrives at the penthouse suite. I step out into a square hallway smaller than the one on my floor, because instead of four doors, there is only one, which I bang on with a clenched fist.

When no one answers, I bang again, longer this time.

The door opens, and Catherine is standing there looking bewildered. "Jordan, dear? What's all the commotion about?"

"Did you call Sam yesterday?" I ask, launching right in without bothering to explain why I'm asking. "Did you tell him to come home?"

"No." Catherine shakes her head. "Why would I do that?"

"He said there was a leaky water pipe in the apartment above us."

Catherine shakes her head again, more slowly this time. "I didn't call Sam, and there are no leaking pipes. If there were, Angelo would have told me. He takes care of all that stuff."

"You're sure?"

"Quite sure. I might be older, my dear, but I'm not senile."

"Unbelievable." I turn and stride back to the elevator, a red haze clouding my vision. Sam lied to me.

Catherine steps into the hallway. "Jordan, wait. Are you all right? What on earth is going on?"

I don't answer. Instead, I jab at the button for the ground floor, because the apartment that I share with Sam is the last place I want to be right now. I can't stand the thought of spending even one second there, surrounded by the shattered memories of our life together. But when I get to the lobby, I come to a halt, because I don't know where else to go.

I could run to my parents' house, but I can almost hear my mother saying that she knew Sam was no good all along. That she never liked him and that I shouldn't have agreed to marry him. I can imagine my father storming out of the house and going in search of him in a blind fury. None of that would do anything to ease my pain or help me figure out what to do next.

I could go to Sam's office and have it out with him—demand answers—but I'm not ready for that, or willing to air our issues in public. I need time to calm down and figure out how I'm going to handle this before I confront Sam.

I could find a coffee shop and sit there wallowing in self-pity, but I don't want to be around a bunch of strangers.

Which leaves me with one option—returning to the apartment where Sam cheated on me with the woman across the hall. I would rather sit in the lobby than do that. Except for Angelo, the doorman. For once, he's right there at his desk, and I can feel his gaze boring into me. Any moment now, he's going to ask if I need help, and then I'll be forced to interact with him.

And then it hits me. There is somewhere I can go and someone who will lend a sympathetic ear.

I reach into my pocket, take out my phone, and call Dawn.

59

"I'm so sorry," Dawn says after I tell her what I've discovered about Sam. "Are you sure about him and Kalina? I mean, that's pretty brazen, cheating on you in your own bed while you're out shopping with your mom. What a sleazebag."

"I'm sure." We're sitting in the living room of Dawn and Jamie's apartment in the building opposite the Glendale. I've never been here before today, but I'm too distressed to take much notice of my surroundings. No sooner had I walked through the door than I burst out in tears. Thankfully, Jamie is at the gym, so it's just us girls.

"What are you going to do?" Dawn asks.

"I don't know." I wipe the tears from my eyes. "He went into work this morning, so I haven't confronted him yet."

"He *told you* that he went into work," Dawn says, "but are you sure that's really where he is?"

"I'm not sure of anything."

"Well, whatever happens, don't let him talk you into giving him another chance. Trust me, it never works out. Once they've cheated on you, they will keep doing it regardless of what they say."

"I have no intention of giving him another chance." The way I feel right now, Sam will be lucky if I don't throw him off the balcony. Forgiveness is not on the agenda.

"Good."

"I should probably leave. Go back right now and pack a bag. Get the hell out of there before he comes home."

"And go where?"

"I don't know. A hotel, I guess." The obvious place would be my parents' house, but I've already decided that I can't face their smug *I told you so* pity. Sure, my mom will say all the right things, but sandwiched between the comforting words will be the passive-aggressive snipes. Also, I don't want to end up back in my childhood bedroom yet again. That would be too much. A couple of nights at a hotel seems like the best solution. "I need time to figure things out, and I can't stay in the apartment with Sam while I do that. I'm not sure I can even face him right now."

"That goes without saying. Honestly, we'd let you stay here, but we only have one bedroom, and the apartment is so small. There just isn't the space."

"I would never impose on you like that."

"Anyway, why should *you* be the one to leave?" Dawn asks. "It's Sam who caused this mess. He's the one who cheated on you. Kick *his* ass out."

"He's also the only one with a steady wage right now. If he leaves, how would I pay the bills?"

"I never said he should shirk responsibility for the apartment. Both your names are on that contract, right?"

I nod.

"Then he still needs to pay his fair share, at least until the two of you come to an agreement."

"Where would he go?"

"Who cares? That's not your problem."

I hadn't thought of that. And unlike me, he does have somewhere to go. His friend Rob. They've known each other for years, but while Sam has focused on his career, Rob has hardly matured since they were college roommates. He lives in a filthy apartment in Allston, a neighborhood on the west side of Boston, and spends most of his time playing video games and eating junk food. But I don't care about any of that. Rob has a couch, albeit sagging and stained. And now my mind is made up. I'm not leaving . . . Sam is.

60

Sam still isn't home when I return to the apartment around noon. I head straight for the bedroom and drag the large suitcase out from under the bed, open it, and start throwing his clothes inside. Fifteen minutes later, I wheel the suitcase to the front door and leave it in the foyer; then I return to the living room and pace back and forth. The earring is still in my pocket. I pull it out and stare down at it, lying in the palm of my hand. My first instinct is to throw it across the room, but that would solve nothing, so I simply close my fist around it, not tightly enough to cause pain this time, and keep pacing.

When Sam finally walks through the door half an hour later, I get straight to the point.

"Don't bother taking your coat off. I packed a suitcase for you."

Sam comes to a startled halt in the living room doorway and stares at me in wide-eyed confusion. "Jordan? What's going on?"

"You know very well what's going on."

"No, I really don't." Sam glances at the suitcase.

I throw the earring. It hits him in the chest and drops onto the floor. "That was on the bedroom floor next to the bed. Recognize it?"

"No." Sam shakes his head.

"Then let me enlighten you. It's Kalina's."

Sam stares at the earring. "I don't understand."

"You said Catherine called about a leak." My voice cracks. "You told me that was why you were home so early, but it was a lie. Catherine didn't call. You were screwing that woman in our bed."

"No. I wasn't. Catherine called. If you don't believe me, look for yourself." He digs the phone out of his pocket, brings up the call log, and holds it out. "See?"

I snatch the phone from his hand and look at the screen. Only one call came in on Sam's phone yesterday. I don't recognize the number. If Sam is to be believed, then this call was from Catherine. My finger hovers over the screen for a moment; then I call the number and put the phone on speaker.

Sam doesn't look worried. Quite the opposite. The smug expression on his face tells me that he expects to be vindicated.

The phone rings. Once, twice, three times. Then a voice comes on the line that I recognize. But not the one Sam claimed it would be.

This is Kalina. Leave a message, and I will get right back to you.

Sam swallows hard. "What the hell?"

I push the phone back into his hand and point at the door. "Get out. I never want to see you again."

"Jordan. Please. I swear—"

"Go!" The word erupts from somewhere deep within me, carrying with it a whirlwind of hurt and anger.

"This is ridiculous." Sam spins on his heel, marches out of the living room and through the foyer, then pulls the front door open so hard it slams back into the wall and leaves a handle-shaped dent. He doesn't take the suitcase. Instead, he strides across the hallway to Kalina's door and hammers on it with a balled-up fist. "Get out here and tell my fiancée that there's nothing going on between us."

Kalina doesn't answer, which I don't find surprising under the circumstances.

"Answer the fucking door, right now!"

I'm not letting Sam back into the apartment. Not a chance. I take the suitcase and wheel it out into the hallway even as he brings his fist down again on Kalina's door with a fury I've never seen from him before.

There's a gasp to my left. I glance around and see our other neighbors, Frank and Jennifer, standing in their doorway and looking on in shock.

Sam finally drops his arm, and his shoulders slump in defeat.

I've seen enough. I retreat back into the apartment, close and lock the door, and engage the dead bolt, leaving Sam stranded on the other side. Then I lean with my back against it, sink down to the floor, pull my knees up to my chin, and cry.

61

Him

Then

I like your new accessory, Raven. A little pepper spray bottle on a rubber coil wristlet. When you walk, it hits against your fitness watch and makes a jingling sound. It's a soothing reminder that thoughts of me are always with you, just as thoughts of you are always with me.

You finish locking the back door of Cindy's Closet, then look both ways before you step out onto the sidewalk and quickly head toward home. The autumn weather has brought with it the earlier arrival of darkness. Perfect for evenings when you work until closing.

You hear a noise and pick up the pace even as you turn and glance behind. As if I'd be so obvious. I know your route. You can't resist taking the quickest route home, even though if you thought about it, you would realize the folly of your actions. It might get you in the door five minutes earlier, but being predictable is so much more dangerous than the three hundred seconds you save.

As you approach the park, I retreat deeper into the shadows. I like it when you can feel me but can't see me. As you pass, I make a small sound, and your breath quickens before you break into a jog. Not an easy feat in your platform boots and short leather skirt. And you are too scared to look back, because you know that I'm always there, watching and waiting . . .

62

Jordan

Now

Sam hammers on the door for a good fifteen minutes after I lock him out of the apartment, begging me to let him back in. He's making such a ruckus that I'm surprised no one has called the police. But they don't, even though he was being so loud that the entire building must have heard him.

After I'm done crying, I haul myself up from the floor and press an eye to the peephole. Sam is still in the hallway, standing next to the suitcase and looking defeated. I watch him for a few minutes before going into the living room, where I sit on the couch and stare into space. But every once in a while, I stand and go back to the door to see if he's still there. More than an hour passes before he finally takes his bag and goes.

I'm overcome by a mix of relief and sadness. This apartment was supposed to have been our dream, the place where we were going to make a new life, but instead, it's turned into the end of us. I don't see how we'll move forward from here, given what Sam has done. To be honest, I'm in a state of shock. Before the Glendale, I never considered for one moment that he would ever do something like this. I thought

I knew him. I guess that you never really *know* anyone, not even the person you intended to spend the rest of your life with.

The afternoon passes at such a slow pace that I begin to wonder if time is moving at all. More than once, I take my phone out. The first time, I bring Sam's number up and almost call, beg him to come back so we can talk and figure this out, because even through the pain, I love him and can't imagine the rest of my life without him. But I don't, because my world is shattered, and Sam is not the glue that will put it back together, no matter how much I want him to be. Then I consider calling my mother, but I don't do that for the same reason that I didn't run to her earlier. I need time to absorb this before I'm subjected to my parents' particular brand of stifling sympathy. There's probably a little embarrassment mixed in, too. No one likes to admit that they got it so wrong.

By six o'clock I can't take it anymore. I go to the kitchen and open the wine fridge. The first bottle I pull out is a Napa Valley pinot, which I quickly put back because it's Sam's favorite. The second bottle is a cabernet, which I decide is good enough. I pour a large glass, then grab the bottle and head back to the couch. Silence presses in around me, heavy and suffocating. I take a large gulp of the wine and reach for the TV remote.

At that moment, there is a knock at the door.

I don't move. Has Sam come back to dissuade me from kicking him out? If so, it won't work. I have no intention of letting him put a foot inside this apartment, tonight or any other night in the immediate future. I don't care what he has to say or how apologetic he is. I don't want to hear his protestations of innocence, because the evidence is overwhelming. As far as I'm concerned, Sam is a nonentity. The next time he steps across the threshold will be to collect the rest of his stuff and get the hell out of my life forever.

Another knock.

It doesn't have the urgency I would expect from Sam.

From the other side of the door comes a voice, soft and concerned. "Jordan? It's Jennifer from next door. I need to know that you're all right."

Jennifer! She and Frank witnessed Sam's enraged outburst in the hallway. They were standing right there when I locked him out. I'm not sure that I want to see anyone right now, but I have a feeling she isn't going to let me ignore her.

I put the glass down, go to the door, and open it.

Jennifer doesn't bother to wait for an invitation. She strides right in. "Thank heavens you're okay. Frank and I were so worried."

I'm not sure that *okay* is the word I would choose, but I don't argue. I also don't bother trying to stop her from entering the apartment, because I'm too emotionally weary to bother with a confrontation. Instead, I close the door and let her follow me into the living room.

"I just opened a bottle of wine," I tell her. "Would you like a glass?"

Jennifer looks at the bottle. "Are you sure that drinking is a good idea under the circumstances?"

"I think it's a fantastic idea." What better way to dull the pain of Sam's betrayal than through copious amounts of alcohol?

Jennifer observes me for a few moments, then shrugs. "Very well. You might as well get me a glass, because I'm not going to let you sit here and drink alone." She folds her arms. "Now, why don't you tell me what's going on between you and Sam?"

63

For the second time, I pour my heart out. I tell Jennifer about Sam and everything that's happened between us since we moved into the Glendale. The only concession I make is to leave Kalina's name out of it. I have no idea how close Frank and Jennifer are to their neighbor, but I know that they've all been living here for many years. The last thing I want to do is start yet another feud with one of the neighbors. But Jennifer quickly guesses who Sam has been having an affair with, probably because of his reaction earlier in the day. After all, you don't hammer on someone's door like that for no reason.

"Kalina has always been flirty," she says, watching me intently over the top of her wineglass. "I'm not making excuses for the woman. Far from it—I don't believe in wrecking relationships—but it's who she is. Still, I wouldn't have expected her to get entangled with one of the neighbors. It's simply unacceptable. I'm so sorry."

"Thank you." I'm overcome by a sudden desire to put this awful day behind me. Perhaps tomorrow I'll be able to think more clearly. Of course, the two large glasses of wine I've consumed aren't helping. I glance down at my phone on the coffee table and see that it's nine o'clock. I've been unburdening myself to Jennifer for more than two hours. I put my glass down. "I hope you don't mind, Jennifer, but I'm really tired."

"Not at all, my dear." Jennifer has been nursing the same glass all night. Now she finishes it off and stands up. "If you need anything, Frank and I are just next door. Don't hesitate to call, day or night."

I thank her and promise I'll keep that in mind, then walk her to the door.

In the hallway, she hesitates, then leans close and wraps her arms around me in an unexpected hug.

"I simply hate the thought of you being in this apartment all alone tonight," she says in my ear, her voice barely above a whisper. "Perhaps you should consider going to stay with your parents for a few days, or maybe a friend."

"I'll be fine," I reassure her, then close the door and make my way back into the living room.

I flop back down onto the couch and turn the TV on, glad for the background noise. Being in the apartment without Sam is strange, like a piece of me is missing. I half expect him to appear in the bedroom doorway as if he's just been changing or taking a shower. But the truth is inescapable, and eventually I drag myself up and head for the bedroom. But when I go to climb into the bed, an image of Kalina lying there naked comes into my head, Sam making furious love to her.

Nope. I'm not sleeping on those sheets. No way in hell.

I drag the comforter back and strip the bed, then take the sheets and pillowcases and dump them outside the bedroom door in a wad. Tomorrow, I'll dispose of them for good in the trash compactor. Next, I go to the closet and find another set and a blanket, then remake the bed. Only then do I feel comfortable. But even after I climb in, thoughts of Sam and Kalina fill my head. I can almost feel the heat of her body and hear the gasps of pleasure.

Stop it! Stop it right now. If I keep on like this, I'll end up sleeping on the couch, or worse, I won't end up sleeping at all. Today has been awful, and God, do I want it over. I pick up the remote, turn on the TV, and go to the Discovery Channel, where I find a documentary that's sure to numb my brain. Then I lie there with my eyes glued to the screen.

And it works.

After about twenty minutes, my eyelids droop, and I fall into a restless sleep.

64

Sunday morning feels weird. Actually, it feels like I'm trapped in a strange alternate reality where everything is the opposite of what it should be. Just a few short weeks ago, Sam and I were moving into the Glendale, and I wasn't even considering a future where he was no longer a part of my life, but now that unimaginable future stretches ahead of me like a long, dark tunnel, and unlike the trite old phrase, I see no light at the end.

Now that the initial shock has faded, I wander the apartment, barely able to comprehend how our perfect future could have turned so toxic in such a short time. Of course, the reason is obvious.

Kalina.

She barreled through our lives like an F5 tornado, ripping apart everything she touched. I feel like marching across the hall and banging on her door just like Sam did yesterday. I want to see the look in her eyes when I tell her what a miserable, home-wrecking bitch she is. Except I'm scared that instead of shame or remorse, I'll see a different emotion in her eyes. Satisfaction. But losing it with Kalina wouldn't accomplish anything, because the truth is that our sultry neighbor comprises only one half of the equation. Without Sam's willingness to be seduced and destroy our relationship, she would have gotten nowhere. If anything, he bears more responsibility than her, because Kalina is a practical stranger and single, while Sam was supposed to love me.

I make coffee, more out of habit than anything else, then sit at the kitchen island. The coffee is awful. I might as well be drinking sludge. It's like even my taste buds have abandoned me. I give up and pour what's left down the sink, then distract myself with housework, because the alternative is to wallow in my pain.

I scrub down the countertops and unload the dishwasher. I vacuum and dust and put stuff away in a mad attempt to keep busy. At one point, my mother calls, but I ignore it. An hour later, there's another call. This time it's Dawn. I ignore that one, too. I'm not in the mood to talk right now. Then, at four in the afternoon, the phone rings again. It's Sam. Needless to say, I let it go to voicemail—if I wasn't picking up for anyone else, I'm sure as hell not answering *that* call. He leaves a message, but I don't listen to it. Instead, I head for the main bedroom's walk-in closet and the stack of boxes in the back corner we haven't yet gotten around to unpacking.

I grab one with *Bathroom* written on the top in black marker and lug it into the en suite.

It might seem like unpacking our belongings right now is futile. After what's happened. I don't even know if I'll still be living in this apartment a month from now. We bought into the Glendale as a couple, and even though we are not officially allowed to sell for five years, there must be some provision for a situation like ours. I remember Jennifer and Frank saying that the previous occupants of this unit were allowed to sell early and move out because their circumstances changed. But I need to do something—anything—to keep myself from falling into a pit of despair, and I've exhausted all the other household busywork.

The box contains towels, washcloths, and other assorted bathroom paraphernalia that we probably won't need. We've collected so many towels since we've been living together that I'm not sure why we even bothered keeping these. Most of them are old, and they're not our favorites. I should probably just bundle them back into the box and take them to Goodwill. But that's a decision for another day. I put everything away, break the box down, then head back to get another.

The next two boxes are full of place mats, table runners, and napkins that belonged to my parents. My mother gave them to us when we moved in here, since we finally had a real dining room. Most of them aren't my style, which is why I've been ignoring this box. The obvious place to store it all is the built-in cabinet that takes up half of one wall of the dining room. The top part of the cabinet has shelves behind glass doors, but the rest is drawers. I heave the boxes into the dining room. I open the first box, grab a pile of place mats, and stuff them in the top drawer, then put a bunch more in the drawer below. The third drawer won't budge when I pull on it. I tug harder but still only manage to get it open halfway before the drawer jams and refuses to move in either direction.

I curse and turn my attention to the lowest drawer before filling it with the last of the place mats. A gold-and-red Christmas set and another, even uglier set with Santa Claus dashing across them in his sleigh. They are ugly, and I doubt I'll ever use them, but at least I can close the drawer and avoid ever looking at them.

Except that I can't, because the drawer refuses to shut. It goes part of the way in and then stops. But it's not stuck like the drawer above. Something behind it in the cabinet is preventing the drawer from closing.

Frustrated, I tug it back out. The cabinet is old and has probably been here since the Glendale was built, so it doesn't take much effort to slide the drawer off its runners and remove it completely. I set it aside and lie flat on the floor, peering into the gap to find the obstruction. And that's when I see the spiral-bound notebook. It must have been in a drawer at some point and fallen down the back of the cabinet.

I grab for the notebook, ignoring the silky touch of spiderwebs on my fingers and something small with too many legs that scuttles away when my hand brushes against it. I suppress a shudder and pull the notebook free from its dark prison.

With a grunt of satisfaction, I push myself up and sit cross-legged on the floor to examine my prize. The notebook looks like it's been there for a long time. A critter, possibly a mouse, has nibbled at the edges on one side. Cobwebs cling to the cover. When I open the notebook, I see a page full of scrawling, hurried handwriting. And at the top is a date—June 4. There is no year. Several small hard black pellets drop from between the pages onto the floor. Roach droppings. Ick. But that isn't what causes me to almost let go of the notebook and scoot backward in fright. It's what I see written below the date in scratchy blue ink.

> *Someone is watching me, and I don't feel safe here anymore.*

65

It's a diary . . . of sorts. Most of the pages are blank. Only the first twenty or so are filled with the jumbled thoughts of whoever owned it, written in a shaky, hurried hand. I can almost feel the author's growing distress as I flick through the pages and the writing becomes more frantic and harder to decipher.

Hi self. It's me. I'm writing to you because I'm freaking out right now. Like, really freaking out! Just got woken up by this loud noise in the apartment. It's the middle of the night and I'm alone and I don't know what to do.

Come on Jackie, pull yourself together! Go take a look . . .

It was a lamp. A stupid lamp in the spare bedroom. The door was open and there's no way I left it like that. I ALWAYS keep it closed because I hate walking past open doorways, especially at night. Yeah, I know. It's a stupid fear but blame that on the closet in my bedroom when I was a kid. I was sure something was hiding in that closet and that it would just reach out and grab me, drag me inside, into the darkness . . . Great, now I'm freaking myself out even more.

Enough already. Stop thinking about that closet.

Deep breaths. Deep breaths.

> *Ok. Back to tonight. So, the spare bedroom door was open and when I turned the light on, the lamp was on the floor. Like, unplugged and off the nightstand and all the way on the other side of the room as if someone had thrown it there. WTF?*

The spare bedroom. That must be the room that I'm currently using as an office. I can't help casting a nervous glance over my shoulder toward the closed door before looking back down at the notebook and turning the page. The next line chills me to the bone.

> *I'm beginning to think this place is haunted!*

I almost set the notebook aside right there and then, because I have to sleep in this apartment all by myself tonight, and the last thing I need is my imagination running wild with thoughts like that. But I don't, because I've been having similar thoughts about the Glendale, and this apartment, so I keep on reading.

> *Seriously . . . Either this apartment is haunted or I'm losing my mind. Or maybe it's both. Because other shit has been happening. I've tried to ignore it, but it just keeps piling up in my mind and I can't stop thinking about it. I don't know . . . maybe it will make more sense if I write everything down, make a list of all the creepy stuff that's been happening . . . or maybe not, but what the hell, it's not like I'm going to get any more sleep tonight, anyway.*

You and me both, sister, I think to myself, turning the page. And there is the list.

> *Came home from work one day last week and the bedroom light was on. I didn't leave it on. I never use*

it in the morning. The sun shines right in and wakes me up. Would the doorman come into my space without permission? Maybe. Still unsettling.

I had seven bottles of wine in the side cabinet. Went to open one on Wednesday and there were only six. I know there were seven because I bought them when I was out with Carrie at the warehouse store on Saturday, so I took advantage of her car and membership to stock up because they are heavy to carry, and I hate having to slog home with them on the subway. I know I didn't drink any. Checked the receipt and yes—seven bottles, not six. Where did the other one go???

A couple of nights ago, I woke up with a headache at like 2 AM. Went to get something for it from the cupboard in the kitchen where I keep my pills, and I swear I could hear whispered voices. It was almost like two people arguing, but they were so faint I couldn't make out exactly what they were saying. It was more like mumbling. Figured there must be someone out in the hallway, but when I looked out the peephole, I didn't see anyone. Opened the door, but the hallway was empty. Couldn't hear the voices anymore, either. But I know what I heard, and it kind of freaked me out. There was no way I was going back to bed. Sat up the rest of the night with all the lights on and the TV playing.

There are other incidents, too. Items going missing and then appearing again later. Things being moved. Noises in the middle of the night. The list is long. I read it with growing concern, not just because the person who wrote it was clearly terrified, but also because it's obvious that the events cataloged on these pages took place right here, *in my apartment*. And worse, they remind me of my own experiences at the Glendale, like getting trapped in the basement, hearing a phantom crying baby, or having the mood board go missing right before my meeting, then reappearing.

I don't want to keep reading, but I can't help myself, because as I turn the pages, the entries are getting more frantic. They start to sound like the ravings of a person who's lost touch with reality. The paranoia increases with each new entry I read. And yet at the same time, I connect with what this mystery woman is going through, especially when I reach the page that initially caught my eye.

> *Someone is watching me, and I don't feel safe here anymore.*
>
> *At first, it was nothing but a faint unease that I could easily dismiss, but now I'm certain that I'm being watched.*
>
> *Last night I was sitting on the sofa in the living room reading a book when all of a sudden, the hairs on the back of my neck stood up. I put the book down and jumped up, feeling that I wasn't alone, but nobody was there—or at least nobody that I could see. But then I noticed the curtains. I had drawn them across the doors leading to the balcony earlier in the evening, and now they were parted as if someone had pulled them open to go outside. I damn near fainted with shock. I even went to the doors and looked out onto the balcony, expecting someone to be standing there staring back at me. Thankfully, there was no one.*
>
> *For the rest of the night, I kept telling myself that it was my imagination, that there was nothing to fear. But after I went to bed, I was overcome by that same overpowering sense that I wasn't alone. I lay there listening to every tiny sound the apartment made. The fridge compressor turning on. A drip of water from the shower in the bathroom. The squeak of my mattress*

whenever I shifted position. And something else. At one point, I was sure that I heard a faint shuffle of footsteps outside my bedroom door. I was so scared . . . I didn't dare get up and look. I just pulled the covers up and lay there staring at the door, praying that the handle wouldn't turn . . . That it wouldn't swing slowly open.

Then, when I came home from work today, my front door was open. I know for sure that I didn't leave it that way. I ALWAYS lock my door. I rushed back downstairs and got the doorman, made him come up, and we searched every inch of the apartment. We even checked behind the clothes in the closet and under the bed. Everywhere anyone could hide. But it was empty. Not that I feel any safer because of that, because the feeling is back and stronger than ever.

Honestly, I don't know what to do. I think I'm losing my mind. I can't keep living like this, engulfed by fear and paranoia. My friends tell me that I'm just jumping at shadows, that I'm nervous because I'm living alone, and I've always had roommates or a boyfriend before. That it's lack of sleep or stress, or something. But I know that it isn't any of those things. This feels to . . . real.

I have the lights on all the time now. I keep the TV running as well, to drown out the silence. But it's not helping. Nothing helps. The fear is always there, lurking. I hope that putting my experiences down on paper will help me make sense of it all, but even as I'm writing this, I can't shake the dreadful feeling that someone is standing there, right behind me . . . and I want to jump up and look . . . but I'm afraid of what I'll see.

66

I've read all that I can take. I slam the notebook closed. Then I sit and stare at it on my lap for the longest time. The notebook stares back at me, too, taunting me with its disturbing contents. Eventually, my curiosity will get the better of me, and I'm sure I'll start reading again. But not now. It's too much, too soon. Those pages have left me with an uneasy knot in the pit of my stomach. But even as I tell myself that it's okay, that whoever wrote this was unstable, and possibly delusional, I don't entirely believe it. Because after all the strange things I've experienced at the Glendale, it could just as easily have been me writing in that notebook. Which makes me wonder about Jackie, and who she was. I also wonder how long ago she lived here, and where she is now.

I need to find out, if only because I sense in this woman a kindred spirit. Maybe she's still local and I can contact her, ask about the notebook and what she wrote in it.

My laptop is sitting on my desk in the office. I jump up and fetch it, then hurry into the living room, turning on all the lights as I go because it's getting dark outside, and I've freaked myself out. I put the laptop and the notebook down on the coffee table, then head into the kitchen and grab a bottle of water before sitting back down and turning my attention to finding the author of the notebook.

There's very little to go on. I only have a first name. Jackie.

I start by typing that into my search browser, along with the address of her apartment—*my apartment*—but come up empty. All I can find are a couple of vague references to the Glendale, but none of them are helpful. A public notice about the renovations of the building when they turned it into a co-op ten years ago. Another notice about a temporary road closure outside the building because of a broken water main from a couple of years later.

But seriously, what did I expect?

I almost close the laptop and give up, but the alternative is sitting here and thinking about Sam and how he cheated on me. Instead, I try a long shot. Jackie is short for Jacqueline, so I type that name in, along with the apartment address. And that's when I score a hit. A newspaper article from eight years ago, and when I read it, I gasp.

> LOCAL WOMAN STILL MISSING
>
> Concern is growing about a Back Bay woman who was reported missing ten days ago after she failed to show up for her shift at work. Twenty-seven-year-old Jacqueline Burke, an assistant manager at Carol's Crystals, a local New Age store, went out for drinks with a friend on the evening of June 5. She didn't arrive at work the next morning and has not been seen in the week since. Burke was an active member of Boston's New Age community, and her sudden disappearance has left family, friends, and customers at the store where she worked deeply concerned.
>
> According to the Boston Police Department, Burke was last seen returning on foot to her apartment around midnight. Security footage from a camera at the entrance of a nearby T station showed her walking past at 12:08 a.m. It is not known if she ever

arrived home because a camera at the entrance to the Glendale—the building where she lived—was inoperable at the time of her disappearance. That camera still has not been repaired.

Detective Neil Meadows, leading the investigation for Boston PD, stated, "We are pursuing all avenues to find out what happened to Jacqueline and bring her home safely. Every lead will be thoroughly investigated. We urge anyone with information regarding Jacqueline's whereabouts, or who saw Jacqueline on the night she went missing, to come forward."

Residents of the Back Bay community where Burke lives have come together to put up flyers in the hopes that someone will provide information about her whereabouts.

"I know that Jackie has been having some problems lately," remarked Jennifer Barnes, who lives in the same building as the missing woman. "She's had some issues in her personal life, but I hope she makes contact with her family and friends and lets us know that she's safe."

For now, all the community can do is wait and support each other until Burke is found. In the meantime, the search continues. Anyone with information regarding Jacqueline Burke's disappearance is encouraged to call the Boston Police Department Crime-Stoppers toll-free tip line.

Wow. The woman who wrote all that stuff in the notebook went missing. I hit the back button and scroll through the remaining search results with a growing sense of dread, praying that Jacqueline didn't just vanish into thin air, but even though I come across a few more mentions of her disappearance, I find nothing to suggest that she was ever found, alive or otherwise.

What the heck?

Now I'm freaking out. This woman lived right here—*in my apartment.*

I go back to the first article and read it again, hoping to see something I missed the first time around . . . because I *have* to know. *What happened to Jackie?*

But the article provides no more information than it did the first time.

Which leaves one place to look. The notebook, which I had put aside because it was too unsettling. Whether I want to or not, I can't ignore it. Not after what I've discovered about its author. With my heart in my mouth, I pick it up and flip to the last page with writing . . .

> *They are watching me all hours of the day and night. They come into the apartment when I'm asleep.*
>
> *I don't know what to do.*
>
> *I'm so scared.*
>
> *I think they want to hurt me. I wish there was someone I could talk to who would take me seriously, but I don't have any evidence except this notebook, and it proves nothing. I'm going to hide it anyway, because I don't want them to take it from me. It's the only record of what has been happening.*

There's a break in the writing, and then it continues in a different color pen as if Jackie wrote it on a different day.

> *I'm meeting a friend tonight to see if I can stay with them for a while. Tomorrow, I'm telling Catherine that I'm*

moving out and I don't care about the contract. I can't live like this. I haven't slept in days. I'm so tired. I just want this nightmare to end.

After that, it's all blank pages. Did she write her last entry on the evening she went missing? Did someone get to her before she could move out of the Glendale? It sure looks that way. Or maybe life simply got to be too much, and she decided to . . . No, I don't believe she took matters into her own hands. Not like that. From what she wrote, Jackie sounds scared and exhausted, not depressed and suicidal. I paw through the rest of the pages, just to make sure I didn't miss anything; then I set the notebook aside and sit there, wondering what to do next.

I should take it to the police first thing in the morning, show them what I've found. It's been a long time, but maybe it will help them figure out what happened to her. Assuming Jackie is still missing, of course. I couldn't find anything online about her being found, but that doesn't mean anything. It was a long time ago. But there is one person who might know. Jennifer. And now seems like as good a time as any to ask her.

67

I knock on Jennifer and Frank's door, with the notebook clutched in my free hand.

When no one answers, I knock again. While I'm waiting, I glance around, my gaze finally settling on the door across the hall. Kalina's door. An image of her and Sam in our bed flits through my mind. Of their bodies locked in passion. My throat tightens. I drag my eyes away and look down, focusing on the floor and trying not to think about everything I have lost.

At that moment, the door in front of me opens, and Frank is standing there. He's leaning on a cane and slightly stooped over.

"Jordan. I'm sorry it took me so long to answer. Dang arthritis. Always plays up in cold weather." A look of concern flashes across his face. I'm sure that his wife told him what happened between me and Sam. "Is everything all right?"

"It's fine. I mean, it's not, but well . . ." I realize that I'm flustered. I take a deep breath and pull myself together. "Can I speak to Jennifer? I have a question for her."

Frank shakes his head. "Jennifer's not here. She's at one of those wine and paint evenings. She goes once a month with a couple of girlfriends from her old job. Maybe I can help you."

I think about this for a moment. I'd feel more comfortable talking to Jennifer because we've gotten to know each other better, but I don't want to wait, so I nod and let Frank lead me into the apartment.

It has a similar floor plan to mine, except that Frank and Jennifer's apartment has accumulated the clutter that comes with living somewhere for a long time. The furniture is dated, and although I spot some pieces that might be antique, most of it just looks old and tired.

Frank leans his cane against the wall, then motions for me to take a seat on a floral-patterned sofa that reminds me of something my grandmother would have liked. "Can I get you a cup of tea or coffee?"

I shake my head. "No, thank you."

"A glass of wine, perhaps?"

It's tempting, since I have to spend the night alone in the same apartment where Jackie disappeared, but I decline.

"You know what, I'm going to make you a cup of tea." Frank starts toward the kitchen, because apparently a drink is required, even if I don't want one. "Jennifer found a fantastic oolong at the organic market a few days ago. You'll love it."

"Honestly, I'm fine." I just want to ask about Jacqueline.

"Nonsense." Frank hurries toward the kitchen.

While he prepares the tea, I look around. The first thing I notice is all the photographs. They sit on the fireplace mantel and on the coffee table in a mix of metal and wood frames. They hang on the living room walls in a variety of different sizes. So many of them that I almost feel claustrophobic. The photos have been taken at different times and in different places, but they share one similarity. The slim, golden-haired girl. In some of them she is a child, in others she's a teenager, then a twentysomething. She's sitting on the floor playing with toys, frolicking at the beach, posing between a much younger Jennifer and Frank as she graduates college. It doesn't take a genius to figure out that this must be the daughter that Jennifer told me had died fifteen years ago.

Frank and Jennifer have fashioned this whole room, and perhaps the entire apartment, into a memorial to her. When I glance at Frank, who's busy on the other side of the kitchen island making our tea, it's hard not to notice the sheets of paper with curling edges pinned to the fridge door. Crude crayon drawings with stick figures and simplistic, boxy-looking buildings and vehicles. The drawings of a child.

I suppress a shudder. This is not healthy.

"Here you are, my dear," Frank says, returning to the living room with two dainty cups resting on bone china saucers. He places one down on the coffee table in front of me and sets the other on a side table next to a wingback chair, which he promptly sinks into with a sigh. Then he goes to get back up. "I'm so sorry. Where are my manners? I forgot to ask—would you like sugar or milk with your tea?"

"No, thank you." I try to ignore the unnerving gaze of their dead daughter from the dozens of photographs surrounding me.

"This is Amanda, our daughter," Frank says, picking up a gold frame from the coffee table. "She died."

I nod and say, "Jennifer told me. I'm so sorry."

"Thank you. It was a long time ago."

"How did it happen?"

"An accident. She was in the wrong place at the wrong time, and . . ." Frank's eyes moisten. His voice cracks. "If you don't mind, I'd rather not talk about it."

"Sure. Okay." I could kick myself for asking such a blunt question. "I didn't mean to upset you."

"It's fine." Frank takes a long breath. "What did you want to ask?"

"There was a woman who lived in my apartment several years ago. Her name was Jacqueline Burke. Do you remember her?"

Frank is reaching for his teacup. He stops and slowly withdraws his hand, leaving the cup on its saucer. "I think you must be mistaken, my dear," he says eventually. "No one of that name has ever lived in this building."

68

I'm momentarily taken aback. I wasn't expecting him to say that. Jacqueline Burke clearly lived in this building, right next door to Jennifer and Frank, in *my* apartment. Jennifer was even quoted in the article I found online from eight years ago. I'm still holding the notebook. I place it on the coffee table and slide it toward him.

"I know that Jacqueline Burke lived here. I found this stuck behind a drawer in my dining room. It's a diary. She wrote it in the weeks before she went missing."

Frank stares at the notebook. From the baffled expression on his face, I expect him to once again deny knowing her, but then he nods slowly and looks up. "Ah. You must mean Jackie. Of course, I remember now." He taps the side of his head with one finger. "Memory's not what it used to be, I'm afraid. Perils of old age, and it was such a long time ago."

"Eight years to be exact," I say. Now it's my turn to look down at the notebook. "I think this might have something to do with her disappearance."

"What do you know about that?" Frank asks.

"I know that she went out for the evening and vanished. That the security camera outside the door of this building wasn't working, so they can't tell if she made it back here that night. Do you know if the police ever found out what happened to her?"

Frank shakes his head. "If they did, I haven't heard anything about it. Poor girl. She wasn't here for that long, and kept mostly to herself, but she always struck me as a bit odd. I recall that she had some issues in her personal life. For all I know, she ran away to escape them. You know, start over fresh somewhere else."

"I don't think so." I tap the notebook. "From the stuff she wrote in here, it sounds more like she was afraid someone was out to get her. She mentioned feeling like she was being watched."

Frank picks up the notebook. He skims through it, stopping on certain pages to read them. Eventually, he looks at me. "Where did you say you found this?"

"Behind a drawer in the dining room cabinet. At first, I thought it must have fallen down the back at some point, but after reading it, I wonder if she hid it there intentionally."

"I guess anything is possible." Frank closes the notebook. "And I can see why you'd think it might be related to her disappearance, but like I said, she had issues. It's also just as likely she was looking for attention. What she wrote in here sounds . . . well, kind of crazy."

"Or maybe there really was someone watching her," I say. "She *did* go missing, after all."

"Then what do you propose to do about it?"

"I'm going to take it to the police in the morning. Turn it in to them. Maybe it will help them discover what happened to her."

"Okay." Frank is still holding the notebook. "I think there's still a card around somewhere from the detective who interviewed us back then. He would be the best person to give this to. I'll see if I can find it. In the meantime, would you mind if I hold on to the diary tonight? I'd like to show it to Jennifer when she comes home. Maybe she'll remember something about Jackie that will be useful."

"Okay." That sounds reasonable.

"Good." Frank sips his tea. He puts the cup back down before speaking again. "Jennifer told me what happened between you and Sam. It must have been very traumatic. Are you going to be all right over there on your own tonight?" He taps the notebook. "You know, after reading this."

"I'll be fine."

"Okay. Because the last thing you need is to be sitting by yourself in that apartment and obsessing over someone who hasn't lived there in almost a decade."

"You don't need to worry about me," I assure him, then stand and glance toward the door. "I've taken up enough of your time. I should go."

Frank walks me to the door. "I'll look for that card from the detective."

"Thank you." I step out into the hallway.

"And remember, if it gets too much over there all by yourself, if you need anything, we're right next door."

"I appreciate that." I return to my apartment, expecting Frank to go back inside, but he doesn't. Instead, he watches me as if he feels that it's his duty to make sure I get home safely, even though my door is mere steps from his. I'm about to reach for the handle when he speaks again.

"Jordan?"

I glance back over my shoulder.

"Remember that you're safe here in this building, regardless of what that young woman wrote in her diary. You hear me?"

"Sure." I nod.

"Good." A faint smile touches Frank's lips. "Now, don't forget to lock your door."

69

I'm on my second cup of coffee, sitting at the island, reading on my phone, and trying to ignore how empty the apartment feels without Sam here, when Frank comes by at eleven o'clock the next morning.

"I found that card and called the detective," he says. "They sent an officer around to collect the notebook already."

"Oh." I thought Frank was going to give me the number so I could call the detective myself, not deal with it on his own. After all, I'm the one who found the diary, and I figured the police might like to know the circumstances of my discovery. Also, I wanted to know if any new leads had surfaced in the years since Jackie vanished. "Did he say anything?"

Frank shakes his head. "Just that they will take a look at the diary. I gave him your phone number so he can contact you if he has questions."

"Can you give me *his* phone number?" I ask. I'd like to know if the diary provides any new clues. Since finding it, I've become invested in Jacqueline Burke and her disappearance. I feel like we're kind of kindred spirits. I also want to set my mind at rest that whatever happened to her had nothing to do with the Glendale or my apartment.

"I don't have it on me. I'll text you later. Okay?"

"Sure."

Then, as if reading my mind, Frank says, "You don't need to worry. The detective said they don't believe she ever made it back here that night. They think something happened to her on the way home."

"Oh." Frank only just told me the detective had said nothing, but apparently he did say *something*. "What did Jennifer say when you showed her the notebook? Did she remember anything about Jackie that might help the police?"

Frank shakes his head slowly. "No, she didn't. Not that I expected her to."

Then why did you keep the notebook? I think.

Frank isn't done. "Honestly, Jordan, I'd forget about it. You have enough to deal with right now, without obsessing over some young woman from years ago who probably had too much to drink and fell in the river or something. Have you spoken to Sam?"

"Not since he left."

"That's too bad." Frank glances toward Kalina's door. "But I suppose he brought it upon himself."

70

The afternoon passes slowly. It's Monday, which means I should be working, but after everything that's happened, I don't have much inclination. And anyway, the only project I have is Catherine's coffee shop design, and I want to show her the mood board—the real one—before I go too much further with that. Having already messed up once, I don't want to do it again.

I slink around the apartment and try not to dwell on all that I have lost. And as I do, I get to thinking. Even though Frank assured me that the police never believed Jackie's disappearance had anything to do with her living at the Glendale, I can't shake the feeling that her experiences in this apartment were in some way connected to it. There are just too many red flags with what she wrote in the notebook. It makes me wonder if any of the other people who lived here had similar experiences? I don't know how many times this apartment has changed hands in the last eight years, but I do know that the last couple who lived here broke their contract and moved out early. Catherine claimed it was because one of them had been offered a job in California. Later, Jennifer said that the previous occupants had only stayed in the apartment for maybe six months.

Jennifer also mentioned their names, but I can't remember them. I do remember something else, though. Catherine had made it sound like they had only recently moved out, but Jennifer later said that she was glad to have new neighbors, that she was starting to think the apartment would be empty forever. Frank corrected her, said that she was talking about how long the apartment might stay empty and not about how long ago the previous occupants had moved out. But thinking back, there was something strange about Jennifer's reaction, almost like she was trying to backpedal on her comment. Which makes me even more curious about the people who lived here before us. Did they really vacate because of a job offer, or was there another, less mundane reason for their hurried departure?

I need to know, and the obvious place to start is with Jennifer. I fetch my phone and tap out a quick message, asking what their names were, how long ago they lived here, and when. I give the message a quick read-through to ensure it makes sense—autocorrect loves to screw with me—then go to send it. Before I get that far, the phone rings.

It's Sam.

I stare at the screen, caught in an internal tug-of-war between ignoring the call—because I know that letting him back into my life right now would only make the situation worse—and answering, because I still love him and being apart hurts more than I could ever have imagined. In the end, the cold, hard voice of reason wins out, and I decline the call. Soon after, the phone notifies me that I have a new voicemail.

I play the message, because hearing his voice is better than not hearing it.

"Hey, Jordan. I just wanted to call and make sure you're doing okay." There's a brief pause. "I'm so confused about all of this, and I really think we should talk. I don't like us being apart. It feels wrong . . . I love you. So, um, text me, or call, or . . . well, just let me know, all right?"

I listen to the message and blink away the tears that moisten my eyes. One bit in particular echoes through my mind. *I love you.* If only that were true, because his affair with Kalina would indicate otherwise. Even so, I play the message again, then close my eyes and wrap myself in the sound of his voice. And when it gets to the part where he says that he loves me, I mouth the sentiment silently back at him. *I love you, too*. But as usual, his betrayal is never far away. An inescapable truth that makes me want to scream with rage, and that is why I do not return his call. Instead, I go back to Jennifer's text message and hit send.

Then I wait for a reply, checking my phone every ten minutes and growing increasingly antsy. Eventually, when my impatience reaches the boiling point, I decide to take a more direct approach and go next door in person. But when I knock, no one answers. Disappointed, I turn back toward my apartment. At that moment, a thought occurs to me. There might be another way to find out the names of the people who lived in the apartment before us. I duck back into our apartment and grab the keys from the kitchen island, then head back out again toward the elevator. When I reach the lobby, it's empty—no big surprise at this point—but I'm not looking for Angelo. Instead, I head straight for the mailboxes, which are in a small room off the lobby. If my hunch is correct, I'll soon know who lived in our apartment before we did.

71

I find our box and open it. I ignore the pile of uncollected mail, and my gaze settles on the white oblong card in a metal slot on the inside of the door. It has our names written on it so the mail person knows who the box belongs to. Behind it, I see the edge of another card. When I lift our card out to reveal the one beneath, there's another set of names written in the same handwriting.

Addison and Mark McGlocklin.

I draw a sharp breath. They must be the previous owners of our apartment, the people who moved to California. I was right. They didn't remove the old card before putting ours in. I take the card out and put our card back, grab the mail, then close the mailbox door and lock it. Back in the apartment, I drop the mail on the kitchen island and hurry to my laptop, where I spend the next two hours searching.

There are plenty of people named Mark and Addison McGlocklin, but I can't find anything about them as a married couple. I come across a bunch of Instagram, Facebook, and LinkedIn profiles for each name, but when I dig deeper, they're either too young or too old (I figure they must at least be in their mid-twenties, and I remember Frank commenting that they were "a polite young couple," so I can disregard anyone over forty), in relationships with other people, live in another country, or have no connections to either Boston or California.

Then I come across a profile for an Addison McGlocklin living in San Francisco. She's the right age, and even better, she's originally from Boston. But when I click on the profile, I'm disappointed. Her relationship status shows that she isn't married and is instead dating a person by the name of Lawrence Siegel. Beyond that, I can't see much, because there are barely any posts on her timeline, which means she has it set to private. Only her friends can see what she writes. But I can see some of her photos, and within them lies a glimmer of hope, because her relationship with Lawrence Siegel must be fairly new. In her older photos, she's with a different man, and they are clearly together. In one image, they're kissing. In another they're standing with their arms around each other and making goofy faces. There are plenty more. And I notice with rising excitement that many of them were taken in and around Boston. And finally, proof positive. A photo of Addison with the same man taken four years ago on the steps in front of the Glendale's lobby, grinning and holding up a set of keys. The caption reads, *Move-in day*.

It's her! I've found the woman who lived in this apartment before us. But despite what both Catherine and Frank said, Addison and Mark McGlocklin didn't move out recently, because the photo is four years old. If they only lived here for six months, their move to California must have happened three and a half years ago. Which means that Jennifer's comment about our apartment being empty for a long time was true. That raises some unsettling questions. Why would the Glendale's executive board let it sit empty like that for so long, when there must have been plenty of people who would have jumped at the chance to purchase a place like this in Boston's scorching-hot property market? And more to the point, why would Catherine and Frank lie about it? I don't have an answer to either question . . . But I intend to find out.

72

I don't have Addison McGlocklin's phone number or email address, but I can contact her on Messenger. I keep it short, explaining who I am and why I'm reaching out—that I'm living in her old apartment and want to know if she ever experienced anything strange there—then I sit and stare at the computer screen. But it's unrealistic to think that she will reply right away. It could be hours or even days before she sees my message, if she sees it at all. There are no posts visible on her timeline because her profile is private, so I have no idea how often she's active or if she even uses social media anymore. Among my own friends on Facebook, plenty of them no longer engage for one reason or another.

All I can do is wait.

With nothing better to do, I turn on the TV and find a suitably distracting movie to watch. When that ends and another film begins, I let it play. I check my messages every once in a while, but there's nothing from Addison. Then, when I'm just about thinking it's time for bed, she replies. And she's willing to talk. Even better, she's given me her phone number.

San Francisco is three hours behind Boston, which means it's only eight o'clock there.

I waste no time in calling.

When she answers, I introduce myself, then say, "Thank you so much for agreeing to talk."

"You're welcome, and honestly, I almost didn't," Addison replies. "I've spent the last three and a half years doing everything I can to forget about the Glendale. It wasn't exactly a happy time in my life. But after what you said in your message . . ."

An image of that photograph on her Facebook page pops into my head. The one of Addison and her husband standing on the steps outside the building. They certainly seemed pleased enough to be moving in.

"Did something happen to you here?" I ask.

"Not me. My husband, Mark," she says, and I can hear the strain in her voice. "I adored living at the Glendale. It was a dream come true. The apartment was stunning, and I couldn't believe our luck getting it for such a cheap price—we shouldn't have been able to afford a place like that. I was the happiest I've ever been . . . at least for the first few months. But then Mark changed. It was subtle at first. He was moody. Withdrawn. He wasn't sleeping well, either. To begin with, I thought maybe he was just overdoing it at work because we'd never taken on a financial commitment this large before and, well . . ."

"I get it," I tell her, although I can't help noticing what she said about being offered the apartment for a surprisingly low price. "It's an enormous commitment, even if the place is undervalued."

"Uh-huh. The apartment was a steal, an opportunity too good to pass up, but it was still right at the edge of what we could afford. But that wasn't the cause of Mark's increasingly dark moods. The longer we were in that apartment, the weirder he was acting. Like I said, at first I didn't think much of it. I put it down to stress. But before long, it was impossible to pass his behavior off as normal. He was irritable. He'd start arguments with me over ridiculous things. His behavior was becoming increasingly . . . I don't know how best to describe it . . . erratic."

"Erratic, how?"

"Well, one incident has always stuck in my mind. I woke up one night in the early hours of the morning, and he wasn't in bed. At first, I thought he must've just gotten up to pee, or to get a glass of water. But after a while, when he didn't return, I got up to see where he was.

I found him sitting on the couch in the living room. All the lights were off, and he was just staring into space. I asked him what was going on, and he said that he was hearing voices and that they wouldn't let him sleep."

"Voices?" I'm not sure what I was expecting when I called this woman, but this is getting just a little too real. I haven't heard any voices, but I have been hearing a crying baby that everyone tells me doesn't live in the building. I need air. I hurry through the dining room to the sliding door leading out onto the balcony and drag it open, then step out into the chilly air of an autumn night, even as Addison is replying.

"Yes. The voices of his dead friends who were killed in a boating accident a few years earlier. One of his friends owned a small yacht, and they decided to take it out, even though it was October, and the weather can turn on a dime. And it did. A sudden storm came in, and they couldn't get back to shore. The boat capsized, and he was the only one who survived. He always blamed himself for their deaths, said he should have talked them out of going that day."

"But he only started hearing the voices after you moved into the Glendale?"

"Yes. He said they whispered to him when he was alone in the apartment, or when I was asleep. It got so bad, he became withdrawn. Moody. I was never sure which version of him I would get. The happy, carefree Mark that I knew previously, or the sullen, angry Mark who emerged after the voices started. It was like a festering darkness had taken hold of him, and I didn't know what to do about it."

I'm silent for a few seconds while I decide what to say next. Then, even though I know that I'm treading on dangerous ground because they are clearly no longer together, I ask, "Is there any way I could talk to Mark? Could you give me his number perhaps?"

"That won't be possible." Addison hesitates. When she speaks again, her voice trembles. "He's dead. He killed himself right there in that apartment."

73

He killed himself right there in that apartment.

I listen to those words, and the world around me tilts as if I've become displaced in time and space. I reach out and grab the balcony railing to steady myself. My voice is croaky when I ask her, "What do you mean, he killed himself?"

"I came home from work one evening, and . . ." It sounds like Addison is weeping. She sniffs. "I'm sorry. You'd think I would be able to handle this better after so long, but—"

"You don't need to apologize." I feel dreadful for pushing her into this. Maybe I should have just let it be. Whatever was I thinking? "If it's too much—"

"No. I'm fine." It's clear that Addison is anything but fine. "Talking about it helps. At least, that's what my therapist says." There's a pause; then she seems to pull herself together. "Anyway, I came home from work and found him lying face down in the foyer. At first, I thought that maybe he'd tripped and fell, that he'd hit his head or something . . . But there was so much blood. It was all over the floor and on the walls. Then I saw the gun lying next to him, and . . . and . . . the back of his head. It was half gone. I could see—"

Again, she breaks down.

My stomach flips. I take a long, icy breath, focus my attention on the glittering Boston skyline beyond the balcony. But in my mind's eye, all I see is one thing. A body sprawled in the foyer of this apartment—in *our* foyer. And I can't help wondering what drove Mark McGlocklin to take his own life. Was he experiencing things in this building, just like I am? I want to speak, but the words catch in my throat, which is fine, because I'm not sure what I'm even going to say. What is there to say?

Addison spares me the uncomfortable moment. "I knew Mark was having problems, that he was struggling emotionally, but I never thought he would do something like that. I don't even know where he got the gun. We had never owned a gun. I don't like them. The police said there was no serial number on it, that he'd probably bought it on the black market specifically to . . . well . . ."

She trails off, which is probably for the best. Right now, I just want this call to be over. I have the answer I was seeking. Catherine and the other residents of this building lied to prevent us from asking why the unit had been empty for so long, because then they would have been forced to tell us what happened here, and they were afraid we might not want to move in. It also explains why the apartment was such a good value. Who knows how long they'd been trying to offload this place before we came along?

I need to say something to fill the heavy silence between us, and only one thing comes to mind. "I'm so sorry for your loss."

"Thank you."

"I had no idea that anything like that had happened here. If I had known, I would never have contacted you. I feel positively awful for putting you through this."

"Don't worry about it." Addison sounds more composed now—barely. "Like I said, my therapist claims that it's good to talk about it. She says that I internalize too much. And I'm glad that you called, because honestly, by the time Mark did what he did, I already hated that place. I loathed it. And even though I never experienced any of the things that Mark claimed to have seen and heard, I always felt there was something not quite right about the building. Who knows, maybe it was just because of the way my husband changed after we moved in, but I felt like it had a dark energy. Like it was capable of sucking the joy right out of the air. When you asked if anything strange happened to me at the Glendale, I knew that I had to reply to your message. I don't want anyone else going through what Mark and I did."

"Thank you. I appreciate that."

"If you don't mind me asking, are you married?"

"No. Engaged," I tell her, without elaborating on the dreadful events of the past few weeks. Addison McGlocklin has gone through enough without listening to my petty troubles.

"I see." There's a momentary silence, as if she's deciding whether she should say anything else. When she finally speaks, there's a harsh note to her voice. "A word of warning, Jordan. Be careful. I really do think there's an evil presence inside that building. A malignancy that's soaked into the walls and floors like rot. If you stay there, bad things will happen. I know, because they happened to me and Mark. The Glendale is not a happy place, and it will destroy everything you hold dear if you let it."

"I'll keep that in mind," I say, caught off guard by her vitriol. But I understand. And I'm not sure that I disagree with her, because the troubles between Sam and me only started after we moved in here. My instinct is to end the conversation now, but I have one last question. "Addison, have you ever heard of a woman named Jacqueline Burke? She went by Jackie?"

"I can't say that I have. Why?"

"No reason. Just curious." Telling Addison what happened to her predecessor in this apartment—that she vanished, and no one knows where she is to this day—feels unnecessary under the circumstances. Like twisting the knife. I thank her for her time, tell her again how sorry I am about her husband, and end the call. Then I linger on the balcony for a few minutes more, shivering against the biting wind as I run through the conversation in my mind, because going back inside fills me with dread. But I can't avoid it forever, and when I do step back into the apartment, I go straight to the foyer and pull back the rug. Then I stand and stare at the dark, uneven stain beneath—the one we discovered on the day we moved in, the one that Sam thought might be varnish—because now I know what it really is, and how it got there.

74

A man died in our apartment. He put a gun to his head and pulled the trigger. He lay in the middle of the floor in our foyer, his blood soaking into the floorboards. I feel like I'm living somebody else's life, because I sure don't recognize this reality. My fiancé is gone and in all likelihood will never be back. My apartment was not only owned by a woman who vanished into thin air but was also the scene of a grisly death that has left an indelible mark upon it. And who knows what else has happened, not just in this apartment but also in the rest of the Glendale, during the last 120 years or so since Catherine's great-grandfather bought a plot of land on the Charles River and built his dream project.

I guess the old adage is true. Be careful what you wish for. Because this place almost seemed too good to be true when we first heard about it, and now I realize that it was.

If only I could turn back the clock and walk away from this place before we ever moved in. Or better yet, dissuade our real estate agent, Jinny, from ever submitting that application for us. But I can't, so I'm left facing yet another dark and lonely night trapped in these four walls along with the ghosts of the past. Except that isn't true. I don't have to spend another moment in this place if I don't want to . . . And I *really* don't want to. I can pack a bag, throw some clothes into a suitcase, and be out of here within the hour. Which is exactly what I plan on doing. But before I can wrench my eyes away from that dreadful stain, my phone chirps.

At first, I assume it must be Addison. That she thought of something else about what happened to her and Mark in this apartment. But it isn't Addison. It's a text from a number that I don't recognize.

> You need to see the apartment on the ground floor. Keys are in office safe behind doorman's desk. Code is 604765. Go tonight, right now. Hurry.

I stare at the message, and for a moment it makes no sense because I'm still thinking about that bloodstain under the rug and packing a bag. Getting out of here. Then, after I read it a second time, the words snap into place. I've been desperate to peek inside that apartment for weeks. And now someone wants me to see it, and they want me to see it tonight.

But who sent it? Almost out of instinct, I reply to the text.

> Who is this?

Three pulsing dots appear under my message, as if someone is typing a reply.

I wait.

The dots vanish, but no response comes through.

This time I call the number.

It doesn't even ring before a generic voicemail message tells me that the person I'm calling isn't available right now. Please leave a message.

I almost leave a message, but something stops me. I end the call instead. Because the sender obviously has no intention of engaging further, and I can't help feeling that it would not be in my best interest to draw attention to myself like that. Call it a gut feeling. Intuition.

But that doesn't stop me from being curious. Angelo finished work at eleven and won't be back again until tomorrow morning. That leaves plenty of time to sneak down into his office, access the safe, and take the keys. Then I can finally find out what secrets lie behind its door.

My curiosity has gotten the better of me. All thoughts of packing a bag and fleeing are forgotten. If this were a horror movie, I'd be screaming at the clueless heroine on the screen right about now, telling her not to follow the instructions of some anonymous text. But this isn't a horror movie, and I've already made up my mind.

I need to know what other secrets the Glendale is hiding.

I'm going to do this.

75

HIM

Then

It's time to finish this. We've had a good run, you and me, but I'm eager to bring our little dance to its long-anticipated climax. And I know you feel the same way, even if you don't realize it. At least, not on a conscious level. Because our destinies have always been entwined. There is an inevitability that weaves through the universe, bringing souls together and pulling them apart, and you and I are just a small part of that celestial game.

When I first encountered you in that coffee shop, I wasn't sure that we would be right together, that you were the one. But now, standing in the lobby of your building at the threshold of your apartment, I've never been more certain. I feel at home here. Content. I step inside and quietly close the door, then slip the lock-picking tool back into my pocket.

Of course, you aren't home. You're out with one of those bratty friends of yours, and she always keeps you out late. It's only eleven thirty, and I doubt that you'll be home much before midnight. Which is fine, because I want to look around a little. Make sure that nothing has changed since I was here last week. That's one of my rules, you see.

You might have gotten yourself a knife or have a gun tucked away in some drawer that I won't know about until it's too late. You could have a baseball bat leaning behind the door. You might even have had an alarm system installed. But you don't have an alarm, not that it would have stopped me. Now I just need to check that you don't have any weapons stashed about the place, either.

I walk through the foyer and into the dark living room. No lights are on. I like that. You don't waste electricity. I bet you're a religious recycler, and you take short showers to save water, too.

I take a flashlight from my pocket with a gloved hand and shine it around. The place is neat, and the smell of pine hangs in the air. It's almost as if you cleaned just for me, but I suspect that you are always this tidy, and good for you.

My flashlight beam sweeps across the room, illuminating a sofa and coffee table and playing across the fireplace and mantel. And that's when I see the photograph in a frame with fine silver filigree, and I can't help myself. I want to look at it again. I cross to the fireplace and pick it up, stare at your smiling face looking back at me from within the frame. You're dressed in a graduation gown and cap, posing next to another young woman dressed the same. A friend perhaps?

I place the picture back on the mantel—I'm getting distracted—then head for the bedroom. I check the drawers in the nightstand, rummage through the clothes in your dresser, and even look under your pillows, because you wouldn't believe the places people hide their guns, and I really dislike surprises. But I don't find anything and that's good. Now nothing will get in the way of our fun.

The bedroom has an en suite bathroom and a walk-in closet with sliding louvered doors. I give the bathroom a cursory inspection, then go to the closet, open the doors, and turn the light on. Clothes hang on both sides of the small room. On the far wall is a tall shoe rack. The closet is well organized and tidy. A laundry basket sits on the floor, half full of dirty clothes. The way it's aligned parallel to the shoe rack, forming a perfect ninety-degree angle to the wall, strikes me as a little compulsive. And trust me, I know all about compulsions. Still, it explains the meticulous precision with which you have arranged everything else in the closet. It's so well organized, in fact, that I hesitate to spoil the perfect symmetry by stepping inside.

But I do, because there aren't many other places in this apartment within which to conceal myself, and it provides a perfect view of your bedroom through the door slats. When you come home, I'm sure you will go straight there because it's late. And even if it isn't, well, we have all night to enjoy each other's company.

I turn off the closet light and extinguish my flashlight, too.

The darkness folds around me.

I reach down and touch the knife at my hip, my fingers grazing the cold, sharp steel. *Just a little longer,* I tell it. *Be patient.* But waiting is hard. The anticipation is almost unbearable, because I've thought about this moment so many times over the last few months—the final thrilling chapter of our love story.

I don't have to wait long.

Because soon I hear the turn of a key, the gentle creak of a door opening and closing.

There are footsteps.

A light snaps on, throwing a rectangle of soft illumination through the bedroom door and across the floor.

More footsteps . . . getting closer.

Closer.

You are in the bedroom now.

I hold my breath, grip the closet door, wait for you to come into view.

And in that brief moment between anticipation and execution, I have never been so happy.

76

Jordan

Now

I leave the apartment and make my way down to the ground floor, taking the stairs instead of the elevator, which is noisy and might attract unwanted attention. The lobby is empty and silent, and no one's around. The lights are dimmed at this time of night to save energy. The chandelier hanging from the vaulted ceiling above me casts long shadows across the marble floor, and it's all I can do not to change my mind and flee back upstairs. There's something creepy about old buildings in the dead of night. They take on a different character, like some bricks-and-mortar Jekyll and Hyde.

A shiver runs through me.

But I have no intention of turning back, because I really want to see what's behind that apartment door. I make one concession that most characters in slasher movies never do. I take out my phone and fire off a quick text to Sam, telling him what I'm about to do, even though I think there's a good chance that he won't see it because he always puts his phone on Do Not Disturb when he's sleeping. Still, it makes me feel better as I creep toward Angelo's desk, step around it, and go into his office.

The wall safe is easy to find, mounted beside the door and hidden from the sight of anyone in the lobby. It only takes me a moment to punch the code in; then I'm rewarded by a click when the lock disengages. I swing the door open to see rows of keys hanging on small hooks. Each one of them is labeled for a room or apartment at the Glendale. I see the key for unit 4C—my unit—and keys for the other apartments on my floor.

A crazy thought enters my head. A notion to forget about the ground floor unit and grab the key for Kalina's apartment instead. Let myself in and suffocate her while she sleeps. Put a pillow over her face and press down until she stops breathing.

It's a fantasy, of course. I would never do anything so heinous, even to a woman like her. But the wicked thought provides me with a brief moment of perverse pleasure before I turn my attention back to the task at hand and find the key for the ground floor apartment.

After closing the safe, I leave the office, looking around quickly to make sure I'm still alone in the lobby. Then I hurry to the apartment and go to put the key in the lock. But now I hesitate. What if it isn't empty? Sure, Angelo claimed that no one lives here, but the residents of this building have lied to me before. After talking to Addison, I have confirmation of that fact. And even if it is empty, do I really want to know what lies on the other side of this door? Am I opening a Pandora's box that I will wish had remained closed? Maybe. But I've come this far, and that text message was clear, even if its sender is still a mystery.

You need to see the apartment on the ground floor.

I slip the key into the lock and turn it. Then I push the door open and step into the apartment. To my relief, it appears to be empty. The lights are off, and a stale, musty odor hangs in the air. I turn and close the door, wincing when the hinges creak, even though I know it's unlikely that anyone will hear it. I can barely see. There isn't even any illumination from the streetlamps and occasional passing cars on Storrow Drive because heavy curtains are drawn tight across the windows.

I fumble for the light switch, snap it on, then hurry through the foyer and deeper into the apartment.

What I see when I enter the living room makes me hesitate, then take a frantic step back toward the door, because it sure doesn't look empty and unlivable, like Angelo claimed when I asked him about this apartment. There's a sofa, chairs, and a coffee table in the living room. Pictures on the walls. A paperback book sits on the kitchen island with a bookmark poking out of it, and several items are next to the sink as if they've just been washed. Plates and a mug and knives and forks. Shit. Someone really is living here, and I'm trespassing.

I backpedal some more, afraid to turn my back on the apartment in case someone appears from the bedroom, groggy and with eyes full of sleep, to confront me. But no one does, and then I notice something else. The entire place is coated in a thick layer of dust. There are dust bunnies on the floor and cobwebs hanging down from the ceiling light. What at first appeared to be signs of habitation now strike me as abandonment. As if whoever lived here got out of bed one morning and walked away, never to come back, leaving everything they owned behind.

My racing heart slows.

I glance over my shoulder toward the foyer. There's a coat closet to the right of the front door. I walk over and open it, to see coats and jackets on hangers and two pairs of boots on the floor atop a plastic shoe tray. A fresh blast of musty air laden with dust wafts out of the small space. I close the door again, then go back into the living room and look around.

Beyond the obvious—that this apartment has been empty for a long time—I see nothing to indicate why anyone would want me to come here. But I do notice other things. For a start, the layout is different from my unit on the fourth floor. The foyer is smaller, the living room bigger, and it's shaped more like an oblong. To the left of the kitchen is a dining area with a wood table and four chairs. The floors are also wood, although nothing like my floors. They're a dark oak color like the floor in the Glendale's library. There's a fireplace with a polished wood mantel. I spot a picture frame sitting on it and cross the room, then lean close to study it. The photo is of two young women at a college graduation. I don't recognize either of them. I don't see anything else of interest.

I go to the kitchen and open cabinets, where I find more plates and mugs and bowls, kitchen appliances, pots and pans. When I look in the pantry, I get a surprise. It's stocked with food: cans of soup and vegetables like corn and beans, boxes of rice and assorted cereals. Like everything else, it looks old. The cereal boxes have been chewed by mice. The labels are peeling off some of the tinned goods. I pick up a can of soup and look at the expiration date. It hasn't been edible for well over a decade. Other items have similarly expired dates.

I close the pantry door again, then leave the kitchen and walk back through the living room to a door on the other side, which I assume must be the bedroom.

That's when I discover what the sender of that text message *really* wanted me to see. Because when I open the door and step inside, I cross the threshold into hell.

77

There is blood everywhere. It's splashed across the floor and spattered on the walls. A trail leads from the bed toward the door, complete with bloody handprints, as if someone was dragging themself along. But it's the bed that I can't rip my gaze from. The sheets are twisted and slashed as if by the blade of a knife and soaked through with even more blood. So much of it that I would never know the sheets were once white if I couldn't see their original color in the folds that hang off the bed. It looks like a massacre took place in this room.

My hands fly to my mouth to stop the scream even as I turn and flee from the room, race through the apartment to the front door, and yank it open. Then I'm running through the lobby in a blind panic, my feet pounding on the marble floor and all thoughts of stealth abandoned. All I want to do right now is to escape this building, and the horrific scene inside that apartment, because something is terribly wrong at the Glendale.

I reach the doors and barrel through them without slowing, then fly down the steps to the sidewalk. At one point I lose my footing and almost trip, but I recover my balance and push forward until I reach the corner of the block, where I come to a breathless halt. When I look back at the building, it looks just like it always has, but now I see it with new eyes. The malignancy that Addison warned me about is real, and I'm not sure I can ever set foot inside that place again. Certainly not tonight. I can't stay here, either.

I take out my cell phone and call Sam. Right now, I don't care what he and Kalina did or if our relationship is over. I need him.

But of course, it goes to voicemail.

I leave a message anyway, because at least he'll get it in the morning. It's garbled, and I probably sound unhinged, but it's the best I can do under the circumstances. Not that it helps me at this moment.

I sum up my options, which aren't many. My parents will probably pick up, but they're at least forty-five minutes away in Newton. I could call an Uber to take me there, but that would also mean waiting out here on the street, and I *really* don't want to do that. I feel vulnerable. I need to get somewhere safe, somewhere that isn't the Glendale; then I can call my parents and have them come and pick me up. There's only one place I can think of to go this late at night. Dawn and Jamie's apartment. They're right here, in the building opposite the Glendale. I make up my mind and call Dawn.

She answers on the second ring.

"Jordan? Is everything okay?"

"No." I'm practically in tears and I can't stop shaking, and when I try to explain what happened, it's hard to compose my thoughts well enough to form a coherent sentence. I'm babbling in between the sobs. "I need to come over right now. The apartment on the ground floor . . . It's . . . Oh my God. There's so much blood . . . I can't go back . . . Please . . ."

"Okay. Take it easy. Slow down. I can't understand a word you're saying." Dawn's voice, calm and collected, slices through my terror. "Come on over to the apartment, and I'll buzz you in."

"Okay." My relief is almost palpable. I have somewhere to go, and it isn't the Glendale. I cross the road and head for Dawn and Jamie's apartment. When I get there, Dawn buzzes me in through the front door, and a couple of minutes later, I'm at their apartment.

Dawn answers the door dressed in a pair of jeans and a sweater that I suspect she threw on after I called. She looks tired . . . and worried. After ushering me inside, she leads me to the sofa and sits me down, then settles next to me. Jamie appears from the bedroom, pulling on a T-shirt and tucking it into his pants. He studies me with narrowed eyes.

Dawn glances quickly at her husband, then focuses her attention back on me. "How about you tell us what's going on."

"I'll try," I say. Then I launch into how I went down to the apartment on the ground floor, which is supposed to be empty, and went inside.

"Wait." Dawn looks at me. "I don't understand. How did you get into the apartment on the ground floor?"

"I took the key from the safe in the doorman's office."

"Wouldn't the safe be locked?" Jamie asks.

"It was. I knew the . . . Look, that isn't the point. Please, just listen to me."

"Okay. Fine. Please, continue."

"Thank you. So, I went into the apartment, and at first, I thought someone was living there. The doorman, Angelo, told me that the place wasn't fit for habitation, but that clearly wasn't the case. There was furniture in there, as if someone had just gotten up one day and walked out. And everything was years out of date, like the food in the pantry. I thought it was strange, but it wasn't a big deal. Then I went into the bedroom, and . . ." My throat closes and the words refuse to come. The panic comes rushing back just thinking about it.

"Hey." Jamie takes my hand. "You're safe here. You know that, right?"

I look at my friends, the concerned expressions on their faces. "I know."

"Now, what about the bedroom?"

An image of that hellish room flashes through my mind. I try to speak, but the words catch in my throat, and all that comes out is a thin croak.

"Hang on." Jamie turns and disappears. After a minute he returns with a tumbler that contains a finger's worth of amber liquid. He offers me the drink.

I shake my head, refusing the glass.

He sits beside me, places a soothing hand on my back. "It's whisky. It will calm you down. Steady your nerves."

He presses the drink into my hand. This time I take it, down the whisky in one gulp, even though I hate the taste of hard liquor. He's right, I need to calm down. My mind is going a hundred miles an hour, making it impossible to think straight.

"There you go," Dawn says. "Now, take some breaths. In and out, nice and slow."

I take several deep breaths, and soon the panic subsides.

"Better?" Dawn asks.

I nod.

"Good." Dawn places her hand on my arm. "Now, tell us what you saw."

"Blood. There was blood everywhere. It was up the walls and on the floor and all over the bed."

Dawn stares at me, wide eyed, then exchanges a glance with her husband. "Are you sure it was blood?"

I mouth a barely audible *Yes*. But even as I say it, I can't help wondering if that is *really* what I saw. Because so many strange things have happened to me since we moved into the Glendale. Like the crib in the basement, and the bumblebee toy that I know moved on its own, which of course is impossible. Or the painting in the hallway outside the apartment. The one of the woman holding her dead baby even as it disintegrated into nothing. By the time Sam came home, the painting was gone as if it had never been there, replaced once more by the original work of art. A much less triggering painting of the Glendale. Sam thought I was seeing things. That the trauma of my miscarriage was rearing its head again. And now, sitting here in the tranquility of Dawn and Jamie's apartment, I wonder if he was right. Which means I could be wrong about the blood, too. Because apart from anything else, I *had* just found a real bloodstain, albeit many years old, under a rug in my foyer. It's hardly surprising that foul play would be on my mind after discovering *that*. "At least, I think it was blood. It looked like it."

"Maybe it was paint or something," Jamie says, echoing my own sudden doubts. He stands back up. "Your doorman did say the place was in a poor state of repair, right?"

I nod, my resolve momentarily wavering. Maybe it *was* paint. But if so, why was it splattered around like that? People don't usually throw paint onto their walls like they're caught in the middle of a Jackson Pollock–style frenzy. They don't leave handprints and smears all over the floor. And it was on the bed, too. The sheets were sliced. They were ripped and slashed. Then there's the text message. Would someone really send me down to the ground floor apartment in the middle of the night just to see a deranged decorating job? No. My conviction hardens even as the obvious occurs to me. Something I should have done before but didn't think of in my blind panic. I fumble to unlock my phone. "It wasn't paint. I need to call the police."

"Whoa. Hold on." Dawn reaches over and gently lifts the phone from my shaking hand. "Let's just think about that, shall we?"

"What? Why?"

"You stole a key and broke into an apartment."

Jamie nods. "You'll probably end up arrested."

"Jamie's right," Dawn says. "Have you talked to anyone else? Like Sam?"

I shake my head. "Sam puts his phone on Do Not Disturb when he's sleeping. I was going to call my parents after I got here and ask them to come and pick me up."

"How about we figure out exactly what you saw before waking people up in the middle of the night. Don't you think?"

"I suppose." As much as my gut is telling me that something is terribly wrong and to get as far away from the Glendale as possible, I have to admit that they're right. I can't be *sure* what I saw. I was already nervous, and the scene in the bedroom shocked me. It *looked* like blood, but now my conviction wavers. After all, the apartment was empty. There was no body, or any other source for what I assumed was blood.

And getting arrested for breaking and entering isn't something I've even considered. That would be beyond awful. But still . . .

Jamie reads the expression on my face. "Look, I understand if you don't want to go back over there, but wouldn't it be better to know?"

"If you want, me and Jamie can go over and take a look while you stay here," Dawn says, standing up. "Then, when we get back, if what you've told us is true, then we'll call the police. Does that sound good?"

"Stay here on my own?"

"We won't be long. Just over and back."

The breath catches in my throat. I don't want to stay here alone any more than I want to go back across the street. I almost say that we should all stay here, that there's no need for them to go and look at that apartment, but I can see by the looks on their faces that they've made up their minds. They don't believe me, or more accurately, they think there's a reasonable explanation for what I saw. After thinking about it, I decide that I'd rather be with them, even if it means facing my fears. And strangely, I'm not afraid anymore. The panic is gone, replaced by a soft and fuzzy sense of calm. The whisky has helped more than I expected. I take a deep breath and stand up. "Okay. I'll go."

"See, that wasn't so hard, was it?" Dawn takes my hand and leads me toward the door. "Come on. You'll be safe with us."

78

The last thing I want to do is go back to the Glendale. But here I am, crossing the street with Dawn and Jamie, walking up the front steps, swiping my key card to let us into the lobby. And there's the apartment, with the front door still standing wide open.

The whisky-induced calmness evaporates, and I'm overcome by a sudden feeling that something isn't right, and we shouldn't be here. I stop halfway across the lobby and try to turn back. "I've changed my mind. I don't want to do this."

"We've come this far," Dawn says, taking my elbow and nudging me toward the apartment. "There's nothing to be afraid of. We're right here with you."

That doesn't make me feel any better.

"Just a quick look. In and out," Jamie says, taking my other elbow.

Every fiber of my being is telling me not to go back into that apartment—to turn and run—and if Dawn and Jamie want to check it out on their own, then that isn't my problem.

Except *all of this* is my problem.

I'm the one who broke into that apartment, when I should have just ignored that text message. I'm the one who ran to Dawn and Jamie for help. And that's exactly what they're trying to do. I got them into this, so how can I abandon them? The answer is simple. I can't. So I force myself to keep going. Because if they see what I saw in that bedroom, they will understand, and we can call the police. And if it isn't blood, if I somehow got it wrong, then I don't need to be afraid.

We reach the apartment and step inside.

Dawn takes her phone out and turns on the flashlight, then points it toward the bedroom door. "Is this it?"

"Uh-huh." I want to say more, but the words won't come. I can barely breathe right now, let alone form a cohesive sentence.

"Okay. Let's go take a look," Jamie says. His hand is still on my elbow, and he steers me forward.

The room is mired in darkness.

Jamie reaches out and clicks the light switch.

The scene before me is no less horrific the second time around than it was the first.

A whimper escapes my lips, because there's no doubt that this is blood. Although now I notice something that I missed before. The blood is dry and crusted. It looks . . . old. And now the expired food in the pantry makes sense. Whoever lived here didn't move out and leave everything behind. They were murdered, and the horrific evidence of that crime is painted up the walls and across the floor and over the sheets of the bed.

"Oh my God. You were right," Dawn says.

I've seen enough. I turn to Dawn. "Give me my phone. We need to call the police. Right now."

"I don't think so."

"What? Why not?" I ask, confused. Then it hits me. I had turned on the lights when I was here earlier, but they were off again when we came back. Something is really wrong. "We have to go. We're not safe here."

"On the contrary, Dawn and I are perfectly safe," Jamie says. "And you would be, too, if only things had gone differently."

"What are you talking about?" I take a step back and turn around, but we are not alone . . . because behind us, appearing out of the darkness like ghosts, are Catherine and the other residents of the Glendale.

79

Catherine stands in the living room with Kalina by her side. Her husband Ron stands behind her, with Dr. Burgess next to him. To my dismay, I also see Frank and Jennifer.

I stare at them in shocked confusion. "I don't understand."

Catherine smiles. "Of course you don't, my dear, and I was hoping it would stay that way for a little longer. We weren't quite ready for you yet. But then you had to go snooping around."

I glare at Dawn and Jamie, who have fallen into line next to the residents of the Glendale. They stand facing me, cutting off any possible escape route. "You're a part of this?" I ask, even though I have no idea what *this* is. I suspect I'm about to find out.

Jamie doesn't react. He just fixes me with an icy stare.

Dawn shrugs but says nothing.

Catherine holds her hand out. "Come along. I think it's time that we finish this."

"I don't think so." I'm not going anywhere near Catherine. I take a step away from her, retreating deeper into the bedroom.

"There's no need to be difficult. You're just delaying the inevitable."

"And what would that be?" I ask.

Catherine doesn't answer. She just stands there as if she's waiting for me to figure it out. And it doesn't take very long, because I've spent the last two days trying to figure out exactly what happened in my apartment. Jacqueline Burke wrote all that stuff in her notebook about not feeling safe and thinking she was being watched. Then she vanished without a trace. Addison McGlocklin's husband, Mark, blew his brains out in my foyer. But did Jacqueline Burke really vanish on her way back from a night out? And did Mark McGlocklin really take his own life? I suspect that the answer to both questions is no. They were murdered, and who knows how many other people have died in this building? Considering the gruesome scene behind me in the bedroom, it's a lot. My blood runs cold. This isn't an apartment building—it's a spider's web, and Catherine is the big fat spider sitting in the middle, waiting for her unsuspecting victims to come too close. Except she isn't the only spider. There's a whole nest of them, and it appears that, for whatever reason, they've set their sights upon me as their prey. But the people standing in front of me aren't the only ones who live in the Glendale. And they can't all be killers. "Come any closer and I'll scream."

A faint smile plays across Catherine's lips. "Of course you will, my dear. That's kind of the point. Which is why the building is soundproofed. No one will hear you."

"The people in the other apartments will hear me."

"No, they won't." Catherine says this with such assurance that it's hard not to believe her.

Shit. I need to get out of here now.

The apartment door is still open, but I'll never get past Catherine and her cronies to reach it. So I go in the only direction I can—deeper into the bedroom, making sure not to turn my back. At least until my legs bump against the bed, stopping my retreat. I glance toward the window, wondering how easy it would be to smash it and climb through. I figure my chances of making it out are slim, but it's better than standing here and waiting for whatever these people have in store for me. Catherine soon shuts down that avenue of escape, however. "The window is reinforced glass. The same kind used in hurricane windows. You won't break it. We spared no expense when we renovated this building. Made it exactly what we needed it to be."

My heart sinks. Apparently, what they needed it to be was a slaughterhouse. And I stepped through its doors willingly and without hesitation. Now it's becoming clear. Everything that's happened here has been carefully orchestrated to push my buttons. The crying baby. The crib in the basement and that bumblebee toy. The hideous painting. It was all because of the miscarriage, which they clearly knew about. Of course, my medical records would be ripe for the picking since they have a doctor in their midst who could easily obtain them. Was the coffee shop project ever real? Probably not. And what about Sam and Kalina? He's been protesting his innocence all along. I look at her. "Sam wasn't cheating on me."

Kalina stares back at me with cold, hard eyes. "No. But it didn't take much to convince you that he was. Honestly, you were so quick to believe the worst of him. He's better off without you."

"Why would you do that?" I ask in a small voice, even though the answer is painfully obvious. I think of Sam, and all I put him through. How could I have doubted him? My cheeks flush with shame.

"We had to get him out of the way," Catherine says.

"So you can kill me, like you killed whoever lived in this apartment."

"My dear, you've got it all wrong." Catherine's voice cracks. A tear runs down her cheek as she gazes past me at the blood on the bed and the walls. "This was my daughter's apartment. She was supposed to be safe here."

Ron puts a comforting arm around his wife, his gaze never straying from me. "But she wasn't. She was brutally murdered instead."

Catherine speaks again. "And the killer got away with it."

Dawn steps forward. "Which is why you have to die."

80

They sit me in a chair facing the bedroom. Jamie closes the apartment door and stands in the foyer, blocking it, his arms folded. The others line up in front of me with their backs to the bedroom door, which throws them into shadow. At least until Kalina turns on a lamp next to the sofa, bathing them all in a soft yellow light that would be relaxing under different circumstances.

Catherine's daughter was murdered in this apartment. That much is clear. What I don't understand is what her death has to do with me. I never even knew the woman. I want to protest, tell them that I have no idea what they're going on about, but I can't find my voice. My throat is as dry as sandpaper. My palms are sweaty against the arms of the chair. The blood thunders in my ears.

Silence falls between us.

At least until the doctor steps forward. He clears his throat and holds up a photograph of an attractive young woman with chestnut hair. "Emma Cerruto. My fiancée. Twenty-six years of age, with her whole life ahead of her."

Next, Frank and Jennifer step forward and hold up a photograph of another young woman, whom I recognize from the framed photos lining the walls and shelves of their apartment. She's wearing a pair of round John Lennon–style glasses and smiling at the camera. "Amanda Barnes. Our daughter. Twenty-four years of age, with her whole life ahead of her."

Kalina goes next. She holds up a photo of a young man. "Aleksander 'Alex' Stefaniak. My brother. Twenty-three years of age, with his whole life ahead of him."

Catherine and Ron lift a photograph of a girl with jet-black hair. "Luna Cole. Our daughter. Twenty-three years of age, with her whole life ahead of her."

Finally, it's Dawn's turn. She steps forward and glances toward Jamie, who's still blocking the door, then takes a photo from her pocket. I recognize it as the same young woman from Catherine and Ron's photograph. Except this time, she's showing off a tattoo on her forearm above her wrist that looks like a blackbird, or maybe a raven. Dawn's hand trembles, and a tear pushes from the corner of her eye. "Luna Cole. My older sister. Twenty-three years of age, with her whole life ahead of her."

I sit through this strange exposition, my terror growing with each person who talks. I'm still confused about why these people want to kill me. I look up at them, searching their faces for any hint of compassion. I see none. Instead, they stand holding the photos up and staring at me, as if to prove some kind of point.

Finally, Catherine speaks again. "Brothers, sisters, partners, and daughters. All snatched away before their time."

Dawn nods. "Murdered by Philip Arthur Munson. The Back Bay Butcher."

"Fifteen victims over six years," says Kalina.

A glimmer of memory ignites at the back of my mind. Because I recognize that name. The Back Bay Butcher. Everyone who grew up in Boston has heard of him, of course. He gave me nightmares when I was a teen. But this memory isn't borne of some detached fear. It's personal, because I remember my father talking about him to my mother when he thought I wasn't around. The memory is hazy and distorted by the passage of time. I force a calm breath, which isn't easy, and say, "I don't understand what any of this has to do with me."

Catherine slides the photo of her daughter to the side to reveal another photograph beneath. I recognize this image, because it's the headshot my father uses for the bio on his psychiatric practice website. She must have printed it from the web. The snatch of memory becomes a little clearer. My dad was somehow connected to the Back Bay Butcher, although the details remain elusive.

Catherine wastes no time in enlightening me. "Michael R. Hollister, MD. Your father, and a forensic psychiatrist for the defense in *The State v. Philip Arthur Munson*. He testified at trial that, in his opinion, the Back Bay Butcher did not know right from wrong when he was torturing and murdering his victims. Your father claimed that Munson was acting under an irresistible impulse and didn't understand the nature of his crimes."

Dawn takes up the mantle, her voice laced with venom. "Which is total fucking bullshit. Munson knew exactly what he was doing. But it didn't matter. The jury was convinced by your father's testimony, thanks to his role as an expert witness for the defense. They found Munson not guilty by reason of insanity."

"Instead of rotting in prison, where he belongs, he's relaxing in some cushy mental health facility and will never face justice for his crimes," Frank says. "Hell, they might even release him someday."

"You've got it all wrong," I say in a tight voice, my throat almost closing in panic. It appears that they blame my father for some perceived lack of retribution for the deaths of their loved ones at the hands of a brutal serial killer. But they aren't right, because I remember now. My father *did* testify in the Back Bay Butcher's trial, and yes, Munson was found not guilty by reason of insanity, which, according to my dad, is an incredibly rare occurrence. But that didn't mean that Munson evaded accountability. My father has consulted on many such cases and has said that being sent to a high-security psychiatric unit is often worse than going to prison because the confinement is indefinite, with no chance of parole. You're completely at the mercy of the doctors, who can keep you locked up forever if they wish, and you're surrounded by other patients with a level of psychosis the same as or greater than your own. And despite what Frank says, it's highly unlikely that the Back Bay Butcher will ever be set free, given the scope and severity of his crimes. But Catherine and my other neighbors don't seem to view it that way. Or maybe, in their warped thirst for justice, they just don't care. My stomach twists in knots as I realize the futility of my situation. Appealing to their common sense is my only hope. I'm not sure it will work, but I don't want to die. "Philip Arthur Munson received a stiff punishment, regardless of whether a jury said he was technically innocent. They will never set him free. He'll be locked up for the rest of his life, and more importantly, he won't be able to hurt anyone else."

"Spoken like your father's daughter." Catherine glances sideways at Jennifer. "I told you she wouldn't understand."

"Even if she did, it doesn't make any difference," says Dr. Burgess. "She has to die. It's the only way her father will comprehend the loss we've all suffered. He needs to learn that actions have consequences."

So that's what this is about? Some kind of sick retribution against my father for his role in the Back Bay Butcher's trial and the subsequent verdict? I'm gripped by sudden panic. "You don't have to do this. If you kill me, you're as bad as Munson."

Kalina glares at me. "We are nothing like that animal."

"Enough talk. Let's get this over with." Catherine turns to the doctor. "Are you ready?"

Burgess nods and walks over to a physician's bag sitting on a side table next to the couch. He opens it with his back to me. Looking at Jamie, he asks, "What did you give her?"

"I put one of those pills you gave me in a glass of whisky," Jamie replies. "Made her drink it."

I stare at Jamie, shocked by this revelation, even though it shouldn't surprise me at this point. No wonder I felt so calm. Why I was so willing to be led back over here. He laced my drink.

Burgess nods and rummages in his bag. When he turns around, he's holding a syringe.

Now I scream at the top of my lungs. I also jump to my feet, because, for some reason, they haven't restrained me in the chair. But it's no use—my captors were expecting this reaction. Jamie leaves his position by the door and rushes forward, grabbing my left arm. Frank, who now appears to move just fine without his cane, grabs the other one, and together they force me back down into the seat and hold me there.

"Get your fucking hands off me," I screech, twisting and thrashing in their grasp. At least until Catherine grabs a bunch of my hair and yanks my head back, almost tearing it from the roots.

My skull slams into the back of the chair.

Dazed and unable to move, I watch helplessly as the doctor approaches with the syringe, then steps around Frank and slips the needle into my exposed neck beneath my ear.

I feel a prick of discomfort, followed by a strange icy chill that worms its way through my veins, and the world fades to black.

81

When I wake up, my vision is disjointed and out of sync. As the drug-induced haze clears, I see that I'm sitting in another chair, this time in my apartment on the fourth floor.

I'm surprised they haven't killed me . . . yet. I'm also surprised to discover that I'm still not restrained.

Jennifer is sitting on the sofa, facing me. She's holding a pistol. We're alone, but Jennifer soon dispels any notion I might have to flee.

"The gun is self-explanatory," she says. "But you should also know that the apartment door is locked, and you won't be able to open it. Likewise, the slider leading out onto the balcony. Catherine and Ron had some unique modifications made to this apartment when they renovated the building, and I assure you that escape is impossible. There's no way out of this room for you."

"Where are the others?" I ask. My throat is dry and a dull ache throbs behind my eyes, which I suspect is thanks to the drug they administered.

"They'll be here soon enough." The gun rests in Jennifer's lap. "You need to be awake for what comes next."

"You drugged me, then waited for me to wake up, just so you can kill me?"

"We need you conscious before you die; otherwise it won't look right."

"You people are nuts." I glance toward the door, even though I believe what Jennifer's just told me. Not that it matters. I'd never make it that far. Unless Jennifer hesitates to shoot me, because I'm not convinced that she has what it takes, but I'm not quite willing to test that assumption. "I'm not responsible for what my father did. And anyway, he was just doing his job."

"Ah, yes. An answer used to justify so many atrocities." Jennifer sighs deeply.

"And how many atrocities have *you* committed?" I ask. "What about Jacqueline Burke and Mark McGlocklin, and who knows how many other people you've killed in this apartment? Because I don't believe for one second that Jackie vanished on her way home after a night out or that Mark killed himself after having a psychotic break. It was you and Catherine and the others, wasn't it?"

"I can't deny my involvement." There's a note of sadness in Jennifer's voice.

"And what was their crime?" Despite my terror, I can't keep the disgust from my voice. "Did you kill them, too, because they were related to someone involved with the Back Bay Butcher's trial?"

"The lead prosecutor's daughter. The judge's son. The jury foreperson's granddaughter. They were all complicit in letting that bastard escape justice." Jennifer won't make eye contact with me as she speaks. "I wanted them to feel the pain of losing someone like that. We all did."

Her admission takes me by surprise. They haven't killed two people. They've killed at least three. This apartment really is a slaughterhouse, and I've been living in it, blissfully unaware of the horrors that have occurred within its walls. Worse, they've gotten away with it by hiding their crimes. A disappearance. A suicide. Who knows how they covered up the other murder. That explains the lack of restraints. A good pathologist might notice the marks from the rope or adhesive from the tape on my wrists and ankles and become suspicious. "What's your plan for me? How are you going to cover up my murder?"

Jennifer looks back up. "They're going to make it look like an overdose. Prescription medication and alcohol. Eventually, someone will come looking for you. Your parents or Sam. They'll find you in the soaking tub. It will look like you ran a bath, climbed in, and washed down a whole thirty-day supply of antidepressants with a bottle of wine. A pretty easy sell, considering the miscarriage and your subsequent struggles. There will be a suicide note, of course. Just a few carefully chosen words typed out on your computer screen to seal the deal."

An undignified scene plays in my mind's eye, of me lying naked and dead in a pool of cold bathwater. Of strangers photographing me and lifting my corpse out of the tub and putting me on a gurney. Of that being my family's last memory of me. Sam's last memory of me. "Why not just shoot me?"

"Two people dying the same way in the same apartment? Too obvious . . . and too messy. The last time we did that, it ruined the floorboards."

If her words were not so chilling, they would be funny. Here we are, talking about a cold-blooded murder, and she's worried about the floorboards. "One problem with your little plan. I don't have a prescription for antidepressants."

"Yes, you do. It comes in handy to have a doctor in the building. He wrote you a prescription last week after you went to him and said that you were feeling depressed."

"Right. Like I'd go to some random doctor I barely know instead of my father. He's a psychiatrist, remember? No one will believe it."

"Yes, they will, because you also told him you were too embarrassed to go to your father. That you didn't want him to know you were suffering from depression."

"I didn't tell him any of those things."

"True, but no one else knows that. Trust me, Jordan, Catherine has this all figured out." Jennifer reaches into her pocket and pulls out the photo of her daughter. She gazes at it for a moment. "Amanda was an only child. I wanted to have another, but I couldn't. After two miscarriages, I gave up. She was our miracle. Smart, too. She loved to read, majored in literature at college. Graduated top of her class. Her dream was to be a writer. She was working on a novel when she died, and it would've been so good. I have the pages in my nightstand drawer. I take them out sometimes and read them, because it helps me feel close to her. That half-finished book is a little part of Amanda that no one can ever take away."

Despite my predicament, a lump rises in my throat. I'm all too familiar with the pain of losing a baby. This woman lost two, then had her only daughter taken away. It doesn't give her the right to do this, though. "You're going to kill me. Why are you telling me all this?"

"Because it's important that you realize exactly what Philip Arthur Munson stole from us when he murdered Amanda. He snuffed a light from this world. Someone who would have made a difference. A beautiful soul who didn't deserve to die. He left a hole in our lives that can never be filled. That's why I'm telling you. I want you to know why Frank and I got involved in this. We aren't monsters. We're just grieving parents, and I need you to understand that."

"Jennifer, what happened to your family is awful. What that man did to Amanda is awful. But killing me won't get her back. It's not going to give you the justice you desire."

"I know." Jennifer nods slowly and meets my gaze. "Which is why you shouldn't have gone to Dawn and Jamie tonight. You should have kept running after you saw that apartment. You should have run as fast as you could and never come back."

82

I sit in stunned silence as the implication of what she's just said sinks in. "You sent me that text message."

Jennifer nods. "I thought I could do this. I thought I could kill again, but I was wrong. I tried to tell myself that it would be okay, but after we spent the evening together the other night drinking wine, I realized that it isn't the answer. I don't want to be a murderer."

Too late, lady, you already are, I think to myself. But that's not what I say, because it appears that Jennifer is on my side, at least for the moment. A faint glimmer of hope that I might get out of this alive breaks through the despair. "Why didn't you just tell me what was going on—or better yet, go to the police?"

"I changed my mind about killing you, but I didn't want to end up in jail for what I've already done. I figured that if you saw the apartment, all that blood, it would scare you enough to leave and not come back. Or maybe you'd be too afraid to live here alone, and you'd figure it out with Sam. They wouldn't be able to do anything with him around."

"I didn't know that Dawn and Jamie were dangerous," I say, because I had no reason to suspect that they meant me harm. As far as I was concerned, we were friends. "I thought they would help me."

"That's what you were meant to think. Catherine wanted someone on the outside. Someone who could befriend you and steer you in the right direction if you got offtrack. Who better to do that than her own daughter?"

"And Luna's sister." Dawn certainly fooled me. She suggested I kick Sam out and I fell for it, leaving me alone at the Glendale and putting myself at the mercy of these people.

"Yes." Jennifer lays the gun down on the couch. "The others will be back soon. I'm supposed to let them know when you wake up so they can finish this. We don't have long."

I look at the gun, calculating my odds of lunging forward and grabbing it, but Jennifer's hand is still right there, resting on the couch next to it. She might be old, but I suspect that she'll still be quick enough to pick it back up and shoot me before I'm halfway there. Besides, I want to see where this is going.

But then she surprises me by standing up and leaving the gun where it is. "My throat is dry, so I'm going to fetch a glass of water. If you have any sense, you'll be gone when I get back."

"What about you?" I want to escape this place more than anything, but I can't do it at the expense of Jennifer's safety, even if she is a murderer. That isn't me. "They'll know you let me go."

Jennifer smiles. "I'm an old woman, and I don't think clearly sometimes. I went to get a glass of water, absentmindedly leaving the gun on the couch, believing you were still out cold from the drugs Dr. Burgess administered. When I came back, you held me at gunpoint until I showed you how to get out of the apartment. Obviously, I'll have to raise the alarm to make it look real, so you won't have long. I suggest you move quickly. Avoid the elevator. It's too noisy. Take the stairs to the lobby, get outside, and don't look back."

"How?" Jennifer already told me that my apartment door is locked, and I won't be able to open it.

"There's another way out. When this place was renovated, they built secret passages in the walls between the apartments. The built-in bookcase on the right side of the fireplace is a door. There's a passageway that leads to another door that opens into our apartment. From there you can get to the stairs."

"What about Frank?" He isn't here, and I don't want to run into him in the apartment next door.

"He's up in the top-floor penthouse apartment along with the others, waiting for me to tell them that you woke up. They have this ritual. Every time we do this, right before the kill, they share a drink from a bottle of whisky that Catherine's daughter bought for Ron on his birthday a few months before she died. That's what they're doing right now."

"But not you."

"No. I've never liked the ritual. It cheapens what we do. That's why I always volunteer to stay with the target until they wake up. Now, for goodness' sake, hurry and get out of here."

"Okay. I'm going." I jump to my feet and head toward the fireplace. On the way past the sofa, I hesitate, then reach down and pick up the gun. If Jennifer is wrong and they aren't up in the penthouse, it might be the only way I'll get out of this building alive, even if I have to kill one of them to do it. But when I get to the bookcase, it occurs to me that I don't know how to open the concealed door.

Jennifer anticipates my question before I even ask. "The ornamental block molding on the top right of the bookcase. Press it in and hold it. You'll hear a click, and then you can swing the bookcase open."

I follow her instructions, and a moment later, the bookcase swings wide to reveal a short, narrow corridor barely wide enough for a person to pass through, with another door at the far end. It has unfinished walls with exposed studs and a rough wood plank floor. There's a light switch to my left, which I turn on. A bare bulb mounted in the ceiling comes on and fills the space with weak light.

"I'll close it behind you," Jennifer says. "Good luck."

"You know I'll go straight to the police when I get out of here, right?"

Jennifer nods. "I figured you would. Maybe it's for the best. But please, do me one favor."

"What?" I'm done with talking. I want to get the hell out of here.

"If you use that gun, please don't kill Frank. He's all I've got left."

"I'll do my best," I tell her, even though I intend to shoot anyone who gets in my way, even if it is Frank. Then I slip past the bookcase and into the cramped space beyond.

83

I hurry through the corridor, which is really nothing more than a tight space between the walls of my apartment and the one next door. Cobwebs fill the gaps between the studs. Here and there, a spider scuttles away, alarmed by my passage. A faint odor hangs in the air, musty and acidic, like a mix of mold and urine, probably from rats. Which makes sense, because they would only use this secret space when someone was living in my apartment. Most of the time, this narrow corridor belongs to the rodents and insects that are impossible to keep out of buildings this old in the city. As I go, it occurs to me that even if Jennifer feigns forgetfulness, the others may still suspect that she let me go on purpose. I wonder if she didn't think about this, or if she's past caring. Not that it matters, because *I* don't care. She's a killer just like the rest of them, and growing a conscience on your fourth murder isn't much of a redemption.

I reach the door on the other side of the passageway and push. It swings open with ease, and then I'm in Jennifer and Frank's apartment, standing next to the fireplace.

I stop and listen, ready to flee back into the walls if Frank is here.

The gun is heavy in my hand.

From somewhere else in the apartment, I hear the steady ticktock of an old mechanical clock, but nothing else.

I turn to the bookcase and push it closed again. I start toward the foyer, hurrying through the living room, but then I stop. The door to the second bedroom was closed the last time I was here, but now it's open. I see a desk against the wall, upon which is an old desktop computer. Mounted above it is a large monitor. On the screen is my living room, and Jennifer pacing back and forth with a phone clutched in one hand.

I don't have time for this, but I can't help myself. I change course, step into the bedroom, and stare at the monitor. The view of my living room is from a high vantage point near the corner of the room, right around one of the recessed lights. Five boxes labeled cam1 through 5 are at the bottom of the screen. I grab the mouse and click cam2.

The scene changes to show the main bedroom, again from a high vantage point, although this time I can't pinpoint the location. I click again. Another view appears, this time of the spare bedroom. Cam4 shows a view of the dining room. One camera to go. I click it, and a view of my kitchen comes up on the screen.

The implications of what I've found leave me reeling. It's no wonder I felt uneasy in that apartment, because even when Sam wasn't there, I was never alone. And with that hidden entrance behind the living room bookcase, anyone could access my apartment whenever they wanted. That's why the mood board went missing. They did it deliberately to leave me questioning my sanity. It's also how Kalina's earring ended up next to the bed. She didn't lose it in the throes of wild passion with my fiancé. They planted it there so I would find it. One last piece of proof that Sam was cheating on me. And all the while, Dawn and Jamie were living in the building opposite, ready to lend a sympathetic ear and steer me in whatever direction Catherine wanted.

I click back to the first camera. Jennifer has stopped pacing. She's talking on her cell phone, presumably letting the others know that I've escaped. There's no sound on the camera, but I can imagine her saying how she stepped away for a moment to get a glass of water, and when she came back, I forced her to let me go. I wish she had given me a little more time to make it to the lobby and get out of the building, but it's also my fault for stopping and looking at the monitor. I should have ignored it and kept running. I need to get out of here right now. But when I turn to flee, my gaze settles on a notebook sitting next to the computer keyboard. Jacqueline Burke's notebook that I found behind the drawer in my dining room. I shouldn't be surprised. After all, was Frank really going to give incriminating evidence to the cops? He probably didn't even have the detective's number. It was all a ruse to get the notebook before I could take it to the police myself. It doesn't matter. My only concern right now should be getting out of the Glendale before Catherine and her sick co-conspirators find and kill me.

I turn and race back through the apartment and out into the hallway. From somewhere below me, I hear the wheezing clunk of the old cage elevator car making its way up to the penthouse apartment. It will take a little while to get there, which buys me some time, but not much.

I reach the door leading out on the fourth-floor landing and tug it open, ignoring how it bangs back against the wall—stealth is pointless now—and then I'm on the stairs.

Above me, I hear footsteps. Someone is coming down from the penthouse.

I pick up the pace, jumping the last three steps to the third-floor landing, then propelling myself down the next flight. The sound of footsteps above me is growing closer. I hear a shout. It's the doctor, which makes sense because he's probably the person most suited to a mad dash down so many flights of stairs. But the others won't be far behind. My only advantage is that the old rickety elevator doesn't move very fast.

By the time I get to the second-floor landing, my heart is practically thumping out of my chest and my breath is ragged. I'm too out of shape for this. And I still feel a little dizzy from the drug they gave me. I make a pact with myself that if I live past tonight, I'm hitting the gym.

One flight of stairs to go.

I fly down it, my hope of escape rising the closer I get to the ground floor. But then my foot misses a step, and I pitch forward, arms flailing. For one dreadful moment, I think I'm going to tumble headfirst down the remaining stairs, but then my hand finds the banister and my fingers close around it, stopping my forward momentum. I teeter for a second, fighting gravity, and then I regain my balance.

Thankfully, I didn't fall, but the mishap has cost me valuable seconds. My pursuer is closer now. I take off again, being careful not to miss another step, until I reach the lobby.

Almost there.

Just another thirty feet to the main doors, and beyond that, the street. If I'm lucky, I'll be able to flag down a passing car, because even at this time of night, there's always someone around in the city. I'm barely halfway across the lobby when a figure steps out from the darkness of the mailroom and blocks my path.

It's Angelo, the doorman.

"Everything okay, miss?" he asks. "It's awfully late for you to be up and about."

I'm overcome by a sweeping sense of relief. This is even better than flagging down some random motorist. Angelo will have a phone. He can call the police. But then a creeping dread replaces my elation, because something isn't right. Angelo finished work at eleven and shouldn't be back until morning. What is he doing skulking around in the mailroom in the early hours? The answer is obvious. He's a part of this.

I stop and raise the gun. "Get out of my way."

"I can't do that, miss." Angelo takes a step toward me.

"I mean it. I *will* shoot." The gun feels strange in my hand. Unnatural.

"You won't shoot me," Angelo says. His face is hard as granite.

For a moment, I wonder if he's right, but then I think about the people in this building and what they plan to do. How they want to wash enough pills to kill a horse down my throat with wine from my own fridge, then dump my naked body in the bathtub for Sam to find.

That's all it takes.

I pull the trigger.

84

I expect a loud bang, and for the doorman to go down, because there's no way I can miss at such short range, even if this is the first time I've ever fired a gun. But what I get is an unsatisfying click. I stare at the weapon, horrified, even as Angelo lunges forward and knocks it from my grip. Then he grabs my arms, turns me around, and marches me back toward the elevator. At the same time, he leans in close so that his mouth is next to my ear and whispers, "Daniela Martínez. My daughter. Twenty-one years of age, with her whole life ahead of her."

85

Another grieving family member. No surprise there. I wonder how many other residents of the Glendale are in on this, and how they've gotten away with it for so long. Not that it matters. I have more immediate concerns, like staying alive.

"Please, you don't need to do this," I beg, even as I realize the futility of my words. These people are blinded by the moral indignation of their own twisted righteousness.

"Shut up." Angelo's fingers dig into the flesh of my arms hard enough that I almost squeal with pain, but I bite my lip. I don't want to give him the satisfaction. And deep down, I'm glad for his roughness, because his fingers might leave bruises that will raise the suspicions of whoever performs my autopsy.

But I'm not dead yet.

I dig my heels in and push back against him, but Angelo is stronger than he looks. And when I finally get some traction and feel his fingers slipping on my arms, he slams me forward into the elevator cage. My head smacks into the bars so hard that I see stars. Then he pins me against it with the full weight of his body.

Satisfied that I'm not going anywhere, he releases his grip on one arm and presses the button to call the elevator, then pulls a phone from his pocket and lifts it to his ear. "I've got the bitch. Bringing her back up now."

The doctor hasn't appeared. He was right behind me on the stairs but must have turned around when he realized Angelo would stop me. It's a small victory amid my defeat, because at least it's one-on-one now. But I'm not sure that it matters, because Angelo clearly has the advantage of size and strength. He's pressing me against the elevator cage with such force that it's hard to breathe. At least until the elevator arrives, and he jerks me back so that he can pull the gate open.

I gulp a long breath, thankful for a momentary reprieve, before he propels me into the car and pulls the gate shut again. He jabs at the button for the fourth floor, and the elevator rises.

I watch the transition between the ground and second floors slide past through the cage—a thick strip of gray concrete. Angelo, satisfied that I'm suitably subdued and have nowhere to go, lowers his hand to push the phone back into his pocket.

At that moment, a jolt shakes the elevator car as it draws level with the second floor. This isn't an uncommon occurrence, given its age. The car shudders whenever it reaches a floor, even if it isn't stopping there. But the sudden bump is enough to make Angelo fumble the phone, which slips from his fingers and clatters to the floor.

He curses and bends down to retrieve it and, in doing so, releases his grip on my other arm. And that's all I need. Before he even realizes what I'm doing, I reach for the elevator control panel and stab the emergency stop button.

The elevator isn't moving fast, but the ensuing jolt as the car slams to a halt is enough for Angelo, already bent over, to lose his balance. He jerks forward with a grunt, his head slamming into one of the glass panels lining the interior of the elevator car.

I smash my knee into his stomach with all the force I can muster.

The breath explodes from Angelo's lungs, and he lets out another longer grunt, but he's not down.

I drop my leg to kick him again, but he's already twisting around to grab me, and my kneecap connects with his face instead. My leg explodes in pain, and I hear an audible snapping sound. At first, I think it might be me, but then I realize it was Angelo's nose. Blood is pouring over his lips and chin. He staggers back with a howl and lifts a hand to his face.

I go for his groin this time, kicking hard.

The howl becomes a warbling shriek, and somewhere deep within me, there's a flash of satisfaction. I'm done being a victim. What happened to the family members of these people was tragic and wrong, but the way they've dealt with it is abhorrent, and they don't deserve my pity.

Angelo is pushing himself up, reaching for me with grasping hands. Blood has soaked into his shirt, and his nose is twisted at an unnatural angle. His movements are slow. He looks dazed. I don't care. My next blow lifts him a few inches before he crumples to the floor and lies there, motionless. I can't tell if he's conscious or not, and I don't bother to check. Instead, I reach for the control panel to press the button for the ground floor. But then I stop. Do I really want to ride back down in this elevator, because Angelo might be playing possum and waiting for me to do exactly that so that he can overpower me again. Besides, Catherine and her little flock of murderers will expect me to run for the ground floor again. Which is why I pull the elevator door open and step out onto the third-floor landing. Then I reach back in and push the button for the basement before sliding the gate closed. The elevator car gives a small groan of protest and starts back down, taking Angelo along for the ride.

I'm free for now.

And then I remember the phone. The one that Angelo dropped in the elevator. I should have picked it up and called for help, but like an idiot, I left it there. Now it's taking a ride to the basement, and there's no way I'm going after it. But someone on this floor must have a phone. I go to the nearest door and raise my fist to hammer on it before I stop. What if everyone in this building is in on this? But if that's the case, wouldn't they have been there for that weird ritual with the photographs? Deciding it's worth the risk, I hammer on the door.

No one answers.

I bang again in desperation. It won't be long before my captors realize I gave Angelo the slip, if they haven't already. When I still don't get anywhere, I go to the door across the hall and do the same. Again, nobody answers. I repeat this with the third door, then the fourth, frantically slamming my fists against them and praying that someone will hear me. But no one does, which is weird, because they can't all be sleeping that soundly. Are they ignoring me? I have no idea, but it doesn't matter, because I'm obviously not getting any help from anyone on this floor. Which means I'll need to make a break for the lobby again.

Abandoning my efforts to raise the alarm, I rush to the stairs. My footsteps echo in the stairwell, much too loud. My breath comes in short, rasping gasps. I reach the second floor and turn on the landing, then take the last flight down toward the lobby. But when I'm only halfway there, Angelo appears at the foot of the stairs. He glares up at me, his face caked in blood. Then he grips the banister and starts to climb.

86

Clearly Angelo wasn't as incapacitated as he looked. He must've stopped the elevator on the ground floor, and now he's climbing back up toward me and cutting off my only escape route. I turn on the stairs and start back up, even as more figures appear above me on the staircase and start down. Three of them. Dawn, Jamie, and Dr. Burgess.

Fuck.

There's only one place left to go. I climb to the second-floor landing and barrel through the door and out to the hallway. If anyone's been disturbed by the ruckus, they haven't come out to investigate. The apartment doors remain closed.

I hammer on the first one but have about as much success as I did on the third floor. This time, though, I'm not giving in so easily. I reach down and grab the door handle, but it's locked. But when I try the second door, it swings open.

From somewhere above me, I hear shouts. The elevator is moving again, too. It clanks and groans, no doubt on its way to the second floor. With nowhere else to go, I step into the apartment and slam the door behind me, then turn and engage the dead bolt.

"Hello? Is anybody there?" I call into the darkness, expecting someone to respond.

When they don't, I call out again.

Still nothing.

Confused, I fumble around for the light switch and turn it on.

And now I see why no one answered, because the apartment is empty, and unlike my unit on the fourth floor, it looks abandoned. The walls are covered in peeling floral-patterned wallpaper that hangs in grubby strips. The plaster has crumbled in places to reveal the wooden laths beneath. Dust coats the floor, along with the dried husks of dead cockroaches and the shriveled remains of a mouse.

I move into the living room, momentarily forgetting about the psychotic mob who wants me dead in my surprise. An old-fashioned brass chandelier hangs from the ceiling. Three of its five bulbs are missing. The walls are in the same sorry state as the foyer. There are more dead rodents. The only piece of furniture is a sagging couch with a torn seat, covered in a thick layer of dust. Where the kitchen should be is nothing but an empty space with skeletal walls. The air is stale and tinged with that same acidic burn of urine that I smelled in the hidden corridor above.

And then I understand. Catherine didn't care if I screamed because there isn't anyone else in the building to hear it. The other apartments haven't been renovated. Only the ones on the fourth floor, the penthouse, and wherever Angelo and the doctor live. Everything else has been left to fall into rack and ruin. The Glendale exists for one reason only. To lure unsuspecting victims into its embrace.

The voices are closer now. It sounds like they're in the hallway, right outside the door.

I rush to the sliding doors leading out onto the balcony, because if I can get outside, I might be able to attract the attention of someone down on the street. But when I tug, they won't open. Then I see the screws driven through the frame and into the wall, preventing the doors from moving.

A loud thud reverberates through the apartment.

I swivel around as a second thud shakes the front door.

Someone is trying to smash their way in.

I look around frantically for a weapon, something with which to defend myself, but all I see are rotting chunks of plaster and a smashed light bulb on the floor that must have come from the chandelier. If only I still had the gun. But it wouldn't do me any good, anyway. The pistol wasn't loaded. Was it just for show, a way to keep me passive, or did they give Jennifer a weapon with no bullets because they suspected that she was having second thoughts about committing murder and they didn't want to risk her letting me escape with it? Which was exactly what she did.

Another thud, followed by a snap of splintering wood, and the door flies open. It slams back against the wall so hard that more plaster tumbles down. Jamie appears, with Dawn right behind. They advance into the room.

"There's nowhere left for you to go," he says. "It's time to finish this."

I have no intention of giving up without a fight. I turn and run in the only direction left open to me—the bedroom. The room is empty. Even the closet doors are gone, leaving an open space with a wooden closet bar that's come loose at one end and now hangs down. It's no gun, but it's better than nothing. I grab the bar and wrench it from the wall, then turn to face the door as Dawn and Jamie rush in.

87

I swing the rod as they draw close. It's an unwieldy weapon and hard to aim, but I land a glancing blow on Dawn, who yelps and jumps back, almost bumping into Jamie.

"Get the hell away from me," I screech and swing again, wielding it like a baseball bat. The rod slices through empty air, missing them both.

Jamie dodges to one side and grasps the rod, tries to tear it from my hands. I hold on tight, but the rod is smooth and slips through my fingers. He tosses it aside with a triumphant cry and lunges forward, grabbing my arm.

I twist free and shove Jamie aside, then try to sidestep him and make a break for the door. But Dawn blocks my path. She delays me just long enough for Jamie to regain his balance. He makes a grab for me, which I manage to evade, but it drives me toward Dawn, who wraps her arms around my waist and holds on tight.

I claw and twist, trying to break free. Her grip loosens. I take hold of her wrist and try to wrench her arm. The sleeve of her sweater rides up. My fingers touch something cold and hard. Metallic. A bracelet. But not just any bracelet. The silver Tiffany bracelet Sam gave me with the angel charm. The opal birthstone in the angel's hands shimmers an iridescent rainbow of colors.

"My bracelet." I spit the words even as I try to snatch it from her wrist, because I don't want my most cherished piece of jewelry—a piece that I thought was stolen and lost forever—on the arm of this psychotic bitch. A white-hot rage consumes me, because I realize what this means. Catherine and the other residents of the Glendale were manipulating Sam and me long before we ever moved into this building. They must have been behind the robbery at our apartment in Jamaica Plain, and I'll bet they also wrecked Sam's credit. All to steer us to the Glendale.

"It's *my* bracelet now." Dawn wraps her other arm around me as Jamie grabs me from behind, and together they drag me from the room and through the dilapidated apartment. When we reach the hallway, I see Catherine and the others waiting there, all wearing blue neoprene gloves, of the sort used in a doctor's office or hospital, no doubt provided by Burgess. Angelo is among them. His face is bloodied, nose crooked. He glowers at me, his eyes flashing with malice. I notice that Jennifer is not with them, and Frank is standing with his shoulders slumped, a sour look on his face. I also notice that Catherine has a gun, but it's not the same one they gave Jennifer. I suspect this pistol is loaded.

"Bring her back upstairs," Catherine orders in a humorless tone. "It's time to finish this."

The doctor steps forward, and for a moment I think he's going to drug me again, but instead he grabs my arm, taking over for Dawn. They pull me toward the waiting elevator, easily thwarting my struggles, and then we're on our way up to the fourth floor.

When we reach the apartment, they sit me in a chair and Kalina goes to the kitchen island, where an open bottle of wine is waiting. She pours a large glass and offers it to me.

"Drink this."

I shake my head. "I'm not doing anything for you."

"We can do this easy or hard." Catherine levels the gun at me. "Your choice."

"You won't shoot me. It will mess up your plan," I say with false bravado, because inside I'm jelly. "And good luck explaining it to the police."

Catherine shrugs. "You wouldn't be the first person we've shot, and the police believed what we wanted them to. Guns are the leading cause of suicide deaths in this country. We stage it right, no one will bat an eyelid."

"Especially since your behavior has been so erratic over the last few weeks," Dawn says. "You even kicked your fiancé out because you thought he was having an affair, which of course was totally untrue. Talk about paranoid."

Kalina pushes the glass into my hand. "Now drink."

I look up at the faces of my neighbors and supposed friends, and at the gun Catherine is pointing at me. Left with little choice, I lift the glass to my lips and swig the wine.

88

I've downed three glasses of wine already, and I'm now on my fourth, but strangely, I'm not feeling the effects of the alcohol. Maybe because the forced drinking session is a prelude to my murder. From the en suite, I can hear the sound of running water. Dawn is filling the soaking tub for my grand exit.

Dr. Burgess stands with an orange pill bottle in his hand. The prescription I didn't know I needed. I wonder if anyone will question the pills that are about to cause my death, prescribed by a doctor who also happens to be my neighbor. Or did he somehow cover up his involvement in acquiring the medication? I guess it doesn't matter, because dead is dead, regardless of what happens to the rest of the people in this room after I'm gone. The slim chance that they'll be caught is scant comfort, under the circumstances.

I linger with the wine, sipping as slowly as I can, because I know what will happen when the glass is empty.

But Catherine is losing her patience. "Hurry up and finish that. This has gone on long enough. We need to get you into the bathtub."

Ah, yes. The final indignity. Being forced into the tub. Then will come the pills, pushed down my throat whether I want to take them or not, and probably followed by whatever remains of the wine. After that, I'll slip away, my consciousness fading into oblivion. At least it will be painless, unlike getting shot.

I take another small sip.

Catherine shakes her head. "This is ridiculous." She motions to Jamie. "Take the glass. She can drink the rest afterward, even if we have to hold her nose and pour it down her throat."

Jamie steps forward and plucks the glass from my hand. "I'll be happy when this is done and I can go back to bed. It's almost three in the morning."

Kalina looks at Frank. "If your wife had done what she was supposed to, we'd all be tucked up in bed by now."

Frank returns her gaze with a glowering look of his own. "I told you Jennifer was having second thoughts. Maybe you should have left someone else down here to watch her."

"We had to know if Jennifer could still be trusted," Catherine says. "Now we have our answer."

"We'll deal with Jennifer next," Dr. Burgess says.

"You're not touching my wife." Frank turns to the doctor, his fists clenched.

"Relax." Catherine steps between them. "Nobody is going to lay a finger on Jennifer; I give you my word. We'll have a little chat, warn her about the consequences of causing any more trouble. We're all in this together."

"Speaking of which, let's get it over with." Dr. Burgess turns toward me.

Jamie grabs my arm and hauls me to my feet.

The sudden movement makes my head spin, and I realize that the wine is affecting me after all.

Burgess takes my other arm, gripping it so tightly that I let out a yelp.

They start toward the bedroom and the en suite, dragging me when I refuse to help them by walking on my own. My thoughts turn to Sam, and a lump rises in my throat, cutting through the haze. If I don't do something, I'll be dead an hour from now, my lifeless nude body sitting in a tub of cold, still water. I don't want him to find me like that. When we reach the door, I somehow manage to grab the frame and hold on for dear life.

"Dammit." Burgess curses and tries to wrench me free, but I've found a strength I didn't know I had. I dig my heels in to stop them pulling me any farther. My fingers curl around the molding, nails digging into the wood. "Let go. You're only making it harder on yourself."

I have no intention of letting go, because the moment I do, it's over.

"Fucking bitch," Jamie mutters under his breath. He grabs my index finger, then pries it away from the doorframe until I cry out. And still I don't release my grip. I grit my teeth and clench my fist, holding on harder with my other fingers, as tears push from the corners of my eyes. But he isn't giving up so easily. He takes hold of my pinkie and yanks it back hard. There's a sudden sharp pain in my knuckle, and I fear he might have broken it.

I cry out and release my grip on the doorframe.

"About time," Jamie exclaims. "We should have killed her first, then dumped her in the tub."

"It has to look like she drowned," Burgess says. "If she was already dead, there wouldn't be any water in her lungs."

"Yeah. Well, this is ridiculous. Even with a bottle of wine in her, she's still a pain in the ass."

"Quit grumbling." Burgess glances toward the en suite, where Dawn is waiting. "Help me get her onto the bed so we can undress her."

The words are like a knife cutting through my inebriation. An image of Sam standing in the bathroom doorway, staring at my watery corpse, flashes through my mind. My arms are restrained, so I use the only weapon I've got. My mouth. I twist and find Jamie's ear, bite down, my teeth sinking into the soft skin of his earlobe.

Now it's his turn to scream. He releases me, one hand flying to his ruined ear.

There's a coppery taste in my mouth. Blood. And something else. A piece of Jamie's skin. I spit it out in disgust.

At that moment, I hear the sound of a dead bolt disengaging. Then the front door swings wide, and Sam is standing there.

89

Sam stares at the assembled group, dumbfounded. Behind him I see a pair of police officers.

Catherine turns around. A look of surprise flashes across her face, to be quickly replaced by one of innocence. The gun is tucked behind her back, out of view. Neither Sam nor the cops appear to have noticed it. Her shoulders slump, as if from relief. "Samuel. Thank goodness you're here. Jordan has been having a hard time. Dr. Burgess believes she may have had a mental break. She has caused quite a ruckus tonight. We're trying to help her."

"Jordan?" Sam glances toward me, still being held by Burgess and Jamie, although they've loosened their grip now.

"Don't believe her. She has a gun," I say quickly. "They want to kill me."

At the mention of a weapon, the two cops push past Sam and into the living room, drawing their weapons.

"Is that true, ma'am?" one of them asks. "Do you have a gun?"

"Why would I have a gun?" Catherine asks, her voice flat and calm. "I appreciate your concern, Officers, but there really isn't any need for you to be here. We have everything under control, and no one got hurt. Dr. Burgess was about to administer Jordan a sedative, and we were going to put her to bed."

"That's right." Burgess clears his throat. He glances toward the wine bottle. "She's had quite a night."

"She bit my goddamn ear off," Jamie says, still clutching a hand to his head. "She's insane."

"They're lying," I say, frantic. "She has a gun behind her back."

"Ma'am, show us your hands," one of the police officers says. "Nice and slow."

Catherine hesitates. Then her face changes. Something seems to snap inside her. Instead of showing her hands, she whips the gun up, aims it at Sam.

"No." I'm overcome by a sudden terror. If she kills Sam, she will inflict a worse revenge than drugging and putting me in that bathtub to drown. I tear free of Burgess, twisting out of his arms with a strength I didn't know I possessed, and lunge forward.

Catherine senses my assault and tries to step out of the way, her finger tightening on the trigger. But we're so close that there's nowhere to go. I slam into her. Grab at her arm.

The gun swings wildly. A loud boom erupts that leaves my ears ringing.

Two more quick blasts split the air.

Catherine staggers backward, her eyes wide with surprise. Her arms fall to her sides, the gun clattering to the floor. Then she crumples to the ground as a pair of crimson stains bloom on her blouse, turning it a dark red.

From somewhere off to my left, there's a grunt.

I turn to see Kalina staring down at her abdomen in shocked disbelief as another seeping red stain soaks through the fabric of her sweater. She wobbles and stumbles forward, and then her legs give out. Of all the places Catherine's errant bullet could have gone, it found Kalina.

I should feel something other than satisfaction at her plight, but I don't.

Ron rushes forward and drops to his knees next to his wife. He cradles her limp body in his arms and screams in anguish. If Catherine's spirit hasn't already taken flight, it will probably be the last thing she ever hears.

Dawn runs from the bedroom and stares at her mother, frozen by shock.

Dr. Burgess bolts for the open door, but one of the cops barks an order for him to stop. He skids to a halt, hands in the air.

Sam rushes forward and scoops me into his arms. "What were you thinking, tackling Catherine like that? You could have gotten yourself shot."

"Better than *her* shooting you," I say, collapsing into his embrace. I'm trying not to cry but losing the battle. Any hint of inebriation is washed away by the adrenaline coursing through me. "I would be dead right now if you hadn't shown up. How did you know I needed help?"

"I got your message, and I knew right away that you were in trouble. Especially after I tried to call you back several times and you didn't answer. That's when I called the police and rushed over here."

"You saved my life. After the way I treated you, after what I accused you of—" I choke back a sob. The last few hours are a blur, and not just because of the alcohol and drugs. I'm clearly in shock. But I'm also more relieved than I've ever been in my life. And right now, I don't want to let go of Sam . . . ever. He's my anchor. My rock. "I'm sorry for—"

"Hey. It wasn't your fault," he says quickly, then holds me even tighter. "And I'm never leaving you alone like that again, even if you try to kick me out."

Right now that sounds like the most wonderful thing in the world. "Promise?"

"I promise." Sam kisses my forehead and strokes my hair, while behind him, out in the hallway, I hear hurried footsteps and raised voices. Then the room is full of cops.

90

I'm sitting out on the balcony of our new apartment, watching the sunset. It's been six months, and we're trying to put our lives back together. We moved out of the Glendale, of course. And not just because of what happened to us there, but also because everyone else in the building is currently in a jail cell. Except for Catherine, who was already dead when the paramedics arrived. Kalina pulled through despite losing a lot of blood. She spent a week in the hospital and then joined her co-conspirators in jail. The whole group face murder charges in the deaths of the three previous occupants of our apartment. They're facing other charges, too, for their treatment of me. False imprisonment, assault, and attempted murder, for starters. We haven't recovered the deposit we put down on the place, but we have retained a top-notch law firm. They're confident we'll get it all back and a whole lot more after the civil suit we filed against the residents of the Glendale, in partnership with Mark McGlocklin's widow and the families of the other victims, goes to trial.

In the meantime, we're back in Jamaica Plain, thanks to a loan from my parents. Because after everything that's happened, taking a loan from them didn't seem so bad. And then there's Sam. Our relationship is better than ever, and he's even forgiven me for accusing him of cheating and then kicking him out, because, well, that's just who he is.

My father isn't consulting on criminal cases anymore. In fact, he's thinking of selling the practice altogether and taking early retirement.

He's only talked about Munson once since the events at the Glendale, because he thought I should know the whole story of the man who started the chain of events that almost got me killed. Fifteen years ago, Munson was a young doctor doing his residency at Mass General. But he was so much more. A depraved killer who believed he was entering into relationships with young women who had no idea he was stalking them—at least, not until it was too late. He suffered from what my dad called a "fantasy-prone personality," among other things. Munson struggled to differentiate fiction from reality, and once a thought entered his head, it didn't take much to create a false memory. He truly believed that the women who became the objects of his affection were willing participants, even as he killed them—or, in the case of Kalina's brother, killed to protect them. Thankfully, Catherine and Ron's daughter Luna was his last victim. He slipped up and left a partial thumbprint on a handle of the Glendale's lobby doors.

He was so careful otherwise, but the police speculated that for whatever reason, he must have peeled his gloves off while walking back through the lobby after killing her. After that, it didn't take much to link the partial to a set of fingerprints taken during the mandatory background check all new doctors undergo before getting their license to practice. And when the police discovered that not only did he match the appearance of a man captured several times on CCTV following victims (including Luna) as they rode the subway, but that he was off work every time a murder took place, they swooped in and arrested him.

The one thing that struck me more than anything with my father's story was that both Munson and Burgess worked as physicians at the same hospital around the same time. Apparently, Munson became fixated with Burgess's fiancée, Emma Cerruto, after seeing her at a Christmas party thrown by one of the other doctors. When I wondered aloud why Munson hadn't killed Burgess the way he had Kalina's brother, my dad said that he wasn't sure, except that Munson might have felt it would be too suspicious, because they were colleagues.

After that, he clammed up and has said nothing on the subject since. But I can tell that his guilt over the consequences of his work all those years ago weighs heavily upon him. He was devasted when he discovered what the residents of the Glendale had done, the lives they had taken in their twisted thirst for revenge. It almost cost the life of his daughter, and I'm not sure he'll ever forgive himself for putting me in that danger, even though he did nothing wrong. Philip Arthur Munson was a monster, for sure, but my dad did his job without prejudice and maintains that he made the right diagnosis, even if he wishes he had never gotten involved with the Back Bay Butcher.

But at least the families of those killed in the Glendale will get some closure, because Ron, Kalina, and the rest of their little band of murderers confessed to killing Jacqueline Burke, Mark McGlocklin, and a third victim, Sandra Prince. They even led the authorities to a local reservoir where they'd dumped Jacqueline's body, because she didn't go missing on her way home from a night out. They disabled the camera covering the Glendale's front doors and waited in her apartment—the same apartment that would become ours many years later—and killed her.

"Hey." Sam appears with a wine in one hand and a glass of chocolate milk in the other. I'm off wine for the moment . . . too many bad memories. But even if I weren't, drinking isn't an option right now, because the two of us will soon be three, which is about the only good thing to come from our time at the Glendale. Even better, our doctor assured us that a miscarriage like the one I previously suffered, so late in the second trimester, is rare, and the odds of a second one are incredibly low. But I was still a nervous wreck until we got to the third trimester, and past the time where we lost the last baby. We're still nervous—that won't change until I'm holding our beautiful child in my arms—but we are also looking forward to welcoming our son.

I take the glass of milk. "I got a call from Detective Meadows this afternoon. The DA is considering another first-degree attempted murder charge because I was pregnant when Kalina and the others tried to kill me."

"Barely." Sam flops down into a chair.

"That doesn't matter." I was only a few weeks along when the residents of the Glendale made their move. We only discovered I was pregnant afterward at the hospital. It was a surprise, because we weren't trying, although we weren't *not* trying, either. When I think back to the copious amounts of wine they made me drink that night, and the drugs Dr. Burgess shot me up with, I realize how lucky we are. Catherine and her cohorts could easily have cost us so much more than they did. Thoughts of our impending new arrival also remind me of the incident in the basement. The cage door that locked itself and the noises I heard in the darkness. That bumblebee toy in the crib that appeared to move on its own. How did Catherine and her cronies pull that off? A removable panel in the cage? A hidden entrance? And how did they rig the latch on the cage door to lock itself? I have no answer to any of those questions and maybe I never will, but it doesn't matter, because somehow, someway, it was them, pushing my buttons.

"After all this time, I still can't believe we were so totally duped," Sam says, breaking my train of thought.

"Me more than you."

"Nah. I fell for Kalina's bull about the Wainwright Building. I should have seen what was going on."

"It wasn't bull," I tell him, because she really did own it. Or at least, she was CEO of the shell company that did. But the truth is more complex, because Catherine's family didn't just own the Glendale; they also owned several other buildings in Boston through a holding company, thanks to her great-grandfather's real estate dealings. One of those was the Wainwright, the renovation of which really has been mired in red tape for at least a decade. All she had to do was create a nested shell company for that building and install Kalina as its head, and voilà. It would look like Kalina, not Catherine, owned the Wainwright. It was the perfect trap for Sam, given his occupation. And it worked.

Sam grins. "Well, it doesn't matter, because when this lawsuit is settled, it might be us who owns the Wainwright. Then I can really get to work on making all that red tape go away, and you'll have your pick of apartments."

I almost choke on my milk. "Absolutely not." We're in a good place right now. Our relationship is stronger than ever, and I intend to keep it that way. We even got married a few weeks after I was released from the hospital—just a small ceremony with close family and friends. Living in the Wainwright would do nothing but stir up bad memories, when we should be looking toward our future. "That's a hard pass."

"Are you sure?" Sam is still grinning. "Just think of the views."

"I'm more than sure," I say, looking out over the Boston skyline as the last golden rays of sun peek between the buildings. Because I like the view from here just fine, and right now, there's nowhere else I'd rather be.

ACKNOWLEDGMENTS

This book did not come easily into the world. It screamed and kicked and refused to do as it was told. In fact, it might be one of the hardest books we've written. From initial plotting to final edits, Jordan, Sam, and the residents of the Glendale gave us fits. We have no idea why; that's just the way it went. But thankfully, we have a wonderful team of people who have our backs, and make sure that everything comes together in the end, which it did. So, without further ado, here we go.

A huge thank-you to our wonderful literary agent, Liza Fleissig, of Liza Royce Associates, for her tireless support and guidance (and for telling us to calm down and get it done).

Thank you to our developmental editor, Charlotte Herscher, who made this book so much better with her keen observations and insightful suggestions. Thanks also to our wonderful editor, Alexandra Torrealba, and Jessica Tribble Wells and the entire team at Thomas & Mercer, including Nicole Burns-Ascue, copyeditor Bill Siever, proofreader Sarah Engel, and cold reader Stephen Schul.

Thank you, Dawn Hills, for your support throughout all the books we've written. It was a pleasure and an honor to feature you and your husband Jamie as characters in this story. Thanks also to all our VIP readers; you truly are very important people.

Thanks to all the influencers, bloggers, podcasters, and everyone else who has helped get the word out on this book. Thanks also to Emily Haynes, who always shouts us from the rooftops.

And of course, a huge thanks to all of you, the readers, without whom Jordan's story would have remained untold.

And lastly, a word from Sonya:

I wish to thank the Moykens family for the story of Archie Hazen, from which we drew inspiration. My best friend, Mary Moykens, lived in an old house with a dirt-floor basement. In that basement, for reasons unknown, was the grave of a young boy named Archie Hazen. When I was sixteen, my parents split up, and while they were working out the separation and living arrangements, I went to stay at Mary's house. They had four bedrooms in the home, but only one downstairs, which is where I stayed. And in that room was the door going down to the basement. I spent a week there, thinking of Archie and that grave on the other side of the door, terrified to sleep and listening for any creak, whisper, or scrape. I still remember staying up all night and reading until the first light of dawn. I even remember the book. It was *Zoya* by Danielle Steel, and it got me through some tough nights! Eventually, I made my way upstairs and stayed in Mary's room with her. I was much happier and better rested for it. But I've never forgotten that grave and little Archie Hazen. It totally creeped out me and Mary as teenagers, and honestly, when I think about it now, it still kind of does. The real grave and inscription are just as they are written in this story. So thank you, Mary, for reminding me of his name and the inscription, and for letting me immortalize Archie here in print.

ABOUT THE AUTHORS

A.M. Strong is the coauthor of ten novels, including *Gravewater Lake*, *The Last Girl Left*, and *I Will Find Her*. He has worked as a graphic designer, newspaper journalist, artist, and actor. Born in the United Kingdom, he currently resides most of the year on Florida's Space Coast, where he can watch rockets launch from his bedroom balcony, and part of the year on an island in Maine, along with his wife and two furry bosses, Izzie and Hayden. A.M. Strong also writes under the pen name Anthony M. Strong. For more information, visit www.amstrongauthor.com.

Sonya Sargent is the coauthor of ten novels, including *Gravewater Lake*, *The Last Girl Left*, and *I Will Find Her*. She has a degree in design; a passion for anything dogs, travel, and the arts; and a love for reading and cooking. Born in Vermont, Sonya now splits her time between the coast of Florida and an island in Maine, along with her husband and two adorable rescue mutts. For more information, visit www.twistedthrillers.com.